CRIME

DENIED

A BUCK TAYLOR NOVEL

BOOK 5

BY

CHUCK MORGAN

Printed in the United States of America

First printing 2020

ISBN 978-1-7337960-9-5 (eBook)

ISBN 978-1-7337960-8-8 (Paperback)

ISBN 978-1-7337960-5-7 (Large Print)

LIBRARY OF CONGRESS CONTROL NUMBER

2020900699

DEDICATION

Dedicated to my Grandsons, Devlin,
Eddie and Ryker

CHAPTER ONE

Alicia Hawkins sat at the end of the long wooden bar and appeared to be focused on the beer in front of her. What no one in the bar realized was that Alicia Hawkins was hunting, and her eyes were slowly and casually moving from seat to seat and table to table in search of her next victim. She had become a predator of the highest level. The top of the food chain, when it came to humans, and the predator needed to be fed. Alicia Hawkins was a serial killer.

She had walked into the bar a couple hours before and found a seat where she could observe the entire room. She was a pretty young woman with purple-streaked blond hair that was tucked up under a straw cowboy hat. She wore tight jeans and a snap-front Western shirt, open just enough to attract the interest of the cowboys and ranch hands who frequented the bar. Being the social person she was, she danced several dances to the local country band and politely thanked the cowboys for their offers to take her home for the night. Tonight, Alicia Hawkins was not interested in casual sex, even though she was attracted to several of the local ranch hands. Tonight, she had a purpose, and had any of the cowboys realized what that purpose was, they would have avoided her like the plague.

Alicia Hawkins had arrived in the middle of nowhere, Oklahoma, a couple days before and had settled into the isolated cabin she'd found on one of those vacation rentals by owner websites. Since all the arrangements were made online, she never actually met the owner, which was just as well, since the fewer people to see her, the safer she felt. The new driver's license and credit cards she'd bought off the dark web worked perfectly, and she was glad she'd spent the extra money to buy the best product available.

She'd left Florida a couple weeks back and was heading, in a roundabout way, towards Colorado to fulfill a promise she'd made to her dying grandfather. In her wake, she'd left several bodies and a task force of federal agents scratching their heads, wondering where her next victim would show up. During the year she had been on the run, she had sliced up seven women in Florida and Colorado, one in Mississippi. Then, to throw off the task force, she'd made a quick trip up to Georgia and left two dead women in that state before heading towards Louisiana and Texas, where two more homeless women died terrible deaths.

She'd lucked out on her second night in Oklahoma when she picked up a young female hitchhiker with no local family. The offer of a place to spend the night and a home-cooked meal was too much to pass up for the young runaway. The sleeping pills Alicia placed in the young woman's wine incapacitated her enough so Alicia could carry her to the basement, strip off her clothes and tie her hands and feet to the wall. Alicia Hawkins then stripped off her own clothes, opened the roll of assorted knives and scalpels she had carefully laid out on the table and spent the next five hours making various-sized incisions all over the woman's body.

She took her time and even stopped now and then to admire the woman's body. She had a thin waist and large, firm breasts, and even though Alicia never reached the kind of sexual pleasure her grandfather had described, she found herself getting aroused as she ran her hands over the woman's body. The drugs started to wear off after the first hour, and Alicia had to gag the woman to silence her screams. Her pleading, tear-filled eyes begged for the pain to stop, which made Alicia increase the speed and depth of the cuts, while using one hand to take care of her own arousal. When the woman's heart stopped beating, Alicia stepped back, admired her handiwork and lay down on the floor and slept. She was exhausted and sexually satisfied. She was also pleased that she was getting closer to her goal of keeping her victim alive until she reached one thousand cuts.

Alicia Hawkins had chosen this cabin because it sat all by itself at the end of a rural lake. The nearest neighbors were almost a half mile away, but she was still fearful that the screams of her victims might attract unwanted attention. For peace of mind, once she settled into the cabin, she took the canoe that was stored in the garage, rowed around the entire lake and noticed one other vacation home that appeared to be occupied. It was late in the season, and she was glad that most of the tourists had gone by the time she got there.

The bar was loud and crowded with cowboys and cowgirls from the local cattle and horse ranches that covered the county. It was Friday night, and they all had money to burn and were looking to let off some steam. Alicia Hawkins was sipping her beer and was about to give up when she spotted her next victim—but she wasn't sure. She'd come into the bar looking for another woman, but across the room, sitting at a table full of well-muscled, tanned cowboys sat a young man who seemed to be the brunt of the jokes that were going around the table. She had already danced with and refused the advances of several of the cowboys at the table, but this young cowboy looked like he might fit the bill. He wasn't well built but was skinny and seemed shy. He didn't seem to be enjoying the razzing he was getting from the others and looked like he wanted to escape.

Alicia Hawkins sized him up. She'd started her career as a serial killer by choosing female victims because they were easier to control and more trusting of going off someplace with another woman. It also made her unique in the serial killer world. She felt she was ready to move up to men, but she needed to make sure it was the right man. She knew she had the skills, and she had experimented with several types of fast-acting sedatives, but she was concerned that she could still be overpowered by a man, especially one of these well-built cowboys. She was not a big woman, but her strength had improved with each victim. Looking at this young man, she believed she could do it. She felt herself getting aroused as she sat there, watching him in the mirror behind the bar.

After several minutes of doubt and internal struggle, she decided that tonight was the night. She watched as the young cowboy picked up some money off the table, stood up and walked towards the bar. He was standing there waiting for his drinks when she walked up and sat on the barstool next to him.

"You don't look like you're having much fun,"

she said. "Maybe I can fix that for you."

The young man looked around as if he was unsure who she was talking to.

"Are you talking to me, ma'am?" His voice
cracked, and he swallowed hard.

"Yes, silly, I'm talking to you. Haven't you
ever talked to a woman before?"

She laughed, and the young man turned a
bright shade of red. He was embarrassed, and
he glanced over his shoulder to the table where
his coworkers had gone quiet and were watching in disbelief, since most of them had already
struck out with the new girl. The bartender set
six beers on the bar, and he looked at her and
then his buddies, tipped his hat and walked the
drinks back to the table. She could hear loud
conversation and a lot of goading, and she sat
there and waited. It was his move.

The laughing continued, and the young cowboy stood up, squared his shoulders and walked
back towards Alicia. She turned to face him.

"You ready to get out of here?" she said. "I
know a quiet place we can go where we won't be
disturbed."

The young cowboy swallowed hard and nodded his head. Alicia set a twenty on the bar,
turned and tipped her hat to the young man's
friends. They could still hear the laughs and the

catcalls as they left the bar.

Alicia Hawkins had an easygoing charm, and she soon had the young man telling her his life story. He'd left home at sixteen after his mother died, and his father fell deeper into the bottle. He'd heard that his dad died a couple years later, which made him an orphan—a lot better than when he had a family. He was trying to make it on his own and had always dreamed of working on a big ranch. He loved horses. He'd been in Oklahoma a couple weeks.

She turned the car down a dark lane, almost invisible between the trees, and drove a quarter mile to the house by the lake. She led him inside and lit a fire in the fireplace. The young man stood in the doorway, not sure what to do, so she walked over and took his hand and led him towards the bedroom. She sat him down and offered him a beer, which he accepted, and she told him to take his clothes off while she headed for the kitchen.

Since this was her first time with a man as a victim, she decided to use the same sleeping pills on him that she'd used on the runaway. Once he was out, she would use the sedative cocktail to incapacitate him. The sleeping pills in the beer would take effect pretty quickly, so she would need to move fast.

She walked into the bedroom and found him

standing next to the bed, naked. It was obvious that he was ready for her, so she handed him the beer, and he took a big, long drink while she stripped off her clothes. She lay down on the bed, took him in her hands and gently guided him in. The first minute or so was pure pleasure, and she found she was enjoying him until she sensed the pills kick in. She reached under her pillow, pulled out the syringe and pushed it into his shoulder. He never felt the needle go in, and within a couple seconds, he stopped moving.

She pushed him off, slipped out of bed and put on a fluffy white robe that was hanging behind the door. She tried to lift him and was surprised that he weighed a lot more than she expected. She needed a plan B, so she went downstairs to the basement and brought back two pairs of shackles, a chain and her knife kit.

Alicia Hawkins clamped the shackles on his hands and feet and chained him to the bed. She typically didn't work on her victims while they were lying down, but this was a new experience and called for a change in her methods. She would need to think about this aspect of her work before she picked up the next guy. Who knows? Maybe if they were lying down, they might stay alive longer. It was something to find out.

She filled a glass with red wine and stood there admiring the young man. For someone so thin, he was certainly virile, and she wished he had been able to stay awake a little longer. She could feel the arousal beginning again, so she stripped off her robe and pulled a beautiful three-inch scalpel from her kit. It was her favorite tool; it made an incision as thin as a human hair. It was a thing of beauty.

CHAPTER TWO

Alicia Hawkins hadn't become a serial killer in the usual manner. She didn't tear the wings off butterflies when she was a kid, and she never killed a neighbor's cat. She even used to volunteer at the Pitkin County animal shelter, and she loved the family dog. For the most part, her childhood was perfectly normal, with no signs of anything strange in her makeup. She was a perfectly normal college student until that summer a year ago when she made the discovery that would change her life.

She'd discovered her grandfather's trophy box a couple months back and wondered about the significance of the baubles. She knew it was her grandfather's because no one in the family remembered the old cigar box that was hidden in a hole in the wall behind her grandfather's big Craftsman toolbox. She had mentioned it one night at dinner, and no one reacted. Well, that's not exactly true. She thought she saw some kind of recognition in her grandmother's eyes, but that disappeared as quickly as it had arrived.

She waited until the family was asleep and entered her grandfather's room. He was sleeping soundly, and she hoped that he might wake up in one of his—getting rarer—lucid moments. She hated to disturb him, so she'd already started to leave his room when a low frail voice stopped her in her tracks.

She approached the bed and stood there with the trophy box held out in front of her. Her grandfather stared at the box in her hands and smiled. She hadn't seen him smile much since she had gotten home from college, and it surprised her. He asked her to open the box so he could look inside.

She opened the box and held it out to him. His heart monitor reacted almost immediately, and she was afraid the change of tone from the monitor might wake someone else in the small house. She closed the box and pulled it away from him, but his expression indicated that he wasn't done. She glanced towards his bedroom door to see if anyone might have heard them, and then she reopened the box, and he looked deep inside. She asked him what all these pieces meant. He smiled and asked her to remove the gold-edged cameo necklace. She held it up for him to see, and he told her that this had been the first one.

She was a pretty runaway from somewhere

up near Chicago. Her family life had been brutal, so she'd headed west to find her own way in the world. The Korean War was over, and many people were leaving their familiar homes to look for financial opportunities out west. The fledgling ski industry and lax laws were drawing people from far and wide, and Aspen was no exception. The young woman found work in a small diner just off the highway, and she found a room with several other young women. Alicia's grandfather befriended the young woman, and they started seeing each other at night. Her grandmother never knew.

After a few weeks, she told him that she was tired of the cold and had decided to head to California. Her grandfather sensed an opportunity about to disappear, so he told her he would drive her to the train in Glenwood Springs. He knew she hadn't told any of her friends about him, so he wasn't worried about getting caught. That night, as she slipped out of her rooming house, he met her up the highway and loaded her one suitcase into the trunk of his car. She was dressed in a long skirt and a pretty white blouse, and she wore the cameo necklace around her neck. A gift from her mother.

Instead of heading north up Highway 82, he turned south and headed out of town. He turned down Route 15, which at the time was a narrow dirt road, and found the old fire road that led to Conundrum Creek. She asked him where they were heading, and he told her that he wanted to show her a beautiful sight before she left. He reached the end of the road, parked the car and reached his arm around her shoulders. The syringe bit deep into her shoulder, and she started to yell, but he put his hand over her mouth and held it there until the sedative had time to work.

The snow was not that deep on the old trail through the woods as he carried her over his shoulder. The old mining cabin had collapsed years before, but it wasn't the cabin he was interested in. When he'd first arrived in Aspen, he spent time exploring his new home and discovered the old cabin a mile or so down Conundrum Creek. It sat back about a quarter mile from the trail along the creek and was completely hidden from view. What interested him most about the cabin was the shaft the old miners had dug under its wooden floor. The shaft went down about thirty feet and then opened into a long tunnel. He found some old, broken-down and decayed wooden shelves and some old mining equipment.

When he'd first found the cabin, he thought it would be perfect for his needs. He spent several weeks tracking down the owner of the property and discovered that the mining claim that the cabin sat on was owned by a man in Pittsburg who had almost forgotten about the old claim.

Through a series of letters and telegrams, her grandfather was finally able to get permission to work the claim and use the cabin.

He spent the next couple of months cleaning out the space and installing the things he knew he would need. Along the walls, he bolted in chains and shackles for hands and feet. He purchased several kerosene hurricane lamps and built a bed with a straw mattress. He was able to make the most significant improvement in the machine shop at the ski resort's maintenance shed. He fashioned a metal hatch door that he installed over the old rotten wooden shaft door and put heavy-duty hinges and a hasp on it.

The old miners had left an old kerosene stove in the tunnel that they had vented up through the ground a few feet behind the cabin. It would help to keep the chill out of the air and make it a more comfortable space to work in. He also placed his pride and joy in the tunnel: over the years working at the ski resort, he had fashioned several beautiful knives and scalpels at the metal shop. Since he'd made them all himself, there was no record of him buying them. His space was complete, and his body tingled at the thought of what would soon be taking place in his secluded little world.

Alicia's grandfather's voice seemed to grow stronger as he told her the rest of the story. He had carried the young woman to the cabin and unlocked the trapdoor. He lowered her down the old wooden ladder and placed her on the bed while he fired up the kerosene lanterns and the old kerosene stove. Once the space got warmer, he stripped off all the young woman's clothes and tied her to the bed frame. She had a beautiful body, young and subtle. Her breasts were small but perky, and she moaned through the gag as he repeatedly penetrated her. Twice he had to inject her with more sedative to keep her quiet. This was the first time he had ever had sex with someone other than his wife, and he was surprised at how much he enjoyed it, but the night was fading fast, and he needed to get home before his wife woke up.

Now that he was totally spent, he untied her from the bed and carried her over to the first set of shackles that he had bolted to the wall. She was still naked, and he hooked the restraints to her hands and feet. She had started to wake up, and the fear in her eyes made him get excited all over again, but he didn't have the time to penetrate her again. He was running out of time. He opened an old cabinet that was hanging on the wall and removed a leather bundle. He carefully placed it on the wooden table under the cabinet and unrolled it, revealing his assortment of custom-made knives.

He chose a thin four-inch-long scalpel from the bundle and admired it in the light from the kerosene lantern. He loved how the blade glowed under the yellow light. He walked over to the young woman and held the scalpel so she could see it. She squirmed hard against the shackles and started to bleed where the metal shackles cut into her hands and feet.

Slowly and almost delicately, he slid the sharp edge of the scalpel along her exposed abdomen. He had used this same technique on several high-ranking German officers during the war. They were a stubborn lot, but eventually, they all talked. He didn't care if the young woman talked or not. This was not an interrogation. This was pleasure.

He could hear her screaming through the gag. He spent the next hour slowly slicing the young woman's torso, legs and arms until she finally passed out. She didn't have the stamina of the German officers, and it was almost disappointing. He walked over to the leather bundle on the bed and, using an old rag, cleaned the blood off the scalpel and his hands. He got dressed and then walked back and turned off the kerosene stove and put his bundle back in the cabinet. If she was still alive when he returned, he would finish the job, but for now, the demons were satisfied. He turned off the kerosene lanterns and climbed out of his workspace. He closed the hatch, made sure the padlock was shut and covered the hatch with the decaying floorboards.

CHAPTER THREE

Alicia could feel the heat rising inside her as her grandfather told her the story of his first civilian kill. She hadn't realized how sexually aroused she'd felt as he described the details of the kill. She felt embarrassed that she was feeling this way and didn't understand what was happening. Her grandfather knew what was happening. He could sense that she had the same feelings he did when it came to taking another's life. He finished his story and looked at the vibrant pink color in her cheeks and the little beads of sweat that had formed on her forehead and her upper lip.

He told her that he knew she was the one who would follow him. He could feel it deep in his soul, and he would help her find her way along the path that had been taken from him so long ago. She stared in disbelief in response to what he was saying. She could never take a human life. She had never killed anything, nor had the desire to do so. Or did she? His description of the kill had certainly stirred something deep inside her. Something scary, but also something wonderful.

Her grandfather started to speak in dribble

and incomplete sentences, and then he closed his eyes and went to sleep. The lucid moment had passed, but she had certainly learned a lot. She looked at the other pieces of jewelry in the little box. Her grandfather had just admitted to being a serial killer. One of the first in modern history, yet there had never been any hint that this was the case. She wondered how many more pieces of jewelry would have found their way into his little trophy box if he had not been injured so many years ago. She also wondered how he had kept the demons from destroying him since he was no longer able to feed their needs.

She was curious whether her grandmother knew about his proclivities. She had definitely noticed the change in her grandmother's eyes when she mentioned the old cigar box she had found in the garage. Yet her grandmother had never said anything about it.

She looked again at the trophies her grandfather had collected. She wondered about the people they had belonged to. Most of the jewelry appeared to be pieces that would have been worn by young women of his time. She wondered if she would ever be able to get their stories from her grandfather. She would need to hurry. She was due back at school in early September. If she was going to act on the feelings that had been stirred up by her grandfather's story, she would need to do it quickly.

She closed the lid of the old box, leaned in and kissed her grandfather on the forehead and left his room. The house was quiet as a church cemetery, and she was grateful. She headed back to her room and, once inside, closed the door and hid the trophy box in the back of her closet. She needed to understand the feelings that her grandfather's story had generated. Was it possible she was a serial killer too?

She had taken psychology classes at school, and she understood that serial killers were psychopaths. She'd always believed they were evil incarnate and that they would stand out in society like freaks at a carnival. Even though she hadn't had the opportunity to see her grandfather in his early years, she never considered him to be odd. He had never spoken before of his craft. But now. His story had aroused something profound inside of her. Something she now both feared and found interesting and exciting.

Could it be true that he could sense in her the things that made him do the evil deeds he had told her about? It made her sick to her stomach, and she ran into her tiny bathroom and vomited in the toilet. No, there was no way she could ever be the evil thing her grandfather had suddenly become in her eyes. But she was also envious of him. If the way she'd felt while he was telling his story was real, the sensation was incredible. She felt more satisfied, sexually, at this moment than she had with any of the college boys she had slept with over the years.

She knew she needed to pursue the feelings to see if they were real. She was afraid of what she might find and of what she might become, but she needed to find out. She lay down on her bed, her head full of strange thoughts and feelings. She decided the first thing she needed to do was try to find her grandfather's old cabin and see if the shaft was still locked. She would check that out first and then decide on the next step.

Alicia Hawkins started slowly. She wanted to savor every minute of her new project. The slices on the young cowboy's chest were long and shallow. She wanted this to last, so she was extra careful. After almost an hour, the sedatives started to wear off, so she put the gag in his mouth and tied it around his head. His eyes grew wider with each cut, and he tried in vain to scream. By this point, Alicia was in the deep end of the sexual arousal pool, so she decided to stop and enjoy the opportunity. She started stroking the young man, and when she felt he was ready, she climbed on top of him and guided him inside. He tried to squirm and buck her off, but all that did was increase her arousal. She rode him like she had never ridden anyone before, and when she looked down, she was covered in blood, his blood. She ran her hands over her body and smeared the blood around her breasts. The sensation grew until she couldn't handle it anymore, and she exploded in ecstasy. It was the most incredible thing she had ever felt. She lost complete control of herself and made several slices in his chest, deeper than she wanted.

The young cowboy screamed through the gag, and his entire body convulsed. She slid off the bed and finished her glass of wine. She now understood the sexual arousal that her grandfather had told her about but she had never experienced. She now realized what she had been missing with the women she had killed. Contentment made her sleepy, so she lay on the floor and wrapped a blanket around herself and fell asleep. This young cowboy had a lot left to give, and she planned to take it all.

The sky was still dark when Alicia woke, and she stood up and stared at the young cowboy. Sometime during the night, he had passed out, but he was still breathing, so she wasn't done quite yet. She continued slicing his body while stroking him, her arousal growing to incredible levels, and she climbed on him again. He'd lost a lot of blood, but he was still able to please her in ways she'd never expected, and she screamed as the climax exploded, but she noticed that he no longer fought like he had earlier in the evening.

Twice more over the next couple hours, she

pleasured herself while continuing to slice him. The sheets and pillows were soaked with blood, and she had so much blood on her body that she looked like she'd been in a fight. He passed out, for the last time, as the sun rose over the tops of the trees, and Alicia put down her scalpel, walked to the window and watched the mist rising from the lake. The scene was so peaceful. Nothing like the scene in the room behind her.

She turned and walked back to the bed. The young cowboy was no longer breathing, and she covered him with the bloody sheet. She was exhausted, but exhilarated, so she climbed onto the bed and fell asleep next to the body. She dreamt about her grandfather.

CHAPTER FOUR

licia's grandfather, Thomas had come to Aspen a few years after the end of World War II. He had been a soldier in the 10th Mountain Division as the war neared its end and had learned how to ski. Some of his fellow warriors were settling in small communities throughout the Colorado mountains and were working to build up the fledgling ski industry. He thought it might be fun to be a part of the movement.

His best friend, Gus Murphy, found a job with the recently formed Aspen Skiing Corporation and offered Thomas a job working as a mechanic on the ski lifts. Having been mechanically inclined all his life, he took to the job like a fish to water. As the years progressed, his life became more and more fulfilling, and he felt he was living the American dream. He met and fell in love with Alicia's grandmother, bought the small Victorian house on West Hallam Street, and raised a son there. It was a perfect life, except that the demons were still working hard in the back of his mind.

The demons had been there as long as he could

remember, and his time in the army had deepened the lust they brought out. He had practiced his craft, as he called it, with great abandon as a young man. Many of the townsfolk around Lynchburg, Virginia, thought he was odd, and many of the neighbors feared him. He had grown up on a very rural farm outside Lynchburg. The family's water came from a pump, and an outhouse served their more personal needs. To say they were dirt poor would have been an understatement. His father was a sharecropper and didn't even own the dirt under their little house.

Life had not been easy growing up. He was constantly picked on when he was able to get to school, which was not often, and as things got worse, his father would take to drinking, and he was a terrible drunk. No one was safe from his father's rage, especially his mother and younger sisters. Numerous times he had watched as his father left his middle sister's room, and he heard her crying inside. As his younger sister got older, the same thing would happen to her. His mother would often come out of her room with a black eye or a bruised lip. However, he wasn't saved from his father's rage because he was a boy. His father would belittle him all the time about not being good at anything and not being a man. He would work him from dawn till dusk and then, if the mood was right, would beat him senseless for even the most minor infraction.

His escape often took him into unknown territory. He chose to follow in his father's footsteps and started abusing the animals on the farm. But it didn't stop there. Many of the neighbors complained to the local sheriff about their pets disappearing. The sheriff had visited the farm numerous times and never found any evidence that anyone on the farm was involved, but the neighbors knew the truth. What they had no way of knowing was how deep the depravity went.

One afternoon one of the neighbors questioned Thomas about a missing goat. The neighbor had seen the goatskin hanging in a tree along the creek behind the farm and confronted him and his father with the evidence, and a fight broke out. By the time the sheriff arrived, the neighbor was dead. His father, who was covered in blood, tried to put all the blame on himself, but the sheriff didn't buy it, and they were both arrested. His father was convicted and died in prison a few years later. Thomas was convicted and given a choice: jail or the army. He chose the army.

The army was a great place for him. They taught him how to kill, a skill he honed with great enthusiasm. He was so good at it that he was often the first soldier called upon when a Nazi guard needed to be dispatched silently. His knife became his friend, and he used it most effectively when an enemy officer needed to be encouraged to talk. He was a skilled craftsman, and his actions often turned the stomachs of even the most hardened soldiers.

Thomas had been able to keep the demons under control for the first couple of years after he moved to Aspen, but they became too strong for him to ignore. He needed to feed the demons, but Aspen was a small mountain town. Missing people would be noticed. At first, he tried to feed the demons with animal sacrifices. He stayed away from family pets—too close to home—and focused on wild animals, which were in abundance in the forests around Aspen.

Killing forest creatures with his bare hands was fun, but it didn't satisfy the demons for long. He needed the sensation and the arousal that came from killing another human being. The incredible satisfaction it would bring as he felt the life slip away from someone who had been a living, breathing person. He also missed the thrill of the hunt. Finding the right person and stalking them until just the right moment. He loved the challenge.

Alicia Hawkins woke slowly, stretched and lay there for a minute, thinking about the incredible night she had experienced. She felt her grandfather would be proud of her. Her skills had exceeded her wildest dreams, and she was ready to fulfill the promise she'd made to her grandfather before leaving for college. She had wanted so badly for him to still be alive when she felt she was ready to deliver on that promise, but that was not to be. Tears formed in her eyes when she thought about her love for him and her desire to live up to what he saw in her. She looked over at the lump under the bloody sheet.

She now believed she was strong enough to include men in her future endeavors. She had proved that to herself with the young cowboy. In all that ecstasy, she lost track of how many slices she had inflicted on him but knew he lasted longer than almost all the women, and she smiled. The more she thought about the previous night, the more excited she got, and she took a few minutes to pleasure herself again.

She couldn't remember ever feeling this satisfied, and she liked the way she felt. Standing up from the bed, she could feel the dried blood that covered her body crack as she moved. She walked into the bathroom, turned on the shower and stood under the hot water as it washed over her body, taking flakes of dried blood with it. The water that collected at the bottom of the shower was crimson, and it continued to amaze her how much blood the human body contained. She was also amazed at how much effort it took to scrub off the crusted blood, but by the time she was finished and stood in front of the mirror, she could see that her body almost glowed. She wasn't sure if it was the sex or the blood, but she liked the way she looked.

Alicia took a few minutes to clean the dried blood off the knives she'd used the night before and made sure they sparkled before she put them away. She had bought the knives at various flea markets while she was in Florida to replace the knives her grandfather had made by hand in his workshop. She'd left the knives in her grandfather's underground lair in Aspen when she made her first kill, and the authorities were on the tunnel so fast, she couldn't get back and retrieve them. It broke her heart and made her angry how things had turned out.

She made herself a huge breakfast because she was starving, and while she ate, she pulled out her laptop and looked at the news. She was thrilled that she had a government task force named after her, and it was fun keeping track of where they were. She laughed at how far behind her they were with the investigation. She had them running all over the Southeast, and they had no idea she was long gone. This was notoriety her grandfather had never achieved during the years he killed.

She liked to think about the number of kills

her grandfather might have accomplished had it not been for the accident that crippled him, but it was okay because she was closing in on his number and had plans to far exceed it. Once she made good on her promise, she planned to head for California. The stories she read made it sound like a good place for serial killers to operate. She stopped and looked up from her coffee. "Oh, my god," she said out loud. "I am also now a rapist, just like my grandfather." She laughed and finished her coffee.

She knew she should get packed and hit the road, but she wasn't concerned. When she'd rented the cabin, she told the owner that she was looking for solitude and didn't want any housekeeping services for the entire week. Since she had gotten so lucky the first two nights she was in town, she still had four days before her rental was up. She also needed to make sure she ended up in Colorado at the right time to deliver on her promise. She couldn't risk getting caught before she delivered.

She washed the dishes by hand and put them back on the shelf. The sheets and towels were shot thanks to all the blood, so she decided to leave them where they were. She knew the evidence techs would do an excellent job of gathering everything up. The person she felt bad for was the housekeeper, who would show up in four days and find a bloodbath. She hoped whoever that person was had a strong stomach.

She wasn't concerned about leaving her DNA. The FBI knew who she was, and she figured that leaving her DNA all over the crime scene would help them know it was her and not a copycat who had committed the crime. It was important to her that they had her kill numbers correct. Mostly because she wanted to surpass her grand-father, but also so they would understand the symbolism of the promise she'd made to him.

CHAPTER FIVE

T he promise began quite by accident on a cool summer night in the Jackpot Bar in Aspen. When Alicia had found the trophy box, there were sixteen pieces of jewelry in the box, but there were fifteen mummified bodies in the tunnel. There was a small jade horse pendant on a thin silver chain in the trophy box that she had admired, and she decided to wear it for a night out with her girlfriends before they all headed back to college.

The thrill of her first kill had started to fade. She had gone home that night and slept like a baby. The next morning, she still felt wired. The response hadn't been sexual, but the kill still excited her. She'd felt better and better about her technique as the night wore on. She'd really got an adrenaline jolt when the girl woke up and realized what was happening to her. If only it had lasted. The cut she had made across her neck must have hit the artery. She'd thought she was shallow enough, but there was a little spurt of blood that wouldn't stop. She would have to remember that for the next time.

She had been hoping there would be a next

time before she had to leave for college, but it was not meant to be. She had been back to the bar every night after work since the first kill; this would be her last night in town, and she had not been able to find her next victim. She finished her drink and told her friends at the table that the next round was on her. Instead of waiting for the waitress, she walked up to the bar.

The woman behind the bar was the owner. Alicia hadn't really met her, but this was where she and her friends had hung out all summer, so they got to know who was who. The owner walked up and asked her what she needed. She gave her the order for three beers and laid a twenty-dollar bill on the bar.

The owner came back with three beers and stared at her for a minute. She was beginning to feel a little self-conscious when the owner finally spoke.

She had admired the necklace Alicia was wearing and wondered where she had found such a pretty piece? She told the owner that she had found it in a pawn shop in Florida. The owner looked at it a little closer and then said something that chilled her to the bone.

The owner told her she had had a necklace very similar to that one, but she'd lost it when she was in a car crash many years before. The necklace belonged to her grandmother, and she had borrowed it—well, actually stole it—when she ran away from home. She was in a crash a couple miles outside of Aspen, and the necklace had disappeared. No one at the hospital remembered seeing it.

Alicia asked the owner if she remembered anything else about the crash, but she said that she must have fallen asleep after she was picked up hitchhiking on the highway. When she woke up in the hospital several days later, she couldn't remember anything about the crash. The police told her that the man who had picked her up was probably going to die and that she was lucky to be alive.

She left the twenty on the bar, picked up the three beer bottles, and walked back to her table. She was too stunned to even talk. Luckily her friends were doing enough talking, so they never noticed.

She had taken the jade necklace out of her grandfather's treasure box. She had admired it since finding the box, and she decided that it would be one thing to remember her grandfather by. He had been slipping in and out of consciousness for the past couple weeks, and the family was not holding out much hope. Since it was her last night in town, and she was certain no one would have any idea where the necklace came from, she decided to wear it out. How in the hell could she have ever guessed that someone would recognize the necklace? What a huge clusterfuck.

She needed some air, so she excused herself and walked out the front door and stood on the sidewalk. The air was fall crisp, and it felt good. Her thoughts turned to the woman at the bar. She didn't remember anyone ever mentioning that there had been a passenger in the car with her grandfather the night he crashed. Was it possible this woman was in the car with him? How could that have gotten missed in the family stories? More importantly, was it her necklace that was in her grandfather's treasure box?

She put her hand up to her open mouth. "Oh, my god." This woman was supposed to be her grandfather's sixteenth victim. That's why there were sixteen mementos in the box, but only fifteen bodies in the mine. He had been on his way to the mine to kill her when the crash occurred. But why had no one ever mentioned a second person in the car?

The owner did not appear to know who was driving the car that night. She had no recollection of the accident. Alicia's grandfather must have already drugged her by the time he crashed the car. Alicia didn't know what he'd used as a sedative, but whatever it was, it had to have been fast-acting and very powerful. Powerful enough to induce amnesia?

She felt a chill run up her spine, and then in a moment of clarity, she struck on an idea. One that would hopefully keep her focused while she was away at school. She would finish what her grandfather had started that fateful night so long ago. She would take care of his sixteenth victim. She would need to devise a plan for this kill. It would take time, and it would need to be perfect. The owner was no slouch. She ran a bar. She would be tough to deal with, and she had a pretty good build, even after so many years. Alicia pictured the woman in her younger days and understood why her grandfather had chosen her. She was probably a real looker in her day, because she was gorgeous now.

This was awesome. What better way to honor her grandfather than to finish his journey? She felt her excitement build like it had the night of her first kill. It was a shame. If she only had more time. But that was okay. She would be back at Christmas. She would start working out the plan in her head, and by Christmas, it would be perfect. She just knew it. Her grandfather would be so proud of her.

She stepped back into the bar and shook off the chill from the night air. Her body was warm and tingling. She sat back down at the table where her friends were still talking away and took a sip of her beer. She looked over the top of the bottle and stared at her next victim.

The next morning her father and mother packed up the car and drove her to Denver for her flight back to Jacksonville. She hugged them and stepped into the security line. She wrapped her hand around the jade necklace and said a silent prayer that her grandfather would live long enough to see her complete his final act. She smiled as she went through security and waved goodbye to her parents.

Unfortunately, the FBI screwed up her plans for coming home at Christmas, but she decided a better way to honor her grandfather would be to kill his sixteenth victim on the first anniversary of his death. That anniversary was now a couple weeks away, which made her timing so important. She wrapped her hand around the small jade horse pendant, and tears filled her eyes.

She was about to close her laptop when a news article caught her attention, so she sat back down at the table and pulled up the story. The article was mostly about her first kill in Aspen, the one that had started it all, and how the discovery of the body coincided with the death of a local wildlife ranger, another anniversary that was fast approaching.

There was a picture below the article, and her anger began to grow as she looked at the picture and continued reading the article. The picture was of Colorado Bureau of Investigation agent Buck Taylor, the cop who'd led the investigation that discovered her grandfather's underground tunnel, and that also led to the discovery of her first kill.

Although her grandfather had already been dying at the time, she blamed Buck Taylor for her grandfather's death, which she had convinced herself occurred sooner than it should have because of all the pressure from the investigation. The truth was that her grandfather had been in a coma before Buck Taylor ever entered his life, but her twisted mind didn't see it that way. She also blamed him because she was unable to get back to the tunnel for her grandfather's knives.

She thought about how awesome it would be if she could find a way to get to Buck Taylor while she was in Colorado. If she could end his life like he had ended her grandfather's life, that would be perfect. She knew getting to a cop would be difficult, but maybe, if she had the time, she could find out if he had any family nearby. She could take out members of his family and hurt him like he'd hurt her and her family.

Her mind was working on a plan when she noticed the other person standing next to Buck in the picture. She looked closer and recognized the person. He was a homeless man who had been around Aspen almost her entire life. The article mentioned that the homeless man had helped Buck with several cases over the years, and a new plan started to grow in her mind. If she couldn't get to Buck, maybe she could take out the homeless man, his friend. After all, how hard could it be to kill a homeless person? He looked old and skinny. It should be a piece of cake.

She closed her laptop, packed her suitcase and backpack and looked around the cabin. From the front door, you couldn't see that anything was amiss. She smiled, locked the door and headed for her car.

CHAPTER SIX

The home invasion team had watched the house for the past couple days, and they decided that the time was right. The dossier their stepmom had put together was thorough, and they found no anomalies. The team didn't understand how she'd gotten all the information, and they never asked. They knew she'd spent a significant part of her life working for the government. They each knew their assignments, and all they had to do was execute the plan.

The family they had been watching followed the same schedule every night. Dinner at six, then there was an hour of homework, and then they all moved into the den for two hours of family time. Tonight was movie night; the lights in the rest of the house went off, and the reflection of the big-screen TV could be seen through the blackout drapes covering the family room windows.

The team figured they would give the family an hour and then make their move. They put on their one-piece spandex suits, placed the hoods over their heads, strapped on their weapons belts and covered the entire outfit with black nylon windbreakers. They looked like ninjas or an elite commando unit, and even though there were only three of them, they were as highly trained as any commando unit.

An hour after sunset, they were ready to make their move. Jessie pulled out her laptop and tapped into the family's digital assistant; she could hear the movie in the background. Typing in the code her stepmom had given her, she asked the digital assistant to turn off all the perimeter alarms and also disconnect the panic buttons. Her final task was to tap into the Sheriff's Office dispatch center and check to make sure she hadn't triggered any silent alarms. Everything was ready.

The team left their nest in the woods and made their way across the field behind the house to the patio door that was on the opposite side of the house from the family room. Slipping out his lockpick set, Earl went to work on the lockset, and within fifteen seconds, the door was unlocked. He slipped the tools back in his jacket pocket and slid open the door.

They waited for a minute to make sure there wasn't a dog they might have missed. Confident that they were good, they walked through the house, pushed open the door to the family room, flipped on the lights and charged into the room with pistols drawn.

The family responded like all the other families had. First, there was confusion, then a sense of fear and finally screams, as Earl and Toby grabbed the father and mother and threw them to the floor.

"What the fuck do you want?" shouted the father as he tried to reach his daughter and son, who were now being held at gunpoint.

"Take what you want, but please don't hurt my children," said the mother. The brothers sat on top of the father, bound his hands behind his back and slipped the gag into his mouth.

Jessie always found it funny that the mother was willing to give up her treasures to save her children, but there was never any mention of saving her husband. She hated these rich fucks, and after she left their houses, she always felt like she needed a shower. She looked over and watched Earl tie the kids to straight-back kitchen chairs they'd carried into the room. Her other brother, Toby, picked up the mother, set her down on the third chair and duct-taped her to it. Jessie could see the fear in the mother's eyes as she repeatedly turned her head to look at the kids. The kids looked petrified.

They positioned all the chairs in a square in the middle of the room and turned down the volume on the movie. Jessie stood watching the movie for a second and then turned to the mother.

"I love this movie," she said. "I hope your kids will still love it after we leave." The two brothers left the room and fanned out through the house. They knew exactly where to find the most expensive jewelry and rare paintings. The family's art collection was impressive. She figured being the CEO of an internet data security company paid well. She also laughed at how easily their stepmom had cracked Mr. Bigshit's home security system.

The brothers walked back into the family room and set down their now-bulging duffel bags. Toby walked out of the room and headed out of the house to get their SUV, which was parked nearby on a side road.

"Did you get the keys?" she asked Earl.

"They were not in the locked drawer in his office. Couldn't find them anywhere," he said.

She walked over to the father and ripped off the duct tape that was holding the gag in his mouth. The gag was soaked, and as she pulled it from his mouth he spit and sputtered.

"Where are the keys?" she asked.

She could see the defiance in his eyes, and he refused to answer. She pulled out her black semi-automatic pistol and rested it on his shoulder.

"Let's try this again. Where are the keys?"

"Fuck you." She was amazed at how calmly he said it. "You don't scare me with this macho bullshit. I will make sure they throw the book at you."

She looked him straight in the eyes and walked over to the mother. She started unbuttoning the mother's blouse, exposing her lacy bra. She could see the fear in the mother's eyes.

"I am going to have my two helpers rape your wife and then your daughter. She's, what? Sixteen? I'll bet she's still a virgin. My boys are going to change that. Now, where are the keys?"

"Fuck you, bitch. I don't have to tell you anything."

She looked at her brother, and he saw something he had never seen before. There was anger in her eyes, and she walked over and hit the father with the butt of her gun, creating a bloody gash across his forehead. She could hear the mother and the children scream into their gags. She looked around the room and spotted what she wanted on a nearby table. She grabbed the metal bowl, dumped out the popcorn and walked over to the father.

"One more chance. Where are the keys?"

He was about to speak when she slammed the side of his head with the metal bowl. Her anger welled up, and she hit him twice more with the bowl. Her brother stood there stunned, as blood flew all over the marble floor.

"Where are the keys?" She hit him again with the bowl. Blood covered the side of his head, and he leered at her.

"Fuck you, bitch. Do you know who I am?"

She hit him once again with the bowl. "Not only do I know who you are, I know what you are. You're a rapist and a sexual abuser."

She hit him twice more and grabbed his shirt. "You think you're a big man because you hurt your wife. Let's see how you like it." She hit him several more times, and his eyes rolled back in his head. His face was a bloody mess, and his head lolled forward, his chin resting on his chest. The floor around the chair was covered in blood.

After a few minutes, her brother walked over and stopped her before she killed him, pulling the metal bowl out of her hand. The mother was bouncing up and down, still strapped to the chair. She walked over to the mother and ripped out the gag.

With tears in her eyes, the mother said, "Please don't hit him anymore. I will tell you where the keys are, just don't hurt him any-more."

She told them where to find the safe in the garage, and Earl walked out to check to see if she was telling the truth. Jessie shoved the gag back in the mother's mouth and stood there pointing her gun at her head.

Toby walked in, looked at the blood all over his sister and saw the unconscious man lying on the floor in a pool of blood.

"Holy shit. What the hell happened?"

"He got in my face, so I took care of him."

He walked over and checked the father's neck for a pulse. He nodded that he found one when Earl walked in with the keys.

"Got them. Let's get out of here. We are over our time."

The brothers grabbed the duffel bags and headed for the garage. Jessie looked around the room to make sure they hadn't missed anything, and then she walked over to the mother, who pulled back out of fear. She leaned down and looked at the mother.

"Your husband is an ass. Everything we took is covered by insurance, but he wanted to sound tough. He is also an abuser, and he has raped you several times. You don't have to stay and put up with that shit anymore. Now, I don't know if he is going to survive or not, and I really don't care. He got what he deserved. You know it, and I know it. We are leaving. We have been monitoring your house for a week and will continue to monitor it until we are safely away. If you try to break free, we will come back, and we will kill your entire family. Once we are safe, we will alert the authorities and have them send an ambulance."

She turned and walked out of the room. The duffel bags were sitting in the back of their SUV, which sat in the driveway next to a shiny blue 2019 McLaren Senna. Her brothers slid into the SUV and started down the driveway. She climbed into the McLaren, fired it up and sat there for a minute, listening to the car purr. She could feel the incredible power between her legs. She pulled off her balaclava, let down her long blond hair, put the car in gear and hit the gas.

CHAPTER SEVEN

Buck Taylor stood on the flagstone veranda outside the family room of an incredible mansion. He estimated that the stone patio was twice the size of his entire house. He looked across the field towards the forest on the other side. The property was huge. In the distance, he could see the green tracks that indicated the ski runs of the Telluride Ski Resort. Soon winter would arrive, and those green tracks would be snow-covered. He turned away from the view as he heard footsteps behind him on the flagstones.

San Miguel County Sheriff Matt Anderson stepped through the multi-panel sliding wall and walked up to Buck.

"Crime scene techs will be done in a few minutes, and then we can go in." He took in the view Buck had been looking at. "Hell of a place, huh? Must have cost a fortune."

"Yeah, but what do you do with all that ground? There isn't a horse or cow in sight. Not an outbuilding to be seen. Kind of a waste."

The sheriff laughed. "These kinds of folks

don't raise livestock. They control all this acreage because they can. It's all about power and the money it takes to buy it, and you know what all that power gets them?"

"Yeah," said Buck. "They become targets for anyone who wants to take it away from them."

The sheriff nodded.

"Tell me about the family," said Buck.

Colorado Bureau of Investigation agent Buck Taylor wasn't an imposing figure, but when Buck was on the crime scene, there was little doubt to anyone around who was in charge. At six feet tall and one hundred eighty-five pounds, Buck was in the best shape of his life. He still looked like he could play football for the Gunnison High School Cowboys, where he and his brother-in-law, Hardy Braxton, were once called the Wrecking Crew, and where they'd broken pretty much every state high school defensive record there was, some of which still stood today.

He wore his salt-and-pepper hair, which had a lot more salt than pepper in it, longer than the style of the day, and considerably longer than when his wife of thirty-four years, Lucy, was still alive. Today he wore a short Carhartt ranch jacket over a T-shirt and jeans. He had the jacket zipped up two-thirds of the way to hold off the chill from the cool north wind. Fall was in the air this morning, and the snow wouldn't be far behind.

The sheriff pulled out his notebook. Buck always felt better when he saw someone else who used a pen and paper instead of a tablet to take notes. He was known around the CBI office in Grand Junction as a technological dinosaur, and he considered himself lucky that his grandkids could help out when he did something to screw up the TV remote.

"The father is Henry Claremont. The mother is Theresa. Claremont is the founder and CEO of Pegasus Data Security. According to Forbes, he is worth about eight hundred million dollars. They bought the land and built this house ten years ago. He also owns several buildings in Telluride. The kids are Michael, age ten, and Sandra, age sixteen."

Buck didn't ask for the details of the case. He liked to walk through a crime scene for the first time unencumbered by the thoughts and opinions of others. It was a process that had worked well for him throughout his thirty-six years in law enforcement.

The sheriff was about to continue reading his notes when a tall, dark-skinned forensic tech wearing a white Tyvek suit and hood stepped out of the patio door and pulled off his surgical mask.

"You're good to go, Buck. We have everything

we need," he said.

"Thanks, Franklin. Any usable prints?"

Franklin Williams was the lead forensic tech for CBI; he'd been assigned to a series of home invasions Buck and his team had been investigating for the past four weeks. So far, the perps hadn't left any fingerprints or DNA at any of the scenes, which was frustrating everyone.

"We ran elimination prints on the family, and we got the dad's prints off a bourbon bottle in his office. The daughter told us he was the only one who touched the bottle. We found two sets of unidentified prints, but there are two housekeepers that work alternate weeks. We'll run them through the system and see if anything pops, but we pretty much got nothing, again."

Buck could sense Franklin's frustration. He was feeling the same way himself. He asked Franklin to have the State Crime Lab put a rush on the samples and told him they could clear out. He nodded to the sheriff, and they stepped through the sliding doors and walked into a bloody mess, literally.

The first thing Buck noticed was the four kitchen chairs sitting in a square in the family room. They still had remnants of duct tape and plastic wire ties hanging off the arms and around the front legs. He stepped carefully around all the blood that had accumulated under one of the chairs. This must have been the chair the father was sitting in. From the amount of blood on the floor, Buck could tell that he was seriously injured.

Buck used his cell phone to take a series of pictures of the chairs, the blood and some close-ups of the tape and wire ties. These would be entered into his crime file once he had a chance to open his laptop. CBI had gone digital a couple years back, so instead of having a blue binder for each case, Buck just had to open a program on his laptop. The new case was automatically assigned a case number, and Buck would list everyone who needed access to the file and send them email invites. All evidence, lab reports, photos, etc. that were part of the case would be uploaded into the file, and anyone who needed access just had to open the file. This was a lot better than the old system where everything was placed in the binder by hand, and Buck would spend half his time trying to track down who had the binder.

For a tech dinosaur like Buck, this made his life so much easier, and he had ready access to anything he needed.

Buck walked through each room of the house and paid close attention to the rooms where items had been stolen. He stepped into the master bedroom and noticed the safe room door sitting open. The door appeared to be part of a bookcase and looked like it was usually closed, but the perps seemed to know where it was and how it opened. Inside he found several shelves with empty slots that at one time held expensive watches. The two jewelry drawers were open and empty as well. Buck made a note on his pad to get a list of everything that was missing from the insurance company. He also wanted to check and see if the cameras he'd noticed throughout the house and the safe room might have captured images of the perps. Whoever these home invaders were, they knew what they were looking for, and they'd taken only the expensive stuff and left the rest behind.

Stepping out of the safe room, Buck noticed the two lighter areas on the walls in the bedroom where pictures should have been. He photographed these and made a note to find out if these had been pictures or paintings.

His final stop was the garage. The safe behind the toolbox was open and empty. There was a hook inside that Buck assumed, at one time, held the key to the missing car. He stood for a minute and looked around the garage. For an amateur car enthusiast, Henry had the space better equipped than the garage and gas station Buck's dad had owned when he was growing up, and his dad had been a professional auto mechanic all his life.

Buck looked out the open garage door and down the driveway.

"How do you get a car like that down the driveway without anyone in the area noticing it? The car had to make a lot of noise," he said to no one in particular.

"You don't," came a disembodied voice from the other side of the garage.

Buck stepped around an MG Spider that was sitting on the lift in the next bay. "Who are you?" he asked the short, dark-haired man in the stained gray jumpsuit, who was removing the front tire from the car.

The man set the tire on the ground, wiped his hands on a dirty rag he pulled from his pocket and stepped up to Buck with his right hand extended.

"Roger Spearman, but everyone calls me Rocket. Pleased to meet you." He shook Buck's hand. "I'm Mr. Claremont's mechanic."

Buck started to say something, then he stopped and stared at the mechanic. "Rocket Spearman, the former NASCAR driver?"

"One and the same," said Rocket.

"I remember your crash in ninety-seven at Daytona. Everyone thought you were dead. How long have you been with Claremont?"

Rocket thought for a minute. "About five years. That's when he bought his first sports car. I keep all his cars running in top-notch condition.

It's a shame about the McLaren. Too bad I wasn't here, or I'd have given those thieves what's for."

"Tell me about the car, I'm told it was expensive."

Rocket dug out his phone and pulled up his gallery app. He handed the phone to Buck. "Expensive ain't the half of it. Mr. C paid over a million bucks for that car. It was going to be the centerpiece of his collection. We'll never see that car again."

"Is there a market for a car like that?"

Rocket put his phone away. "Sure as hell is. Cars like that, they only make a couple hundred, if that many. I'm told there are folks in Asia and the Middle East that will pay serious money to get their hands on one. That car is probably already on a boat heading out to sea."

Buck made a couple notes in his notebook. "Do you live on the property?"

"Nah. The Mrs. and I have an apartment in Telluride. Last night we were home. The sheriff called me this morning when they got the call about the break-in, and I came over to check on the family and make sure nothing was stolen. My heart sank when I saw that the McLaren was gone. Damn shame about Mr. C getting beat up. Wish I would have been here to stop the bastards."

Buck thanked Rocket and went in search of the sheriff, who met him at the entrance to the house.

"I see you met Rocket," said the sheriff. "I have the kids sitting in the kitchen, figured you'd want to talk to them next."

"Any word on the father?"

"Flight for Life took him to St. Mary's Medical Center in Grand Junction. It's the closest trauma center. He's in surgery, and his wife is with him. He took a hell of a beating."

"How come they didn't take him to a Level One trauma hospital in Denver? St. Mary's is a Level Three."

"They weren't sure he would survive the trip, and St. Mary's has one of the best neurosurgeons in the country."

Buck nodded, and they walked towards the kitchen to talk to the kids. Ten-year-old Michael had his face in a video game and headphones on. His sister, Sandra, was sitting on the floor with her back against the cabinet, her legs pulled close to her chest.

Buck tapped Michael on the shoulder, and the kid almost jumped out of his seat. Buck asked him to turn off the game for a minute. He set the game on the table next to him.

"Michael, my name is Buck, and I'm going to

try to find the people who hurt your dad, but I'm going to need your help. Can you tell me what happened?"

Michael looked like he would rather be any-place else than sitting there with Buck. He squirmed and shifted in his seat and poked at his game tablet. When he spoke, his voice was low, and Buck had to listen carefully to hear him. There were also tears and sniffles.

He told Buck about the people in black clothes who came into the house while they were watching the movie, and about watching the girl beat up his dad with a popcorn bowl. Buck asked him if he could describe the people, and he said they had on masks. He did mention that the girl talked like his Uncle Mike, but he couldn't really explain what he meant. By this time, Sandra, still crying, had joined them at the table and had her arm around her little brother.

"The girl had a Southern accent," she said. "Our Uncle Mike lives in Louisiana. Her accent wasn't as heavy as his. More soft and gentle. She seemed to be the one in charge, because she ordered the other guys around, and she was the one who beat my dad." Tears flowed down her face, and Buck handed her a paper towel off the roll on the island.

Buck made notes in his notebook and asked them if there was anything else they could remember about the attack.

"The alarms didn't go off," said Sandra.

"Do you know if the alarms were set?" Buck asked.

"The system is automatic. Once 7 P.M. chimes, the entire house locks down. Dad set it up that way so we wouldn't have to remember to set it. We each have our own access code."

She led Buck over to a console on the wall and punched a couple buttons, bringing up a history page. Buck looked where she was pointing. According to the alarm history, the system armed automatically at 7 P.M. every night, like she said, but at seven forty-five the night before, someone had entered a code and deactivated the alarm.

"That's not one of our code numbers," she said.

Buck wrote the code number down and took a picture of the console. He then pushed a button on his phone and waited for the person on the other end to answer.

"Hey, Buck. What's up?"

"Hey, Bax, I'm sending you a picture of the alarm console. Can you contact the alarm company and see who might have entered the last code at seven forty-five? According to the daughter, the number does not belong to anyone she knows."

"Sure thing, Buck. I'll get right on it."

"Thanks, Bax. I'll call you in a little bit."

Buck hung up. "Good work, Sandra. This could help us out a lot."

"What's a rapist?" They both turned and looked at Michael, and the sheriff stepped away from the door and stood next to him.

"Where did you hear that word?" asked Buck.

Michael looked embarrassed, and he hung his head as if he'd done something wrong. Sandra looked at Buck.

"The woman said it to my mom before they left. She said my dad was a rapist and an abuser." Tears flowed like water. "Why would she say that? Our dad loves us."

The sheriff tapped Buck on the shoulder and nodded for him to follow. Buck left Sandra with her arms wrapped around her brother. Out of earshot, the sheriff pulled out his phone and opened a message.

"This came in on my private email account about ten minutes after we received the nine-one-one call about the break-in." He pushed play, and Buck held the phone up to his ear. A deep furrow formed across Buck's forehead as he listened to the call. He took the phone away from his ear.

"The email message said it was recorded at

this location this past weekend, while the kids were staying at a friend's house. That sure sounds like a rape to me, and those voices are definitely the Claremonts'."

Buck played the message one more time. "Do me a favor and forward that to my email. You know these folks. Do you think what we heard is possible?"

The sheriff thought for a minute. "I've been in this business a long time, and I have come to believe that anything is possible. What troubles me is, if this is true, how did someone get a recording of it, and where did they get my private email address?"

"Good questions, for which I have no answer right now," said Buck. "These kids going to be all right here alone?"

"Rocket and his wife are going to take care of the kids until their grandfather can get here."

Buck handed the phone back to the sheriff when his own phone rang. He looked at the number, frowned and put the phone back in his pocket.

"Look, Buck. I read the reports on two of the other break-ins. The physical violence went way up on this one. You think it's the same group?"

"Everything else fits, Matt, except for the violence. This team has no trouble terrorizing their victims during the attack, but they have never hurt anyone. I hope this isn't an escalation."

Buck thanked the sheriff for his help and headed for his car. His mind was wrapped around the violence he'd heard on the sheriff's phone.

CHAPTER EIGHT

B uck drove away from the house, followed Raspberry Patch Road and turned onto Route 145, heading towards Telluride. He was hoping to get to Grand Junction today so he could interview Theresa Claremont. The voice recording from the sheriff's phone played heavy on his mind. He was hoping he could get her to talk with him about what had happened. He also thought more about how the perps had gotten hold of the voice recording in the first place.

A mile or so north of Telluride, Route 145 took a hard left turn, and Buck headed north. His phone rang, and he frowned as he pulled it from his pocket. Recognizing the number, he answered.

"Hey, Hank. What's up?"

Hank Clancy, the special agent in charge of the Denver office of the FBI, barely let him finish.

"Where are you?"

Buck saw the sign for the Telluride airport. "Just passing the Telluride airport. Why?"

"Good. Pull in and wait at the fixed base operator there. I'm sending a helicopter for you."

Before Buck could answer, Hank hung up. Buck wondered what this was all about, but he knew if Hank was diverting a helicopter to pick him up, it must be important. Hank was a straight shooter and a consummate professional when it came to his duties with the FBI.

Buck pulled onto the road to the airport and climbed the hill to the parking lot. He found a space outside the FBO and pulled in. Telluride Regional Airport sat on the top of a mesa, north of the town of Telluride. In the early days, the local pilots called it the USS Telluride because landing at the airport was like landing on an aircraft carrier. There were steep drop-offs at both ends of the runway, so your approach had to be perfect, and you didn't want to miss it and have to abort your landing because the end of the runway took you straight into a box canyon. Landing at this airport was always an adventure.

Buck pulled out his phone and called Bax. CBI agent Ashley Baxter worked with Buck on a lot of interesting cases, in between working on her own cases. At thirty years old, she was one of the youngest agents in the Grand Junction Field Office, and she valued the time she got to spend with Buck because she learned so much about running an investigation. Bax was also a whiz at doing deep background searches, a talent Buck did not share, so he relied on Bax to help him out. They worked well as a team and had found themselves collaborating more and more as the years rolled by.

Bax answered on the second ring. "What's up, Buck?"

"Hey, Bax. You in the middle of anything right now?"

"No," she said. "I'm waiting for a call back from the alarm company. What can I do for you?"

Buck explained about the short, cryptic call he'd gotten from Hank Clancy. "I was planning on interviewing the wife today, but now, with this, I am not going to be able to get to St. Mary's, and I have no idea when I will be back."

"No worries, Buck. I can cover the interview. What do you think is up with Hank?"

"Not sure, Bax. I'm wondering if it has something to do with Alicia Hawkins."

"You think they found her, and he wants you in on the bust? Wouldn't that be great?"

"Don't know. Listen, Bax. Something else. I am sending you an audio recording the sheriff received. Listen to the audio and then call me back and let's talk about it."

Buck hung up, pulled up the email and forwarded it to Bax. He grabbed his backpack off the back seat and checked to make sure he had a change of clothes and his laptop. He was closing his bag when Bax called back.

"Oh, my god, Buck. Is that what I think it is?"

"The sheriff and I both think so, which means my going on a trip might be a good thing. I hate to put this on you, but a woman doing the interview might be less embarrassing for her."

"That's not a problem, Buck. How do you want me to handle it?"

"We need to know if the recording is real and if that is her and her husband. If it is, we need to try to figure out how the perps got the recording. We also need her thoughts on what happened last night. You okay with all this?"

"You can count on me, Buck."

Buck smiled at the phone. "Of that, there was no doubt, Bax."

"Buck, you might want to call Jane and see if she can meet me there. Mrs. Claremont might need some moral support."

"Great minds, Bax. She's my next call. I will call you once I know where I am headed with Hank. And Bax. Thanks."

"Travel safe, Buck."

Buck hung up and looked at his watch. He had a few minutes until the helicopter arrived, so he hit another speed dial button and waited.

"Judge Morgan's chambers, Janelle speaking. How may I help you?"

"Hey, Janelle, it's Buck. Is the judge in?"

"Hi, Agent Taylor, please hold on for a second, and I will see." Buck liked talking to Janelle. For someone so young, she was very poised and professional on the phone, and equally so in person. Of course, at Buck's age, everyone seemed young.

"Hiya, Buck," said Judge Morgan. "What can I do for you on this fine day?"

"Well, today, I need to talk to Jane, not the judge."

Judge Jane Morgan, besides being a municipal court judge for Grand Junction, was also the chairwoman of a family trust that helped counsel and find housing and services for women and children that were on the receiving end of sexual violence. With the help of her husband, they had set up a safe house outside Grand Junction and had gathered together a staff of volunteers who were willing to work with these women and children to find the help they needed.

Buck explained the situation with Mrs. Claremont, and the judge listened without interrupting. When Buck stopped to take a breath, she said, "Buck, forward me the audio file. I want to hear it myself."

Buck forwarded the file for the second time

and waited while the judge put him on hold. A couple minutes went by, and Buck checked his watch. He heard the helicopter in the distance, and he was about to hang up when the judge came back on the line.

"Buck, if this is real, this woman is going to need our help. I have one more case to hear this afternoon, and I will head over to the hospital to meet Bax as soon as I'm done. Don't worry about a thing. Bax and I can handle this."

The sound of the helicopter was loud as it settled onto the tarmac behind Buck. He covered his one ear and turned away from the craft.

"Jane, I have to run. You're the best. Thanks."

Buck hung up and put his phone back in his pocket, picked his backpack off the ground and headed to the helicopter and his flight into the unknown.

CHAPTER NINE

The copilot handed Buck a headset as he climbed aboard and pointed to a console on the bulkhead behind the seat, indicating where he could plug in the end.

"Welcome aboard, Agent Taylor. There's water and a couple sandwiches in the cooler next to your feet. Agent Clancy wasn't sure if you had eaten. We will be in the air for about an hour and a half. If you need anything, hit the red button on the mic."

"Where are we heading?" asked Buck.

"Oklahoma. Agent Clancy will fill you in once we arrive. Please sit back and enjoy the flight."

Buck grabbed a bottle of water and what looked like a roast beef and cheddar sandwich out of the cooler and sat back as the pilot lifted off. He had never been a big fan of flying, especially in helicopters. He didn't like the noise and the vibration, except this helicopter was much quieter than the ones he'd flown in during his time in the army. Surprisingly, he dozed off about halfway through the flight and only snapped awake when the pilot touched down on a road in the middle of nowhere. The last vestiges of daylight were fading over the horizon as he stepped out of the helicopter and looked around. All Buck could see for miles in any direction were yellow fields.

A black FBI SUV was parked along the paved road about a hundred feet from the helicopter, so Buck headed in that direction. A tall, fair-skinned FBI agent with short blond hair stepped out of the car and opened the rear door. He extended his hand.

"Agent Taylor, Agent Tom Corwin. Please climb in, and we can be on our way."

"Nice to meet you, Tom. Please call me Buck." He looked around. "Where in the hell are we?" he asked.

"We're about twenty minutes from the location. Agent Clancy will explain everything when we get there."

Buck slid his backpack across the back seat, shut the door and climbed into the front seat. Agent Corwin pulled off the shoulder and headed west until he reached a dirt road in a wooded area that seemed to appear out of nowhere. After fifteen minutes of driving on the bumpy road, Buck saw, in the distance, the flashing lights of emergency vehicles. He could make out the outline of a decent-sized lake in the distance.

The SUV pulled behind several other black SUVs, and Buck opened the door, grabbed his backpack and slid out. He was standing in front of a log cabin, colored gray from prolonged exposure to the hot sun. The cabin was lit up like an amusement park, but he sensed that nothing about this scene was going to be amusing.

Agent Corwin directed him towards the front entrance, so Buck slung his backpack over his left shoulder and headed for the door. Hank Clancy stepped out of the front door as Buck approached. The two men shook hands. Buck noticed how tired Hank looked. It had been a while since they had seen each other in person, and Hank looked thin and drawn.

"Sorry about all the cloak-and-dagger stuff, Buck. We're trying to keep this low profile."

"What's going on, Hank? From the number of cars in the lot and the number of suits I see, I'm betting this has something to do with Alicia Hawkins."

Hank led Buck into the cabin. At first glance, it was a warm, cozy cabin with rustic wood furnishings and several good-sized fish mounted on planks of old barn wood and hung on the walls. This was obviously a well-cared-for property.

Hank spoke as they started down a hallway towards, what Buck assumed, were a couple bedrooms.

"The cabin belongs to Jack Pendleton. Been in his family for years. He rents it out on one of those vacation rentals by owner websites. Sight unseen, I might add. He never sees the tenant or has any personal contact with them. Everything is done online. Two weeks ago, he rented it to a woman named Susan Carson. She gave him a credit card number in that name, and the deposit went through with no issues. A week later, he collected the rest of the fee for the one-week rental. Susan Carson requested no cleaning service for the week she was here, which was fine with the owner since it saved him a lot of money. This morning the cleaners showed up and discovered a mess."

Hank stepped aside and let Buck walk into the bedroom. The first thing Buck noticed was the smell. Had it not been cold the last couple days, Buck imagined the smell would be a lot worse. The body was lying naked and exposed on the blood-soaked bed. There was blood on the walls, and the carpet was soaked with blood. There were bloody footprints heading into the bathroom connected to the bedroom. Buck looked inside the bathroom as they passed, and there was blood everywhere.

Buck stepped up to the bed as one of the FBI evidence techs stepped aside. His expression said it all.

"This is a male," he said. "If Alicia Hawkins

did this, she's stepped up her game. I'm gonna assume the cause of death is exsanguination. It looks like she drained every ounce of blood this poor kid had. There are also a lot more cuts than the last case." He looked at Hank. "She's getting better at this. She's keeping them alive longer while she slices. How long?"

"Medical examiner figures three, four days max," said Hank.

"One more thing you need to see before we leave this body. Go ahead and turn him over, Doc."

The medical examiner and his assistant reached across the body and turned it on its side. Buck had no problem seeing through all the blood. Carved into the young man's back was Buck's name.

"There doesn't seem to be any doubt who did this, Buck. She left you a message," said Hank.

Buck stared at his name carved in the young man's back. He had no idea why she would single him out, but there was no doubt she had.

Buck nodded. "You said 'before we leave this body.' Is there another?"

Hank led Buck out of the bedroom and down a flight of stairs at the end of the hall that led to a finished basement. The scene here was almost as bad. The walls and floors were covered in blood, with the same bare footsteps leading into another bathroom, this one also covered in blood. The young woman hanging from two chains screwed into the wall, with her feet shackled, dangled like a butchered piece of meat in a slaughterhouse. The look in her clouded-over eyes told of a horrible death.

"Fuck, Hank. Two in one week. How many does this make?"

"Thirteen and fourteen, if everything we found so far is hers." Hank turned and headed up the stairs.

Hank and Buck stepped out onto the front porch and watched as the ME's gurney was lifted into the back of a hearse.

"Any identity so far on either body?" asked Buck.

"Not so far. We've only been here for seven hours. What do you make of her carving your name into the male victim?"

Buck thought for a minute. "I think she is sending me a message that this is not over yet. Maybe she's blaming me for sending her down this road. Who the hell knows with crazies like her?"

"You don't think it's a warning that she's coming after you? Maybe I need to get you protection," said Hank.

Buck looked at him with an intensity Hank hadn't seen before. "Don't even think about sending your agents to watch over me. I've got too much going on right now, and I don't need your people in my way."

"What about your family? You should, at the very least, tell them to watch their backs."

"My kids can all take care of themselves, but if it keeps you off my back, I will send them her picture and let them know to be careful with strangers."

Hank held up his hand in surrender. "Okay, Buck, but watch your ass, and if you see her, you make sure you call me. We're going to be here for another day or two before we regroup in Denver and see if we can figure out her next move. You get any thoughts, give me a call. Corwin will drive you back to the chopper."

Buck shook hands with Hank and headed back to the SUV. He slid onto the seat and didn't look back as they headed back to where the helicopter was parked. Buck thanked Corwin and climbed aboard the helicopter. He put on his headset and was asleep before they were airborne. Buck had been threatened before and would handle this threat the same way he'd handled all the others. He would do his job, and when the time and the opportunity presented itself, he would arrest Alicia Hawkins.

CHAPTER TEN

Ashley Baxter walked up to the front desk at St. Mary's Hospital, and the same thing happened that always happened when Bax walked into a room. Men noticed her, at least until they saw the badge and gun that were clipped to her belt. Bax wasn't supermodel gorgeous, but she would be considered pretty by most people's standards. She had long blond hair that she wore in a ponytail that hung through the back of her CBI cap and amazing jade-green eyes.

She had a nice figure—not thin, but not heavy either. What used to be called a "mountain girl" figure. A little stocky, but with curves in all the right places. She carried herself with the grace of an athlete, and she moved with a certain fluidness that came from being a track star in college and years of running marathons with her dad. She stepped up to the desk, flashed her badge and asked where she could find the Claremonts. She was directed down the hall to the surgical waiting area. She was told that Henry Claremont was still in surgery. She thanked the volunteer at the desk and headed down the hallway.

She found Theresa Claremont sitting all alone in the empty waiting room, staring into space, the tear stains on her cheeks marking the passage of time. She looked up as Bax entered the room, surely wishing instead that it was the doctor coming to tell her that Henry was going to be all right. She gave Bax a half-hearted smile and went back to staring at the wall. Bax sat down next to her and opened her cred pack, so Theresa could see her CBI identification card. She slid the wallet back into her back pocket.

"Mrs. Claremont, I'm Ashley Baxter with the Colorado Bureau of Investigation. First, I want to tell you how sorry I am about what you are going through. A situation like this is never easy. We are investigating the home invasion at your place, and I'd like to ask you a few questions while things are still fresh in your mind. Would that be okay?"

Theresa Claremont gave her a tiny nod.

"If at any time this becomes too much for you, let me know, and we can stop and sit for a while. Can you tell me what you remember about last night?"

Bax sat back in the chair and let Theresa Claremont tell her story in her own way. Sometimes she would go on for a while talking with clarity, and then she would stop, the tears would flow and the conversation would lag. Bax didn't mind. One of the things she'd learned from working with Buck all these years was patience. On several occasions, she'd watched Buck sit in an interrogation room for hours with a suspect and never say a word. Just sit there and stare off into space. Never ask a question or even talk to the suspect, just sit there. She was amazed at how often the suspect would blurt out a confession just to break up the silence. Buck was the best interrogator she had ever seen, and patience was a huge part of his success.

Theresa Claremont was able to confirm the information Buck had gotten from the children. She did remember the southern accent, and she agreed with her daughter's assessment that it wasn't harsh like her brother-in-law's accent but was smooth and soft. She agreed that the woman seemed to be in charge, and she didn't understand why the woman had given her husband such a beating. She confirmed that her husband did mouth off to the woman and called her a bitch at one point. The tears began to flow.

Bax held off on asking about the audiotape Buck had sent her. Instead, she asked Theresa a series of conversational questions. Nothing about the case, but about her family and her life in Telluride. After a while, the conversation seemed to get more relaxed, and Theresa started to get comfortable talking to her. She was trying to figure out how to broach the subject of the tape when Judge Morgan walked into the room.

Bax stood up and met Jane at the door, and they shook hands.

"Hey, Bax, how are you doing?"

"Good, Jane. Nice to see you. I've been sitting here with Theresa, having a nice conversation about her family. Maybe you could sit with her for a while, so I can make some phone calls and see how her children are doing?"

Jane smiled. She was wearing jeans, a flannel shirt and boots, and she looked nothing like a judge, which was what she'd hoped for. Right now, she was just Jane and was here to help. Her petite figure and amazing smile helped her look younger than she should after almost thirty years on the bench.

Jane had listened to the tape a second and third time on the way over from the courthouse, and she knew what information Buck needed for his case. Her priority, however, was to help the victim, and even though she wasn't acting in her capacity as a municipal judge or as an attorney, she still held herself to a higher standard, and that included confidentiality. Buck knew, when he involved her in his cases, that she would invoke attorney-client privilege to protect the victim. She would do her best to get the victim to a point where she would feel comfortable telling Buck her story, but she would never tell

Buck anything confidential without the victim's consent. Buck accepted that, and in all these years, he had never crossed that line.

Jane watched Bax walk down the hall and then sat down next to Theresa Claremont and introduced herself. At first, their conversation was very casual and was designed to help Theresa relax. At one point, the surgeon came out, dressed in his light blue scrubs, and sat down next to Theresa. Jane offered to leave, but Theresa grabbed her hand.

The surgeon told her that they had repaired as much of the damage to Henry's brain as they could. He would know more once the swelling went down, which could take a few hours or a few days. He told her that if her husband survived the next forty-eight hours, his chances of surviving would improve dramatically, but there was still a chance that he would suffer some brain damage. How much, there was no way of knowing, until he came out of the coma. He said that her husband would be in recovery for a couple of hours, and then they would take him to intensive care. She would be able to see him there.

The doctor put his hand on her shoulder and told her that he was available if she needed him. He bid them both a good night and walked back towards the surgical area.

Jane sat with Theresa and held her for a while until she sensed that Theresa might be ready to talk. She started the conversation slowly and ran into the same resistance she usually got from abuse victims. Nothing had happened. Her husband would never. People didn't know. Their marriage was a happy one. Lots of love. Jane had heard it all before over the twenty years that she and her husband had run the shelter. She listened and let Theresa talk and argue and cry, and then she played the tape for her. Theresa sat there, stunned, and all of a sudden, she started to tell Jane a story, and it all came out, every lurid detail. When she was finished, she sat back, exhausted, and closed her eyes. She had never told anyone the story before.

Jane pulled out her phone, called Bax and asked her to come back to the waiting room. And to bring some coffee.

CHAPTER ELEVEN

PIS pushed through the back door of the Celtic Club, one of his favorite bars, and stepped into the alley between East Hopkins Avenue and East Hyman Avenue. As he let the door close behind him, he looked up and down the alley. It was late, and the alley was deserted. There was a fall chill in the air, and he felt warmed by the nightly glass of brandy he had just finished in the bar. He buttoned his linen coat, snugged down his black beret and turned up his collar against the chilly breeze. It was a beautiful night, and the sky was full of stars.

PIS had lived in Aspen for the past twenty-some years and was considered one of its most colorful characters, in a city filled with colorful characters. Everyone in Aspen either had heard of or knew PIS, except that no one really knew much about him. PIS was tall, about six feet two and gangly, as folks used to say. He probably weighed one hundred fifty pounds soaking wet. He had long gray hair pulled back in a ponytail, piercing gray eyes and a three-day growth of stubble on his face. The odd thing was, no matter what day or time you encountered PIS, his stubble was always the same. It never seemed to grow out or look untidy.

Unlike most of the homeless characters in town, PIS never smelled like a homeless person. He wore the same clothes every day but never looked dirty or unkempt. His outfit hadn't changed in over twenty years. He wore calf-height brown leather lace-up moccasin-style boots, light gray tuxedo pants with a dark gray stripe down each leg and a worn white dress shirt, frayed and yellow with age. Around his waist, he wore a bright red cummerbund, and around his neck, he wore a bright red ascot.

No matter what time of year or what the temperature was, PIS always wore the same tattered brown linen coat and a black beret. He looked rather elegant for a homeless person. His only other possession was a well-worn leather backpack that looked like it had traveled the world. The initials p.i.s. were stamped on the flap, and since no one knew his name, everyone called him PIS, which he never seemed to mind. His demeanor was always jovial and friendly, and no one ever complained about feeling threatened by his presence. Most striking was his British accent. Not the harsh Cockney accent you associate with street people, but a silky smooth accent that exuded sophistication.

No one ever saw him panhandling for money, yet he always seemed to have enough to visit one of the local pubs for his nightly glass of brandy. As it turned out, PIS also had an incredible talent, which helped him generate some income on a regular basis. PIS was an amazing tracker. There wasn't anything he couldn't find, whether it be an animal or a missing child, and his abilities had come to the attention of many of the local hunting guides, who paid him a daily fee to help them find game for their out-of-town clients. PIS's tracking skills had also come to the attention of the local police and sheriff, and over the years, he had been involved in finding many lost hikers or missing persons in the rugged mountains surrounding Aspen.

Early on, when he'd first arrived in Aspen, many people tried to engage him in conversation to try to determine his real name or his background. It was rumored that several times, people had tried to follow him as he left the downtown area and headed for the forest at the end of the day. No one was ever successful. Within minutes of entering the forest, PIS would completely disappear, leaving his followers bewildered. No one had any idea where he went at night or where he slept, but every morning he was right back downtown walking the alleys between East Hopkins Avenue and East Hyman Avenue, rummaging through trash dumpsters. If you asked people to guess PIS's age, you would get answers from forty to eighty. He truly was a mystery.

The sheriff had run his fingerprints once when an overzealous deputy tried to arrest PIS for vagrancy, and his prints came back as flagged, meaning some agency had restricted access to his information. PIS had become furious at the intrusion into his privacy, and ever since, there had been a truce between local law enforcement and PIS. He would provide his tracking services for free to any agency that needed such services; in exchange, local law enforcement would no longer try to determine his true identity. That truce had lasted almost twenty years.

PIS turned towards South Galena Street and started walking. Even though you couldn't see it, PIS was always aware of his surroundings. Passing the midpoint of the alley, PIS heard what sounded like someone whimpering. Never one to pass up someone in need, especially one of his homeless brethren, he started checking behind and alongside the bear-proof dumpsters he passed. The crying grew louder.

Almost at the end of the alley, PIS spotted a brown lump lying next to the back door to the bookstore. His senses on full alert, he looked up and down the alley to see if there might be some help available if needed, and slowly he approached the lump.

"Hey, fella, are you okay?" he said softly.

The lump moved and made a moaning noise. PIS, sensing that this person was in serious trouble, stepped forward and knelt next to the lump. He was worried that this might be a drug overdose, which had become a serious problem amongst the homeless population.

With the opioid crisis in full swing, PIS had helped countless people in the shadows, and the Pitkin County sheriff had supplied him with several doses of Narcan, since he was the first responder for a lot of these folks. Knowing that fast action was essential in a drug overdose case, PIS had already pulled a Narcan dose out of his coat pocket as he approached the lump.

He reached out and touched the shoulder of the lump and pulled the person flat so he could evaluate them. The first thing he noticed was the purple-striped blond hair and the smell of vomit.

"Hey, young lady, can you hear me?" The only response was a long moan, and the young girl pulled her legs up tighter into her abdomen and rolled onto her side.

"Sweetie, what did you take?" PIS asked, his concern for her well-being growing.

The young girl started to moan louder, and PIS dropped his guard, grabbed her by her shoulder and pulled her, so he could lay her flat on her back. He barely felt the thin blade of the knife as it penetrated his coat, sliced through his faded white shirt and slid deep into his chest cavity. Momentarily stunned, he just stared as the young girl looked into his face with those piercing jade-green eyes.

She started to pull out the knife and then drove it into his heart even deeper, and then she smiled.

"When you see Buck Taylor in hell, tell him Alicia says hello."

She pushed PIS away, and the knife slid out of his chest. He was leaning back on his arms and was losing blood fast. Alicia Hawkins stood up and looked down at him, deciding whether it was worth it to slit his throat. No, she decided. It was better if he died slowly.

Suddenly, a voice came from down the alley.

"Hey, what's going on down there?"

Alicia Hawkins spotted a short man running down the alley towards them and decided it was time to go. She wiped the knife on PIS's coat, walked around the corner and disappeared down Galena Street.

Hector Martinez reached PIS just as he fell onto his back. He pulled back his coat and saw the blood seeping through the white shirt.

"Oh, my god," he said with a thick Mexican accent. He made the sign of the cross and pulled out his phone.

"Nine-one-one, what is your emergency?"

"This is Hector Martinez. Someone stabbed Mr. PIS. He is bleeding very badly. Please hurry!"

"Hector, where are you?" asked the 911 operator.

"The alley off Galena by the bookstore. Hurry!"

He dropped the phone on the pavement, pulled off his jacket and pressed down hard on the bloody wound in PIS's chest. He heard sirens in the distance and said a silent prayer that they would get there in time.

CHAPTER TWELVE

The home invasion team sat around the table, playing cards and drinking beer. The downtime felt good, as they had pulled off six major jobs in the last seven weeks. The time off was good for morale, and it was good to keep them off the radar for a while.

Their dad grabbed another beer from the fridge and sat down. "Good job on the watches and jewelry, guys. Our take was almost half a million dollars after service fees."

Everyone at the table high-fived, and they toasted their success. They knew from listening to the police networks across the state of Colorado that they had gotten away clean. They also knew that their last male victim was in the hospital in critical condition.

Jessie didn't feel bad about beating him to a pulp. He was a pig and had abused his wife on more than one occasion, and they had only been monitoring the family for a week. Who knew how many times in the past he had done the same thing?

Jessie was a tough woman. She had been a star

softball player in high school and college, back when she and her family had lived an almost normal life. They knew about hardship growing up poor in North Carolina, but that all changed when Victoria Larsen entered their lives. The kids didn't know a lot about her past before she married their father, but they knew a lot of her life was still classified. They knew she had retired early from the Central Intelligence Agency, and they knew she was a master hacker of the highest order. The rest they didn't care about because they had more money now than they had ever seen before and were having a wonderful time with their new careers as home invaders and car thieves.

Jessie's brother Earl was dealing the next hand when their stepmom walked out of her office and sat down at the table with a new manila folder in her hand. She had a big smile on her face.

"First off, I got a call from our friend in Europe. They deposited six hundred thousand into our account for the McLaren. It's safely on the boat and will be in Germany by the end of next week. Great job all around."

She opened the manila folder and handed everyone at the table a copy of the dossier for their next victim. They each took a minute to look over the information.

"We may have hit the jackpot with this one. Our friend in the Middle East has a buyer already standing by if we can deliver." She slid a printed page over to Jessie. She read the paper and said, "Wow."

Victoria continued. "If we can pull this off, our split for the car alone will be two point five million dollars, and the money is already in the bank waiting. We will also be famous for stealing one of the most expensive cars in the world."

They all laughed and high-fived again.

"This will not be easy," she said. "I found one available here in Colorado. If we can take this one, we can pull out of here and head towards Montana for a couple weeks of rest before we head out to California. I already have several clients lined up in California who have what we need to keep our customers abroad happy for a long time to come."

Jessie's youngest brother, Toby, asked Victoria about security. He had heard about this next victim and knew this man could pay for some of the best protection available.

"You're right, Toby," she said. "This one is not going to be a walk in the park. Everything will need to go like clockwork. I have already started monitoring his location, and I am running software to try to crack his internet encryption. Besides the car, this guy has some incredible jewelry pieces in his collection. This could be a huge payday if we don't get sloppy. Now let's get some rest. We still have one more order to fill in Colorado before we try for the big prize, and you guys need to be on-site within the next two days. We promised the buyer that this would be in his collection by the end of the month, so we don't have a lot of time. While you are sitting on this next project, your dad and I will be heading to Aspen to start our surveillance."

They were too wired to rest, so Jessie and her brothers decided to hit the Rodeo Bar and Grill and listen to some of Telluride's best country rock.

CHAPTER THIRTEEN

B uck was sitting at a booth by the window in the Elkhorn Diner on Main Street in Telluride. Because of the lateness of the helicopter flight, he'd decided to stay and rent a room for the night at the Elkhorn Lodge, a quaint twelve-unit B&B a block off Main Street. He'd stayed here once before when Lucy was still healthy. That seemed like a long time ago, even though she'd passed away a little over two years ago.

He thought about his life with Lucinda Torres, Lucy to everyone who knew her, and how she'd decided, during senior year in high school, to take a chance and date a jock. She'd always assumed he was conceited and would spend their entire date talking about his prowess on the football field. What she found was a soft-spoken, sensitive gentleman who was interested in her. After that first date they were inseparable.

Buck cut into the French toast he had ordered for breakfast, took a bite and washed it down with a swallow of Coke, his first one of the day. There would be several more before the day was over. His Coke drinking was legendary around the CBI office in Grand Junction. He was about to take another bite when his phone rang. He looked at the number, frowned and slid the red button to the left, sending the call to voice mail.

Buck finished his breakfast, left a nice tip for the waitress and headed for his state-issued Jeep Grand Cherokee. His plan for the day was to head to the office in Grand Junction and meet up with Bax. He wanted to see how her interview with Theresa Claremont went and to see if the judge had had any luck getting her to talk about the possible assault. He was sliding into the car when his phone rang. It was CBI Director Kevin Jackson. This time he answered.

"Yes, sir," said Buck.

"How did your trip to Oklahoma go? Is this Hawkins woman gonna be our problem again?"

"It might be, Director. It was definitely her kill, and it appears she's heading in our direction."

The director was silent for a minute. Jackson had become the youngest person ever appointed to head up the Colorado Bureau of Investigation when he was tapped by Governor Richard J. Kennedy to run the agency. He spent the early part of his career on the administrative side of the Colorado Springs Police Department and was highly regarded by the law enforcement community. He was not only an effective manager, but a seasoned investigator in his own right. Buck held the man in high regard.

"I understand she left a personal message for you, Buck. You okay with that, or do we need to send you on a long vacation?"

Buck knew the director wasn't serious about the vacation, but he wondered if maybe there wasn't a little bit more to his offer. The director held Buck in high regard as well. He'd almost lost Buck a few years back, during a drug investigation Buck was running in Durango against the Sonoma Cartel out of Mexico. In the end, it wasn't the cartel that tried to kill him, but two suspects in a triple homicide that Buck was also working at the time. The director didn't want to face the prospect of losing him again.

"No, sir. Won't need a vacation. I doubt she would try to come after me, and there is little information about my family available in the public record. Besides, they can all take care of themselves, and I'm going to give them a heads-up that she's on the loose."

"Okay, Buck. You need anything, you let me know. How are you coming with the car theft cases?"

Buck filled him in on the limited information they had so far, and he told him that he would get back to him once he had a chance to talk to Bax. The director thanked him, told him to yell if he needed anything and hung up. Buck went to put his phone away when it rang again.

"Hey, Bax. I was just leaving Telluride for Grand Junction. What's up?"

"Wanted to fill you in on the time we spent with Theresa Claremont. We wrapped up the conversation about an hour ago. Jane headed home to get ready for court, and I got Mrs. Claremont situated in a hotel near the hospital. By the way, Jane was awesome. Once she got her talking about her life with Henry Claremont, we couldn't stop her. She did confirm that the audio file is her and her husband, and it was not the first time it happened. It seems her husband has a short fuse and doesn't accept no for an answer."

Bax took a breath, and Buck asked, "Does she have any idea how the recording was made?"

"No. She was as shocked as we were when she heard it. She can't imagine how it happened, but I had an idea, and I wanted to catch you before you left Telluride. Can you run back to their house and see if they have a digital assistant?"

"Sure thing. Are you thinking someone hacked into their internet feed?"

"Possibly, or there could be electronic bugs in the house. It's the only two things that make sense."

"If I have the digital scanner in my backpack,

I'll run a quick sweep of the house while I'm there and see what turns up. Why don't you go home and crash for a while and let's meet this afternoon in the office and compare notes? How is her husband doing?"

"Not good," said Bax. "According to the surgeon, if he survives the next forty-eight hours, he will be out of the woods, but he could still be a vegetable. The damage to his brain is extensive. Oh, how was your helicopter ride last night? Do we have anything to worry about?"

"Maybe. I'll fill you in later. Go rest."

Buck hung up, called the sheriff and asked him to meet him at the Claremont house. Then he started his car and followed the route he had taken last night.

The sheriff was standing by the front door when Buck pulled his Jeep into the driveway and parked next to the sheriff's SUV. He opened the hatch, grabbed his backpack and headed towards the front door.

"Hey, Buck. How's Henry Claremont doing?"

"Not good, Matt. The next forty-eight hours will tell the tale." Matt Anderson nodded.

Buck explained to the sheriff what he was looking for, the sheriff unlocked the door and they entered the front foyer. Since the house was huge, they decided to separate to cover more ground. As the sheriff headed upstairs to the private space, Buck pulled out a portable scanner from his backpack and started scanning the ground floor for electronic bugs.

After two hours, they met back in the kitchen. The sheriff hadn't found any recording devices in the private spaces on the second floor, and Buck's scan of the ground floor came up empty. It was possible that the home invasion crew had removed any bugs that were in the house, but Buck thought that was unlikely. He was putting the scanner back in his backpack when he spotted the white tower sitting on the counter next to the coffee maker.

Buck walked over to the counter, picked up the device and faced the sheriff.

"Is this what they call a digital assistant?"

The sheriff walked over and looked at the device in Buck's hand. "I believe that is. My son has something like this in his house. Gives him the weather and traffic in the morning. I think it does other stuff too, but technology is not my thing."

"Do you think this could have picked up sound from the bedroom, sitting here on the counter?" asked Buck.

"I'll bet not, especially in a house this size. I know my son has a few—I think he calls them pucks—spread out around his house, so he can talk to this thing from anywhere. Let's take a quick look and see if we can find something like that."

By the time they got back to the kitchen, they each carried a half dozen pucks they'd found in various rooms. They laid them on the kitchen counter and looked at the small pile. Buck took a picture of the tower, the information tag on the bottom and the information that was printed on the pucks. Once he got back to Grand Junction, he would have Bax contact the manufacturer to see how vulnerable these things were.

Buck thanked the sheriff, stowed his back-pack in the back of his Jeep and headed for Grand Junction.

CHAPTER FOURTEEN

J essie and Toby drove by the target house and slowed down as they approached the drive-way. The gate was imposing: at least ten feet tall, solid wood, with two massive brick columns on either side. They couldn't see the house from the road, but Victoria had included a Google Earth picture in the dossier. The property wasn't as big as the place outside Telluride, but the house was huge. This was some serious money.

As they passed the driveway, the two sections of the gate started to swing open. Jessie pulled to the side of the road and looked in the rear-view mirror. She hoped that once whoever was pulling out of the driveway went by, they would have time enough to turn around and get a view of the house before the gates closed.

The sound of the car was the first thing they heard. The throaty roar of pure power imme-diately kicked their adrenaline into high gear. They watched in awe as the lime-green car pulled through the gate, stopped momentarily at the edge of the road and then blasted out onto Highway 34, flying past them. All they could see of the driver was long blond hair blowing in the wind and mirrored aviator sunglasses, and in a flash, she was gone, leaving a cloud of dust behind her.

Jessie pulled off the shoulder and swung the car around. The gates were still standing open as she drove by. Toby took pictures of the inside of the property as they went, concentrating on the area around the gate, where they could see a security camera mounted to a pole. There were no signs of any guards or a keypad. It looked like the only way to open the gate was to be seen approaching the gate by the camera. It must be monitored from somewhere in the house. This was going to complicate things.

She turned the car around and risked one more pass in front of the gate. She was looking for something she didn't see. There were no cameras on the street side of the gate. She wondered how someone driving up to the gate could notify whoever was watching from inside that they needed entry. It was possible there were cameras mounted in the trees surrounding the gate, or it could be a sensor in the ground in front of the gate. Whatever it was, they were going to have to do a lot more research.

Pulling away from the gate before she attracted any unnecessary attention, she headed down 34. The plan was to meet Earl at a small restaurant in Estes Park and start to put together a game plan. Victoria, as always, provided them with all the access codes and passwords they would need to access the house. They had a complete dossier on everyone in the house, as well as the domestic staff. They would watch the house, both electronically and visually, for a couple days until they could get a feel for how the family went about their daily business, and they would focus on the perfect opportunity to strike.

Jessie cruised down Highway 34 and turned right onto West Elkhorn Avenue. She slowed down as they approached the center of town and looked for a parking space. She was stunned when she spotted the Lamborghini parked in front of the same restaurant where they were meeting Earl. What were the odds? They had never been to Estes Park, yet of all the places to eat, they'd chosen the same place as the driver.

Jessie found a parking space half a block down from the restaurant, and she pulled in. There was a crowd of what she assumed were mostly tourists standing on the sidewalk, gawking at the car. Even standing still, it looked like it was traveling at two hundred miles an hour.

Jessie and Toby strolled by, looking like locals with their dark brown Stetsons, jeans and cowboy boots. Toby even wore a large Western-style belt buckle. They stepped into the restaurant and removed their sunglasses to let their eyes adjust to the light. Earl was sitting at a table for four in the back corner with a view of the dining room, and he waved as they walked in. He was dressed like his brother and sister. Since there were several other people having lunch who were dressed just like them, they felt comfortable.

Earl casually nodded and shifted his chin slightly to the left. Jessie followed his movement and spotted an attractive blond woman sitting at a table for four with three other women. They were drinking wine, laughing and giggling like schoolgirls. Jessie and Toby sat down at the table, with Jessie taking the chair that gave her the best view of the woman.

They made small talk while the server took their orders, and then they got down to business. They discussed the wooden gates and the fact that they could not see any active surveillance equipment anywhere near the property. They decided to give Victoria a call after dinner and ask her to look into possible security systems that matched what they had been able to see. It was agreed that Earl would take the first surveillance shift, and he told them he'd found a spot down the street where he could watch the gate. As for inside the house, the information would have to come strictly from what they could pull off the internet, but they were lucky there. Victoria had spotted a vast number of cameras showing almost every area of the interior.

The woman and her friends laughed out loud at something one of them said and ordered another bottle of wine. They didn't seem to care that they were attracting attention, which Jessie thought was typical of people like that. She pulled out her phone and opened the dossier from Victoria and perused the pictures. She looked from her phone to the woman.

Based on the pictures, the woman was Constance Fontaine. She was the wife of almost-billionaire Jerry Fontaine, industrialist, philanthropist and recently announced owner of the Las Vegas Knights, NFL team and current Super Bowl champs. The car, according to Victoria, had been a gift for his wife to celebrate their fifteenth wedding anniversary. According to the dossier, they did not have children, which led Jessie to wonder what they did with all that space in the house.

The women were still laughing when Jessie paid the bill for dinner, and they headed for their cars. They would head out in different directions and make their way back to the RV parked in the Mary's Lake campground. As they walked past the car, Earl stopped to look in the dark-tinted windows. It was hard to make out anything with all that shading. He stepped up on the sidewalk and whispered in Jessie's ear.

"Why don't we stop her on the road when she heads home? The way she's been drinking, her reaction time would be way out of whack. We could take the car and leave her on the side of the road. That would save us a lot of work trying to figure out how to get through the gate."

Jessie looked at him. "We've never taken a car without doing a lot of research before we struck. You know Victoria doesn't like spontaneity. Every contingency must be accounted for. You think we could put this together before she leaves the restaurant?"

Earl nodded. "All we need to know is how close Dad is. If he's within a half hour or an hour of here, we could meet on a dark road and make the transfer."

"That would get us to Aspen four days before we were planning to be there," said Toby.

Jessie thought about it, stepped away from the car and pulled out her phone. Victoria picked up on the second ring, and Jessie told her what they had seen so far, and then she told her about the start of a plan she had formed in her head. Victoria listened without comment until Jessie was finished.

"It makes sense, especially based on what you saw at the gate. I would hate to miss out on an opportunity that's right in front of our faces, but I'm worried about the logistics."

"Logistics is my job, yours is information. I think we can set it up and execute it, as long as Dad is close by."

"Okay," said Victoria. "Let me call your dad and see where he is and discuss it with him. I need to make sure he's ready to make the long drive on such short notice. Give me a few minutes, and I'll call you back."

Victoria hung up, and Jessie walked back to her brothers. "Victoria is calling Dad. Earl, why don't you head back along the highway and see if you can find a good spot to make the stop? Start working out how we're going to do it. Toby and I will wait for Victoria to call back."

Earl nodded and headed towards his SUV, while Jessie and Toby sat on a wooden bench a block from the car. They were discussing the approach when Jessie's phone rang.

"Your dad is on the Peak to Peak Highway. He said he will meet you a mile north of Allenspark; it should take you about twenty-five minutes to get there. He said there's a wide spot in the road near a picnic area. He'll be ready for you. One last thing. Don't force it. If it doesn't look good, abort, and we will try to figure out the gate issue. I'll monitor the police bands and the house and keep you apprised."

Jessie hung up the call from Victoria, smiled at Toby and called Earl.

"It's a go. Toby will stay here and watch the car until she leaves. I will head your way so we can set up the approach."

Jessie hugged Toby and headed for her car.

CHAPTER FIFTEEN

Buck was sitting at a table near the back wall of Santini's Italian Restaurant on Main Street in Grand Junction when Bax walked in and grabbed the chair opposite him.

"Hey, Bax."

He slid the menu across the table. Bax picked it up and, before looking at it, ordered a glass of pinot noir from the waiter, who had appeared, almost ghostlike, at the table. This was one of Buck's favorite spots to eat when he needed to be at the CBI office in Grand Junction.

While Bax looked at the menu, several people stopped by to say hi and chat for a minute with Buck. Bax looked over the top of the menu.

"Is there anyone you don't know?" she asked.

Buck smiled and picked up his glass of Coke. His phone rang before he had a chance to take a sip, and he looked at it and frowned. He slid the red button to the left and put the phone back in his pocket.

"Do you need to get that?" she asked.

"Nah, I'll deal with it later."

The waiter appeared, and Bax ordered the cheese ravioli with vodka sauce. She handed the menu to the waiter and picked up a piece of Italian bread off the plate on the table and dipped it in the seasoned olive oil.

"So, tell me about Oklahoma. It's not every day you get to ride in an FBI helicopter. Was it Alicia Hawkins?"

Buck looked around the restaurant to make sure no one was listening.

"Yeah. This time she left the FBI two bodies, and one was a male."

Bax stopped chewing and looked at him. "Is she stepping outside her comfort zone? So far, she's only done women. This is a new wrinkle."

"And not a good wrinkle. She appears to have honed her craft to a new level of sick. It also appears she was able to keep the male alive a lot longer than any of her previous victims. The number of cuts was astounding."

Buck lowered his voice and looked around the restaurant. He didn't want to be overheard, giving gory details in an Italian restaurant.

"Do they have an ID on either victim?"

"Yeah, the male was a young cowboy. No family they could find. He worked on a cattle ranch about a half hour from the cabin he was found in. I talked with Hank on the way here. The

FBI spoke to the other cowboys from the ranch. They were all together in a bar and that's where she picked him up. The other cowboys were shaken up, since most of them had tried, at some point during the evening, to pick up the pretty girl with the purple-striped blond hair."

"Are they certain it was her and not a copycat? I heard she has quite an internet following."

"Yeah, Hank wouldn't have dragged me out to Oklahoma if he wasn't sure this was her. Her DNA was everywhere. She doesn't try to hide her identity anymore. I think she believes she is smarter than all of us, and so far, she might be right. The FBI is chasing their tails."

"Do you think she's coming here? Back to Colorado?" asked Bax.

Buck finished his mouthful of food. "I don't doubt it for a minute, but I can't figure out why she would risk it. In almost a year, the FBI hasn't even gotten close to her. Why now?"

Bax thought about it while she ate some of her ravioli. She held off answering until the waiter walked away from the table. The second glass of wine went down too easy.

"Maybe the FBI got it wrong. You said yourself that her DNA was everywhere, but if the FBI hasn't processed it yet, assuming it's her, then maybe they're wrong."

"They didn't get it wrong."

"Then maybe this is a fake-out, like Georgia. Fuck, Buck. From Oklahoma, she could be heading anywhere."

Buck set down his fork and looked at Bax. "It's not a fake-out." He hesitated a second. "She left a message."

Bax looked surprised. "What kind of message?"

"She carved my name in the kid's back."

Bax almost dropped her glass of wine. "Seriously? But why your name? You're not even involved in the investigation and haven't been since the Feds took over. She must know that?"

Buck's frown said it all. "Yeah, that's the problem that has the FBI confused. The profilers have no idea what it means."

"Well, it sounds to me like she's calling you out. Do you really think she would come after you?"

"Hank's worried she might try to go after my family. None of it makes sense."

"Have you called your kids to fill them in? They need to be on alert."

"I was going to make those calls tonight to give them a heads-up."

"Buck, are you all right with this?"

Buck smiled. "She comes after me, and her life as a serial killer will end abruptly."

"Okay, tough guy." Bax smiled. "What do you need me to do?"

Buck thought for a minute. The FBI was running a nationwide manhunt, but Colorado was Buck's world, and he had no intention of sitting back and waiting for the FBI to do their job. This was where knowing a lot of people might come in handy.

"Can you pull her college photo from the file and somehow add purple streaks to her hair?"

"If I can't, we have an entire building of talented people. I'm sure someone can. What do you want to do?"

"Let's put out an APB to all of Colorado, and let's cover Wyoming, Utah, Kansas, Nebraska and New Mexico, just in case she did decide not to come here. Let's also get the CBI Public Information Office to circulate her picture to all the TV, radio and newspaper outlets, here and in those states as well."

"How about hotels, motels, VRBOs and social media?"

Since the internet was not Buck's friend, he didn't even know how that stuff worked, but if Bax could do it, then why not? He nodded in agreement.

"On the VRBO sites, let's mention single woman looking for an isolated location," he added.

"What are you going to do?" she asked.

"Tomorrow, I'm heading to Aspen to talk to her family, to see if any of them have heard from her."

Buck finished his dinner. While they waited for dessert, he switched gears.

"Were you able to get ahold of the company that manufactured the digital assistant to see if they think someone could hack their machine?"

"I did one better. I subpoenaed their records. The judge mentioned that she read a trial transcript from another state, and these machines can record the conversations that take place around them. The companies keep those recordings. She signed the subpoena and suggested we get all the records for that individual unit and see what it has to say. The hard part will still be trying to see if someone was able to hack the unit and listen to the recording, but one step at a time."

"Great idea. It's good to have a judge on our side. Once the records come in, get them over to the techs and see what they can find. In the meantime, let's proceed with the plan as we discussed."

They paid their bill, and they each left a hefty tip since they had occupied the table a lot longer than most of the surrounding diners. They grabbed their backpacks and headed out into the night. Bax zipped up her vest against the chill. They turned down Main Street, and Buck walked Bax to her car, which was parked on the next street over. Buck was a dinosaur in many respects, and even though he knew Bax was as tough as they come, he still felt it was his duty to escort her safely to her car. Chivalry was still alive in Buck's world.

They said goodnight, and Bax slid into her Jeep and headed for home. Buck walked two blocks over and stepped into the lobby of his hotel. He had some calls to make before he crashed for the night. It had been a hell of a couple of days.

CHAPTER SIXTEEN

B uck got back to his hotel room, clicked on his laptop and grabbed a Coke from the refrigerator. He sat down at his desk and signed into the case file for the home invasion–car theft case. Carefully and with precise detail, he entered a synopsis of everything that had transpired during the past couple days, read the entries and saved the file. He then went into the folder labeled Lab Results and reviewed the latest information from the crime lab. There wasn't much.

Other than prints and DNA from the family and the staff, there was no other DNA to be found. He closed the file and opened the files for the other home invasions. He read through Bax's case notes and looked over the lab reports. It was like he was reading the same report each time, except for the violence. With the information he'd gotten from Bax about the conversation with Theresa Claremont, he felt he understood where the violence stemmed from, but he wasn't sure what had set it off.

He clicked out of the file, sat back in the chair and put his palms against his temples.

"These folks are stealing high-end cars that should stand out like a sore thumb, yet no one sees or hears a thing. How is that possible? How are they moving the cars without being noticed?"

He looked around the room and said out loud, "This is great. Now I'm talking to myself. Sometimes I think I'm getting too old for this shit!"

He took another sip of Coke, grabbed his phone and dialed his oldest son. David was a police officer with the Gunnison Police Department. He looked a lot like his dad when his dad was his age. Slightly taller than Buck and slightly heavier, but the resemblance was striking. Unlike his father, David still moved with the ease of a young man.

David was a sergeant and was now the night shift supervisor. He liked working the night shift and had been a patrolman on that shift for many years. He enjoyed the calm and quiet of a small mountain town in the early morning hours.

David answered on the second ring. "Hey, Dad, what's up?"

"Hey, yourself. Do you have a minute to talk?"

"Yeah, it's a good time. I'm covering the desk for a while, and so far, it's been quiet. What's going on?"

Buck filled him in on the home invasion case,

and they bounced around a couple ideas, but nothing that made a lot of sense. He then got to the point and told David about the new information they had on Alicia Hawkins and the message she'd left for Buck.

David listened carefully. "Hold on a minute, Dad." He could hear the printer running in the background.

David picked up the phone. "Just got an APB from your office. Pretty girl. Doesn't look like a serial killer."

Buck looked at his watch. Bax hadn't gone home after they left the restaurant. She must have gone back to the office and spent the last hour putting together a current picture of Alicia Hawkins. Buck's email alert chimed, and he opened his laptop. There she was in all her glory, purple streaks included. Buck left the email open and went back to his call.

"Yeah," he said. "Pretty girl who has already killed fourteen people in less than a year. Do me a favor. Give Judy and the kids copies of her picture, without the description of her crimes, so they can have it with them for the next couple weeks. Let the kids know that if they see this girl, they need to get to the nearest adult and call 911."

"No worries, Dad. Do you think she would really come after you or us?"

"I don't know, David, but I don't want to take any chances. This girl is extremely dangerous, and I don't have a clue what her next move is going to be."

They talked for a few more minutes about the kids, and then Buck hung up. He reopened the email from Bax, read the information and was pleased. He couldn't have done a better job. He forwarded the email to Jason and Cassie and closed his laptop.

He dialed his youngest son and Jason answered the phone. Jason was an architect, and he lived in Boulder with his wife, Kate, and their three children. He listened in silence as Buck told him about Alicia Hawkins. Buck knew Jason would take it differently than David had. Jason was more sensitive, and he tended to take things to heart and worry a lot more than his brother or sister. Of all of Buck's kids, Jason was the one who had continued to follow Catholicism, just like his mom, and he'd seemed to get more involved in his church after Lucy died. They had the same conversation, including talking about the kids, but it took a little longer to convince him that the email was just a precaution. Buck hung up and took another sip of Coke. He wasn't worried about the kids being able to take care of themselves. He'd made sure when they were growing up that they knew how to handle a weapon, and they each had concealed carry permits. He'd also spent a lot of time on the range with his older grandchildren, and he was confident in everyone's abilities.

His last call was to his daughter. Cassandra, or Cassie to everyone she knew, was the middle child, and she was every bit a middle child. In high school, she'd played soccer, ran track and played volleyball. She lettered in all three sports. She was also the one who got in trouble for violating curfew, drinking and getting into whatever other mischief she could find. Buck was surprised when she was accepted to the University of Arizona with a full scholarship for volleyball. He was even more surprised when she was accepted into law school. Cassie had never been one for regimented education.

Three years ago, she suddenly dropped out of law school, and her career path took a different track. She joined the Forest Service and was now working as a wildland firefighter with the Helena Hotshots, one of the country's elite firefighting teams based out of Helena, Montana.

Buck had not been surprised by any of this. He never saw her sitting behind a desk as a lawyer. She loved the outdoors, and she was as tough as they come. Lucy wasn't pleased that she quit school without any discussion, and she always worried whenever Cassie was called out on a fire, but she also knew her daughter, and if this was where she was happy, then so was her mom.

Cassie's phone went straight to voice mail, so Buck assumed she was out on a fire line somewhere. He left her a message about the email he'd forwarded to her and told her to call when she had a minute. He hung up and decided to call it a night. He closed his laptop, set his alarm for six and climbed into bed. He knew tomorrow was going to be a busy day, but he had no idea how soon tomorrow was going to start.

CHAPTER SEVENTEEN

Toby sat on a wooden bench across the street from the bar and licked his chocolate ice cream cone. Most of the shops on the street had closed, and the street was almost vacant of tourists. The sounds coming from the bar meant that there was quite a party going on, and he wished he could be inside having a drink with a pretty girl instead of sitting outside in the cold watching a car, but this was his job, and he would do as he was told.

He pulled up the collar of his jacket and settled into the bench when the door to the bar flew open, and the four laughing women stumbled out the door. Toby didn't need to use the microphone app on his phone to hear what they were saying. Anyone within half a block could have heard. They all promised to get together again, and then they hugged and each headed for their cars.

Toby figured that women who looked like that never worried about getting a DUI. All they would need to do was slide up their miniskirts a little, and most cops would turn a blind eye. He figured it must be nice to be rich and gorgeous, and these four women had the whole package.

He watched Constance Fontaine fumble with her key fob, and then she threw her purse onto the passenger seat, climbed in and fired up the turbocharged engine. He was certain the noise must have woken up half the people in town. She put the car into reverse and pulled away from the curb, never looking to make sure she wasn't going to hit anyone. She threw the car into drive and stomped down on the gas. The car took off like a shot, her blond hair flying wildly in the wind.

Toby speed-dialed Jessie and looked around to make sure no one was watching. "She just left the bar and is heading your way." He hung up, sat back on the bench and settled in. Once Jessie and Earl were done, one of them would be back to collect him.

Jessie hung up her phone and called to Earl, "She's on her way, get ready."

Jessie had changed into a miniskirt that showed a lot of leg, high heels and a sequined blouse. They'd decided that a woman would be more inclined to stop to help another woman, especially a woman who was dressed similarly to herself. Jessie also had on a long brown wig to cover her blond hair and dark sunglasses to hide her eyes.

Earl, in the meantime, had positioned Jessie's

car in a conspicuous spot and opened the hood. He was walking back into the woods along the road when he heard the throaty roar of the approaching car. He could tell from the sound that she was really moving, and he yelled to Jessie to get ready.

Jessie leaned into the engine compartment as Constance Fontaine blew through the stop sign and blasted onto Highway 34. From down the road, all you could see were these beautiful long legs leaning into the car. It was a sight that would have made any guy stop, but would it be enough to stop Constance Fontaine?

That question was about to be answered. Constance blew past them. They thought they had miscalculated, then the red brake lights came on and the car stopped. The white back-up lights popped on, and the car flew backward, making them worry if she was going to stop, but she did, right in front of Jessie's car.

The door flew open, and Constance bounced out of the car, long blond hair flying in the air. She stumbled, stopped, reached down and slipped off her high heels and walked barefoot back to Jessie.

"Hey, girlfriend, what's going on?" she slurred. She stumbled again and almost went down but caught herself and walked up next to Jessie.

Jessie told her she had no idea what was wrong

with the car and would she be kind enough to call a tow company? Constance never even questioned why Jessie didn't have a phone of her own, but she nodded and then leaned into the engine compartment like she had some idea how to fix the imaginary problem.

Earl walked up behind her and jammed the needle into her exposed thigh. Between the sedative and the excessive alcohol, she barely flinched. She fell over the side panel and didn't move.

Jessie pulled two pairs of flex-cuffs off the front seat and looked up and down the highway.

"Okay," she said. "Like we planned. Carry her back into the woods, tie her hands and feet and then follow me to Dad, then we can run back and get Toby. She should be out for at least an hour, if not longer."

Earl lifted Constance over his shoulder and headed back into the woods. He had picked out a good spot where she would be comfortable and couldn't be seen from the road. Victoria would alert the authorities once the car was secure and they were on their way.

Earl carried her to the spot he found and laid her on the ground. As he did, her skirt slid up, and Earl couldn't help but notice that she wasn't wearing anything under the skirt. He found himself getting aroused, and he knew he had a minute or two before Jessie was changed into her jeans and ready to leave, so he pulled down his pants and slid into Constance.

He was almost finished when he heard a car pull to a stop on the road, so he pulled up his pants, secured her hands and feet and silently approached the road. The car was an older Ford Explorer, and a guy in a dark suit was standing next to it.

"Excuse me, miss, where is Mrs. Fontaine, and who are you?" he asked.

Jessie froze. She had already gotten dressed in her jeans and a T-shirt and was leaning into the car, pulling her shoes out when the car stopped.

Thinking fast, she said, "I'm Ashley Rivers, we were together at the bar tonight. Constance is on the other side of the car, throwing up. I stopped to give her a hand."

The guy in the suit reached into his jacket and pulled out a phone, keeping a close eye on Jessie. As he dialed, he heard someone step onto the gravel behind his car, and he did the most foolish thing he could have done: he momentarily glanced behind him. He didn't see Earl, but when he turned back, he dropped his phone on the ground and pushed back his jacket, revealing a holstered pistol. He pulled his gun, but that momentary glance was all Jessie needed. She had reached into the car, pulled her silenced pistol and fired as he turned. In the quiet of the highway, the silenced shot still sounded loud, but her aim was true. The bullet struck the guy in the forehead, and he fell back and slammed into the ground.

Earl came around the corner of his car, looked at the body on the ground, picked him up and headed into the woods. He placed the body next to the now-immobile Constance Fontaine and headed back for the car.

Jessie grabbed the phone and pistol off the ground with gloved hands and threw them into the woods. She looked at Earl. It had been almost five minutes since they had drugged Constance, and they were behind schedule. They needed to move.

Earl mentioned that he'd spotted a dirt road about a half mile down the road, and he would take the guy's car down there and hide it and then come back and retrieve Jessie's car. He told Jessie to take off in Constance's car, and he would catch up with her. She nodded, headed for the car, jumped in and put the car in gear.

Earl was worried. He had taken longer with Constance than he should have, and it had almost cost his sister her life. He wouldn't let that happen again. He pulled the guy's car back into the woods on the narrow dirt road, ran back to Jessie's car, slid in and headed towards Allenspark.

CHAPTER EIGHTEEN

Buck wasn't sure if it was the ringing in his ears or the nightmare that had woken him, but whichever it was, he was not happy. The nightmare was the same one he had been having over the past couple weeks, and it always ended the same, with his late wife, Lucy, being sliced up by Alicia Hawkins. He didn't understand why he was having this nightmare. He couldn't remember ever having them before, about any of the cases he had worked, and he had worked some pretty gruesome cases. There was something about Alicia Hawkins that he seemed to be having trouble dealing with, but he couldn't put his finger on it. He knew one thing for sure when he woke up. The bug that ran around in his brain when he got involved in a case was bouncing around wearing combat boots, and that got his attention.

The other thing that got his attention was the phone ringing next to the bed. He turned on the bedside lamp, checked the number and answered.

"Hey, Bob. What's up?" Buck wiped the sleep from his eyes and took a long drink from the warm Coke bottle sitting on the nightstand.

Robert Brady was the Aspen, Colorado, police chief, a position he had held for nearly fifteen years. He and Buck had worked together on several cases over the years, but the most noteworthy was a case involving a missing thirteen-year-old heiress that had happened twelve years ago. Every investigator had that one case that got away or that kept them up at night, and that case was the one that Buck carried with him everywhere he went. The old dog-eared file had a special place in Buck's backpack, and he reviewed it weekly.

The young girl had disappeared from what, for all intents and purposes, was a safe, happy home. Her wealthy parents—her father being an heir to an international shipping company—were vacationing in Aspen at the time with the young girl and her brother and sister. The family had several security guards they traveled with, and the house had the latest in security technology, yet no one saw anything, and the security system didn't catch anything unusual.

Buck was called in when the locals ran into a brick wall, and he wasn't able to make any headway. He followed up on a couple potential suspects, but nothing panned out, and a nationwide Amber Alert led nowhere. It was as if the girl had vanished into thin air. Buck and his friend PIS, a member of the Aspen homeless community and one of the best trackers Buck had ever met, spent countless hours in the woods around the house, trying to find any sign of the girl, but to no avail.

Buck still spoke with the girl's mother periodically. Her father had passed away a couple years back, never knowing what happened to his little girl.

Buck hadn't spoken with Bob Brady in several months, so when he saw the name on his phone, he wondered if something in the case had broken open. He couldn't have been more wrong.

"Sorry to call so early, Buck, but I thought you'd want to know." He hesitated for a second. "PIS was stabbed tonight. He's in critical condition at Aspen Valley Hospital. They are getting ready to take him into surgery. He lost a lot of blood."

Buck had to clear his mind to make sense of what Bob Brady said. "Is he going to be all right?"

"Too early to tell. Doc says the blade went in deep, and whoever stabbed him knew what they were doing."

"Bob, any idea who did it? Was it another homeless person?"

"We just started investigating, so we have no idea. We know he was at the Celtic Club, and that he left a little after midnight, and we know Hector Martinez called nine-one-one at twelve twelve a.m., so it happened right after he left the bar and started walking down the alley."

"Do you have Hector in an interview room?"

"Right now, he's here in the hospital with the rest of us. He went in the ambulance with PIS. Doc says he probably saved PIS's life. You can talk to him when you get here. I've got to run. Get here as soon as you can, before it's too late."

Buck hung up his phone, grabbed a quick shower, got dressed and clipped his badge and gun to his belt. He threw some clean clothes in his go bag, grabbed his coat and then stopped to pull out his phone and send a text to Bax.

PIS STABBED. HEADING TO ASPEN. I'LL CALL WHEN I KNOW SOMETHING

He ran out of the hotel, jumped into his Jeep and hit the gas. As soon as he pulled onto I-70 Eastbound, he called the state police dispatcher and told the woman who answered that he was enroute to a crime, where he was heading and that he had his emergency flashers on. He didn't want to blow by a state trooper and end up in a chase, especially this early in the morning. He flipped the switch on his dash that activated the red, white and blue flashers that were buried in his grill and rear window and punched it.

It was typically a two hour and fifteen minute

drive from Grand Junction to Aspen, but Buck made it in a little over an hour and twenty minutes. He pulled into the parking lot and sat for a minute to calm down.

The last time he had been at this hospital was when PIS was brought in to remove a five-inch chunk of wood from his shoulder. A year ago, PIS had helped Buck and the Pitkin County sheriff search for a missing Parks and Wildlife ranger after her dog was found shot in a parking lot near the Maroon Bells trailhead.

The female ranger, Susan Corey, was found murdered, her body concealed in a ravine several miles from the trailhead. PIS had used his tracking skills to find the body, which was no easy task. After finding the body, he led Buck and two Pitkin County sheriff's deputies on a search for the killers. They found an old cabin and were ambushed by the killers, who turned out to be two young boys. They were living in the woods with an old Vietnam vet and several younger kids, all of whom had been kidnapped by the one young killer's mother. The cabin had been rigged to explode, and PIS was able to push Buck out of the way, just in time, but he ended up getting a chunk of wood driven into his shoulder. Both young boys were killed during the gun battle that took place around the cabin, as was the older vet.

It was while PIS was being worked on by a

Gunnison County deputy who had EMT training that they noticed that his back was covered with deep scars. It was another interesting piece of information to add to the mystery they all called PIS.

PIS had survived that encounter, but Buck was concerned about his chances of surviving this encounter. He would hate it if PIS died without anyone knowing his real story. He was also worried about who would want to hurt him. He didn't know any of the details, but he did know that everyone who knew him thought the world of him. He was soft-spoken and easygoing and didn't act like any homeless person anyone had ever met.

Buck slid out of the Jeep, grabbed his backpack and headed into the hospital. The sun was coming up over the mountains, and he knew this was going to be a long day.

CHAPTER NINETEEN

J essie pulled the Lamborghini to a stop at the end of the ramp. Her dad stood to the side and watched as she slowly drove up the ramp into the back of the semi, pulled to the front end of the trailer and shut off the car. She climbed out, walked back towards the ramp and closed the intermediary doors behind the car. Her dad was in the process of sliding the cargo racks back into place.

The cargo racks could be slid out of the back of the trailer and swung aside. This had been an expensive addition to the trailer, but well worth it. Before they had the racks installed, they had to unload the boxes by hand and then put them all back, in the correct position, to hide the hidden compartment. This took a lot of valuable time that they could ill afford.

Now, all they had to do was push a button on the controller to slide them out of the way, fully loaded, and when they were ready, push another button to slide them back. The entire process took less than five minutes, and any inspector or cop on the road would only see full boxes of clothing as far into the trailer as they could see.

The company that had built the system was one of Victoria's contacts from her CIA days and had performed the same kind of work for several government agencies and private contractors. The system was designed initially to hide human beings that needed to be moved from one location to another without being seen. According to Victoria, many of the world's dictators had escaped their countries using the very same system. She also said the system was used by Tier 1 operators, SEALs and Delta Force, to get into locations too hot to use conventional insertion techniques.

They were putting the last rack in place when Earl pulled into the picnic area parking lot.

Jessie was not happy. "What the fuck were you doing when that security guy showed up?"

Earl looked surprised. "What? You told me to make sure she was tied up, so I was working on that when I heard the car pull up."

Their dad walked up after closing the trailer doors. "What's going on?"

"Nothing," said Earl.

"Nothing, my ass." Jessie turned to face her dad. "I had to kill a guy who stopped on the road. He showed up as we were getting ready to pull out. I had to wait for Earl while he dumped the woman in the woods. The guy heard Earl coming out of the woods and went for his gun. I had no choice."

"What did you do with the guy?" asked their dad.

Earl turned. "I put him next to the woman; she was still out cold. When she wakes up, she's going to be freaked out." He laughed.

The scowl on their dad's face said it all. "Did you put your sister in a compromising position while you fucked around? She asked you a question."

"And I answered her. I was securing the woman. I took her back a ways from the road so no one would see her. I was finishing up when I heard the car pull up."

Jessie looked at him with laser-focused eyes and started to say something. Their dad put up his hand for silence. "We're losing time. Go get your brother and head for Aspen. Victoria will text you the location of the RV."

He turned and walked towards the cab, climbed up inside and put the transmission in gear. He pulled out of the picnic area and headed south. In less than an hour, he would be turning onto I-70, and in two days, he would be at the warehouse in Long Beach, California. Three days total and the car would be on its way to Asia, to some wealthy media mogul, and their bank account would be a lot fuller.

Jessie punched Earl in the arm. She could tell by looking at him that he was not telling the truth. She had been able to read him like a book since they were little kids. She wanted to say something, but they were wasting time. In a couple hours, the sun would be up, and she wanted to be out of Estes Park and on the way to Aspen. Just another group of tourists enjoying Colorado.

They pulled into Estes Park and found an empty parking space on Main Street. They spotted Toby sitting in a small restaurant having breakfast, walked in and sat down. The waitress came over with a coffee pot in one hand and two menus in the other. She poured the coffee while they read the menus, and they ordered.

Toby leaned in closer. "Three cop cars went by about ten minutes ago. I called in, and Victoria said she made the call a few minutes before that. She said Dad called and told her you guys had a problem."

Jessie looked across the table at Earl, who diverted his eyes to his cell phone. "Nothing we couldn't handle. It's all good," she said.

She glared at Earl, and Toby could sense the tension, but he let it go. The restaurant was no place to discuss this issue. They were almost finished with breakfast when two sheriff's department cars blew by with lights and sirens, followed by an ambulance. They paid their bill, left a decent tip and stepped out into the morning air.

They made their way down Main Street, looking in some of the shop windows as they went. They looked like all the other tourists that were starting to congregate on the sidewalk. Once they reached their SUV, they climbed in, pulled out of the space and headed back the way they'd come. In a couple hours, they would be in Aspen, ready to start their next project.

CHAPTER TWENTY

Buck walked into the surgical waiting room, looked around and spotted Bob Brady, the Aspen police chief, sitting against the back wall next to a short, older Hispanic man with black wavy hair. Hector Martinez was still wearing his blood-covered janitorial company shirt and pants. Bob Brady looked up from his phone, spotted Buck and met him at the door; they shook hands.

"Thanks for coming, Buck."

"Any word?" asked Buck.

"No. Still in surgery." He looked at his watch. "Been about four hours."

"Bob, what happened?"

"Not sure. I've got everyone I can spare working on this." He waved over Hector, who walked up and shook Buck's hand.

"Hector, this is Buck Taylor, from the Colorado Bureau of Investigation. He is a friend of Mr. PIS, and he could use your help."

Buck smiled at him. "Hector, first, thanks for

helping PIS. They tell me you saved his life." Hector shuffled his feet and looked embarrassed.

"I hope I did enough. Mr. PIS is always good to me." A tear formed in his eye.

"Hector, would you mind answering a few questions for me? I know you've already told the chief everything, but I'd like to hear it for myself if that's okay?"

Hector nodded, and Buck pointed towards a couple chairs. They sat down, and Hector wiped his eyes.

Buck put his hand on Hector's shoulder. "It's okay. Can you tell me exactly what you saw and did last night? Don't leave out any details, no matter how small."

Buck clicked on the voice recorder on his phone and set it on the arm of the chair.

"I had just finished cleaning the bank building, like I do every night. I stepped out back into the alley to have a cigarette. I cannot smoke at home. Maria, my wife, does not allow it." He smiled. "I had just lit up when I looked down the alley and spotted someone leaning over a pile on the ground. Something did not seem right, so I started walking down the alley. That was when I saw it was two people. I yelled to see what they were doing, and the person kneeling next to the person on the ground looked up, saw me, said something to the person on the ground and stood up and walked around the corner."

"I ran the rest of the way down the alley and spotted Mr. PIS on the ground. I reached down to see if he was okay, and my hand came away covered in blood. I used my phone to call the police. There was so much blood."

Hector's hands started to shake, and he looked at the bloodstains on his pants. Tears filled his eyes, and he looked up at Buck. "Who would do such a thing? Mr. PIS, he never hurt anyone."

Bob Brady handed Hector a bottle of water, and he took a long drink.

"Hector, did you recognize the person who was kneeling next to Mr. PIS?"

"It was dark, and I did not get a good look at the face. The person was wearing one of those sweatshirts with the hood on it like all the kids wear."

"Could you tell if it was a man or a woman?"

"It could be a man, but he would be very short, I think shorter than me, so maybe it was a woman. I wish I could help."

Buck told him he was doing fine and gave him a minute to take another drink and compose himself.

"You said the person said something to Mr. PIS. Could you hear what was said?"

"No, I was too far away. I saw the person lean down to his ear, and I saw his mouth move, but I could not hear the words."

"Hector, did you notice any kind of weapon in the person's hand?"

Hector squinted his eyes and thought back on the events of the night. He nodded. "I think I saw a knife."

He looked surprised as he squinted a little harder. "Yes, something flashed in the light from the street when the person stood up." He looked at Bob Brady. "I do not know why I did not remember this when I spoke to your detective."

Bob Brady told him it was okay and explained that he was probably in shock and that he might have new memories pop up over the next couple of days, and it was important that he contact the police if that happened.

Buck continued. "Hector, you said the person stood up and walked around the corner. He didn't run, he just walked away? Are you sure?"

Hector thought for a minute. "No, I am sure. He walked away like he was not in a hurry." He looked puzzled.

Buck nodded his head to Bob Brady and stepped out into the hallway. The chief followed.

"Anything about his story seem odd to you?"

asked Buck.

"Yeah, probably the same thing that's bothering you. The guy was spotted by someone running down the alley, and he took the time to say something to PIS and then walk away like he had nowhere to be."

Buck thought about this for a minute. In his career, he had seen criminals do a lot of weird things, but this seemed odd.

"Anything at the scene that might cast doubt on Hector's story?"

"Can't say for sure. I'll check in with my detectives and see what they've found. What are you going to do?"

Buck looked at Hector, who was sitting alone in the waiting room. "I'm going to stick around a while and wait for the doctor. Can you get Hector home and have someone collect the clothes he's wearing? I want to get them down to the State Crime Lab as soon as possible."

Bob Brady nodded and walked back into the waiting room. He spoke with Hector for a minute, and then they both stood up and walked out the door. Hector stopped and reached out his hand to Buck.

"I will stop by the church and pray for Mr. PIS. I hope you will find the person who did this."

Buck shook Hector's hand and watched as

Hector and Bob Brady walked down the hall towards the front entrance. Buck grabbed a seat along the back wall, sat back and closed his eyes.

CHAPTER TWENTY-ONE

Bax pulled her Jeep in behind a Larimer County Sheriff's Department SUV, grabbed her backpack and headed for the group of cops standing along the road. She presented her ID to the officer at the crime scene tape and asked for the officer in charge.

Detective Lawrence Boyd was an average-height black man with a bald head and a thin mustache. He had been with the Larimer County Sheriff's Department for fifteen years and was a seasoned investigator. Detective Boyd was talking with two crime scene techs when Bax walked up and introduced herself. The detective dismissed the techs and turned to face Bax.

"Detective Boyd, Ashley Baxter, CBI, nice to meet you."

"You as well, Agent Baxter. The sheriff said you'd be arriving. So what can I do for you?"

"The first thing you can do is call me Bax; everyone does." He nodded. "Secondly, can you run me through the scene?"

Detective Boyd nodded, stepped off the shoulder of the road and headed into the woods. They ducked under the crime scene tape and walked back about fifty yards until they came to a group of technicians working in various locations around the body, which was lying near a tree. Boyd asked one of the techs if it was okay for them to approach, and he said it was.

Bax pulled a pair of black nitrile gloves out of her backpack and pulled out her cell phone. She approached the body, and about five feet out, she started to circle it, using her phone to record her progress. The body was a middle-aged man of average height with brown hair and a good build. She figured he was about forty years old. He also had a bullet hole above the bridge of his nose.

She knelt next to the body and took a couple still photos of the wound.

"Caliber?" she asked.

"Nine mil," said Boyd.

She asked the tech to roll the body and noticed minimal damage to the back of the head. She'd expected more.

She looked up at Boyd. "No exit wound. Any idea how far away the shooter was?"

"We found blood on the gravel on the shoulder, next to tire marks. We found another set of footprints about twenty-five feet in front of those. The techs think the gun might have had a silencer, which slowed the bullet down. That's why it didn't blow out the back of his head. We'll know more once the pathologist can dig it out."

Colorado was one of about a dozen states that still used the coroner system, instead of the medical examiner system. The coroner for each jurisdiction was an elected official, and that person did not have to have any experience or even be a medical professional. Anyone could run for coroner. The system was gradually evolving so that the coroner was required to complete a formal training program in death investigations, but it was a slow process. Unlike in the medical examiner system, and since the coroner did not have to be a doctor, coroners would contract with a licensed forensic pathologist to handle any investigations that required an autopsy. These forensic pathologists were highly trained doctors who split their time among several jurisdictions to keep costs down. Many of the forensic pathologists were current or former medical examiners, and several were retired, working part-time to keep their hands in the game.

Bax stood up, turned off her phone and stepped back from the body.

"Tell me about the other victim," she said.

Boyd pulled up his notes on his iPad. "The victim is Constance Fontaine." Bax let out a low whistle, and Boyd nodded.

"From what we were able to get out of her before we got her to the hospital, she was out drinking with some friends in Estes. She was still pretty wasted when we found her, and we think she might have been drugged as well. Anyway, she said something about pulling over to help a girlfriend and not remembering a thing after that until she woke up in the woods with her hands and feet bound, lying next to a dead body."

Boyd looked a little uneasy. "Something else, detective?" Bax asked.

He looked down at his tablet. "The first officer on the scene thinks she might have been raped. She is missing her underwear, and the female officer who checked her over said it looked like she had dried semen on her thigh. The officer accompanied her to the hospital, and I called the hospital and asked them to do a rape kit."

Bax looked down at the body. "Who's this guy, and how does he fit in? Good Samaritan in the right place at the wrong time?" she asked.

"His name is James Woodbridge. He works on the security detail for her husband, Jerry Fontaine. He was on his way to work. All we can figure is he saw her car on the side of the road and stopped. We don't know what happened after that, except that he was shot on the road, carried in here and his car was driven about a half mile down and pulled into a dirt road. Techs are going over it now for prints."

"How did you find her?"

"Nine-one-one got a call at two twenty-five a.m. about a possible kidnapping attempt. It was odd. The caller's voice sounded disguised, and the operator was given coordinates, instead of street information, like it came from someone unfamiliar with the area. The first officer on the scene followed the coordinates with a handheld GPS and found the body. Mrs. Fontaine was starting to come around, and she started screaming when she saw the body next to her. According to the officer, her miniskirt was pushed up to her hips, and she was without any underwear. That's when she saw the dried semen."

Bax and Detective Boyd walked back to the shoulder on the road, and she used her phone again to take pictures of the bloodstains, the tire tracks and the footprints. She got down on her knees and took a closer look at the prints.

"These are high heel marks, and if I'm not mistaken, there are two different sizes here." She moved a few feet back. "These look like a man's shoe," she said, pointing her camera at the print. Boyd knelt next to her and looked at the footprints she indicated. He called over a tech and told him to photograph all three prints. They stood up.

"Good catch, Bax. Looks like we have a male-female team. How did you see those?"

"I got lucky with the light. Where is her car?"

"We think the car was the target, that's why we called you guys. The sheriff read about your home invasions, and even though this didn't fit, it was the car that attracted our attention."

He looked down at his notes. "Car was a 2019 Lamborghini Aventador SVJ. I was told that there were only eight hundred made, and the base cost is about six hundred thousand."

"The car cost a little over a million dollars."

Bax and Boyd turned around. The man approaching them was six feet tall and had a little paunch, but otherwise looked in good shape. He had a full head of blond hair and a dark tan. He walked up to the officers and reached out his hand.

"Jerry Fontaine," he said.

Bax and Boyd shook hands and introduced themselves.

"Is this where it happened?" he asked.

Bax nodded and pointed out the approximate location of the car.

"I bought that car for my wife as an anniversary present. I've been so busy lately with the team that I think she felt a little neglected. We only took possession a month ago, but she loved to show it off. Do you think whoever did this was after my wife or the car? She is a beautiful woman, and I always worry about kidnappers."

"We don't know for sure, but we think they were after the car. Does your wife travel with a bodyguard? Is that what James Woodbridge was doing here?"

"No. We live here because it's a small town and everyone knows her. We felt it was safe, so when she was going into town to meet her girlfriends, she didn't take security. James was a member of my detail and was on his way in late because we were leaving for Vegas first thing this morning. I need to call his wife." He wiped the tears from his eyes.

"Mr. Fontaine, this may seem like an odd question, but do you guys have digital assistance devices in your house?" asked Bax.

Jerry Fontaine looked at her with a suspicious look. "No. I won't allow them in the house. We have enough security issues to deal with. May I ask why you want to know?"

"It's possible your wife was the victim of a group of very sophisticated car thieves, but we won't know for sure until we finish our investigation. I would like to speak to your security chief. Can you arrange that?"

"Whatever you need, Agent Baxter." He pulled out his phone and called the house.

CHAPTER TWENTY-TWO

B uck woke up with a start and looked around the surgical waiting room. Several people now occupied seats, waiting on word about their loved ones. The surgical waiting room was not a place of good memories for Buck. He had been dreaming about the long wait he'd experienced while his wife, Lucy, had her double mastectomy. It was one of the longest days of his life, waiting for word from the doctor that they had gotten all the cancer. And when the doctor finally walked into the waiting room, Buck almost broke down.

The good news that day was that Lucy had survived the surgery. The bad news came from the lab a couple days later, when they discovered additional cancer in her spine and lung. Devastating was the only word Buck could think of to describe that day.

Buck stood up, stretched and checked his watch. PIS had been under the knife for almost seven hours. He knew PIS was one tough son of a bitch, but seven hours is a long time, and he

152

started to worry. He checked his messages and saw that Bax had called and was about to call her back when the doctor, dressed in blue scrubs, walked in and signaled for him to follow.

Buck walked into the hallway and shook the doctor's hand.

"Good to see you again, Buck."

"Good to see you too, Doc. How is he?"

"He survived the operation, but he lost a lot of blood. If he survives the next twenty-four hours, he should be okay. Whoever did this was very skilled and knew exactly where to put the knife for maximum effect."

"Bob Brady said he was stabbed in the heart. How did he manage to survive the initial attack?"

"The blade penetrated the chest wall, exactly where his heart should be."

Buck looked up with surprise. "If he was stabbed in the heart, why isn't he dead?"

"You didn't hear what I said, Buck. He was stabbed where his heart should have been if he was a normal person, but he's not normal."

"What are you talking about?" asked Buck.

"I thought you knew from the last time he was here, when we pulled out that chunk of wood. PIS's heart is on the right side, not the left. As a matter of fact, all his organs are on the opposite side."

Buck was astonished and speechless, something he had never been accused of. He looked at the doctor, trying to comprehend what he was saying. He finally gathered his wits about him and asked, "How is that even possible?"

The doctor explained that it was not a common condition, but that it was also not uncommon. PIS had survived because his heart was not where the knife-wielder expected it to be. He'd lost so much blood because the blade nicked an artery, and they had trouble getting the bleeding to stop.

"Truth is, Buck, if PIS were normal, we would be having a very different conversation. He has a condition called situs inversus totalis. In simple terms, all the organs in his body are reversed. He is a mirror image of most of the rest of the population. The doctor explained that situs inversus totalis affects about one in ten thousand people and is a genetic condition, so although rare, it is not uncommon. It could happen to anyone but is most common in mirror-image identical twins.

Buck was having a hard time grasping what the doc was saying. He had never heard of this condition and was finding it hard to believe that someone could live with all their organs on the opposite side.

"I studied this condition in medical school, but until we operated on PIS last year, I'd never seen an actual case. Since then, I have been doing a lot of research, trying to figure out why he has the condition. The only conclusion I can come to is that . . ."

"He had a twin sister, an identical twin sister, and she did not have the same condition."

Buck and the doctor turned to see who was talking, the heavy Scottish accent surprising them both. Walking down the hall was a mountain of a man with a balding head of red hair and a neatly trimmed red beard. He looked to be several inches over six feet and close to three hundred pounds, and he walked with a limp, using a wooden cane for support.

Buck looked him up and down. "I'm sorry. Did you say something?"

"Aye. I said he had a twin sister. We weren't sure when we saw his picture that he was our comrade, but hearing that he survived another attack because of his heart thing means he probably is."

Buck looked at the doctor, who shrugged his shoulders. "Who would you be, sir?" he asked.

He stepped up to Buck and reached out a huge right hand. "My apologies for eavesdropping. I'm Sergeant Major Michael MacDonald, SBS retired. Please call me Mac."

Buck introduced himself and the doctor. "You say you saw a picture of the person who was attacked, and you think he might be a friend of yours?"

"Correct, but we didn't know he had been attacked. We were on a military tour in Washington, DC, when Devlin spotted an internet story about you, and in the picture was a gentleman with long gray hair wearing a costume. Could have knocked us over with a feather when he showed us the picture. It's been over thirty years since the last time we saw him."

The doctor asked, "How do you know PIS?"

Mac laughed a hearty laugh. "That's what he calls himself now? PIS. What kind of name is that? The man I knew would have killed anyone that called him something like that."

Buck interrupted. "PIS is the only name we know him by. He's never told anyone his real name, and the only thing the people in town had to go on were the letters p.i.s. stamped on an old leather backpack."

Mac scratched his chin, his mind deep in thought. "His father gave him that backpack when he entered the Royal Marines. That was a long time ago."

Buck could have sworn he saw a tear form in the corner of Mac's eye. He asked Mac how he had tracked them to the hospital.

"We weren't sure where to start, so I stopped by the local constabulary to inquire about you. We figured if we found you, we might find him, since the article said you worked together on cases."

He told them that when he and his two comrades saw the picture online, they were stunned. They had no idea he was in the United States. They weren't even sure if he was alive, but they figured, since they were here, they should try to find him, so they ditched the tour group, took a cab to the Greyhound station and bought three tickets to Aspen, Colorado. They'd spent four days on the bus and arrived in town about an hour ago.

"My traveling companions needed to take a rest, so I dropped them off at the motel and walked around a little. I asked a gentleman sweeping the sidewalk in front of his shop if he knew where I might find the man who dressed funny and worked with the police. He gave me directions to the police station. Based on the description I gave them, they said I should come here, and here I am."

Buck suggested they sit down in the waiting room, but the doctor offered up his office, and they followed him down the hall and into a small but comfortable office. The doctor sat behind his desk, and Buck and Mac took the visitor's chairs. Buck felt uneasy, remembering the day he'd sat in an office very similar to this one with Lucy, listening as the doctor said those three horrible words: metastatic breast cancer. Buck shook off the memory.

The doctor asked, "Can you tell us your friend's real name?"

"That's easy. His name is Pheasant Iverson-Smythe. He was a captain in the Special Boat Service during our last posting. It's very much like your Navy SEALs. We've been friends since we were kids." This was a name Buck had heard before.

Mac asked if it would be possible to see his friend, to make sure it was the same person he knew as Pheasant, but the doctor said that wasn't possible since he was in recovery in the intensive care unit. Mac looked disheartened until the doctor clicked a couple keys and brought up a picture of PIS that had been taken by the ER nurse. He turned his computer to face Mac, who took a pair of glasses out of his pocket, put them on and looked carefully at the picture. Buck could see a light shine in his eyes as he removed his glasses, sat back and shook his head.

"That's him, all right. I'd recognize him anywhere."

He smiled, but Buck could see that there was a pain behind the smile. Mac pulled out his phone. "I need to call my friends, if you'll excuse me."

He stood up, opened the door and stepped out of the office into the hallway. Buck and the doctor looked at each other, not saying a word.

CHAPTER TWENTY-THREE

Buck and the doctor caught up to Mac in the waiting room as he hung up his phone.

"My companions will come by tomorrow since we can't see him anyway. Would it be possible to see where he was attacked?"

Buck had made plans to head over to the alley, so he nodded, but before he could answer, the doctor asked. "Mac, what can you tell us about PIS . . . sorry, Pheasant's medical condition? Any information might be helpful as to how we treat his wound."

Buck smiled. He knew the doctor was sincere in his quest for information, but there was also a little bit of bullshit in that statement. The doctor was as curious as Buck was about PIS's past, but he used medicine as a pretext for asking the question Buck was trying to figure out how to ask.

Mac stepped to the back of the waiting room and sat down, and Buck and the doctor did the same. Mac got a serious look on his face. It was obvious he was struggling with how much he was willing to tell these folks about Pheasant's life, especially since he had lived amongst them for over twenty years and they knew almost nothing about him. He sat deep in thought for a minute before finally answering.

"Pheasant's mom died during childbirth. His dad never gave us much detail, but I guess the strain of delivering twins was too much on her heart. Pheasant is younger than his sister by a minute or two, and she used to love to tease him about being his older sister. According to things we learned over the years, no one knew Pheasant was different until he broke his arm when he was three or four, falling out of a tree. They knew he wasn't like the other babies, right from birth, but it wasn't until they took a bunch of X-rays that they discovered that all his organs were reversed. The doctors did some tests on his sister, and Sparrow was perfectly normal. According to family lore, the doctors told Pheasant's dad that he probably wouldn't live more than a year or two. I guess he surprised them all."

"Did his condition affect him while he was growing up?" asked the doctor.

"Not a bit. I've known him since he was four, and he did everything the other kids did and usually better than any of us. He was as tough as they come, and he had no fear."

"Is his sister still alive?" asked the doctor.

"No. She died about ten years back. They said it was a brain tumor. It was the first time anyone could remember her being sick. She was as tough as Pheasant and just as fearless. Spent her entire adult life at Scotland Yard. She was so proud of Pheasant when he graduated from SBS training. It was a huge achievement for someone who wasn't supposed to live a year or two at most."

"What can you tell me about his wounds? We couldn't help but notice that his back is covered with scars, as if someone whipped him. There's also an *X* carved in his chest where his heart should be, with a scar from a bullet right in the middle."

"Doctor, I think I've said enough right now. Agent Taylor, I'm getting tired, so if we can head for the alley, I would appreciate it."

Buck could see the disappointment in the doctor's face. He was hoping for more insight into PIS than he got from Mac. Buck understood where Mac was coming from. He was not about to reveal any of PIS's secrets and violate his friend's trust, even a friend he hadn't seen in over thirty years.

Buck left his business card with the doctor and led Mac down the hall to the hospital entrance and out into the parking lot. They reached Buck's Jeep and slid onto the seats. Buck pulled out his phone and called Bob Brady to let him know he was heading to the alley to look around, and he would report back later. He pulled out of the parking lot and headed downtown.

Buck was always amazed at how much the little mining town had grown over the years. The first time he'd visited Aspen as a kid was with his dad. They had driven up in his dad's tow truck to pick up a car for one of his dad's customers. Buck's dad owned the only gas station in Gunnison back in the day, and everyone came to his dad's station when they needed gas, an engine repaired or a tire fixed. It was also the neighborhood gathering place, where the town's old-timers could hang out, drink a couple beers from the old cooler and shoot the shit about politics and the troubles of the day. It was nothing like the new travel centers that now dotted the landscape. This was a down and dirty mechanics garage. A place for working men to get together, out of earshot of the womenfolk. There was no convenience store attached to it, only two old greasy repair bays and two restrooms located out back, which would have been condemned by the Board of Health today but were perfectly fine back in the day.

Buck's thoughts turned back to Aspen and how, even since his last major crime in the city ten years before, the little town had grown up even more. More mansions were being built than middle-class homes, and he wondered how the average Aspenite was able to survive in the place now. It was also apparent, he noticed as he turned down the alley, that the homeless population had grown. Several small groups and individuals were scrounging through the dumpsters that lined the alley, looking for tonight's dinner, or possibly scouting out a better place to live once winter arrived, which wouldn't be too much longer.

Buck's phone rang, and he looked at the number and frowned. He pushed the red button to the left and put the phone back in his pocket.

The drive over from the hospital was quiet, and Mac sat and looked out the window. Buck could tell that Mac was trying to work something out in his mind, so he decided not to press him. He imagined that the sudden reappearance of Pheasant in his life was a hard thing to deal with. Buck didn't know the particulars, but it was evident that something had happened a long time ago that led PIS to leave the life he knew as a soldier, disappear into the world outside Britain and lose contact with those who had been his friends. He wondered if, now that they had located him, Mac thought it might have been a mistake to make the journey to Aspen. After all, it had been over thirty years, and PIS had had no contact with his friends and comrades in arms. What if this visit was not something that PIS wanted?

Buck pulled up behind the bookstore and stopped the Jeep. They climbed out, and Buck asked Mac to hang back for a minute. The smell from something rotting in the dumpsters in the unusually warm weather was unpleasant, but Buck put it out of his head and walked to the back of the Jeep. Since Buck hadn't been here before, to him, this was a new crime scene, and he needed to handle it like he dealt with any crime scene, even though he knew the local forensic team had already scoured the area. He pulled a pair of black nitrile gloves out of his backpack, put them on and stepped up to the yellow crime scene tape that still hung between the power pole and the dumpster.

He walked along the perimeter of the yellow tape, looking at the overall scene. He noticed Mac out of the corner of his eye, looking at the homeless as they wandered about. He wondered what was going through his mind.

Buck focused on the job at hand and slipped under the tape. He knelt next to the bloodstain that had dried on the pavement and scanned the surrounding area. As far as crime scenes went, this one was pristine, except for the blood. He stood up, looked around and spotted cameras on several of the buildings. He made a mental note to call Bob Brady and see if his detectives had pulled the tapes from the cameras. He realized as he thought it that most of these cameras didn't use tape anymore, that everything was stored in a cloud somewhere in digital space. He didn't have a clue how to find this cloud, but he knew a lot of people who did, including his grandkids. Maybe he really was a technological dinosaur. He cleared away that thought. He looked over towards the edge of the dumpster and spotted a dried pile of something on the ground next to one wheel. He stepped over and pushed the dumpster out of the way enough to see that the pile was vomit. He had no way of knowing if it was connected to PIS's attack, but for the moment, it was evidence.

He pulled his phone out and dialed Bob Brady. "Bob, did your detectives take a sample of some vomit that is next to the dumpster?"

"Yeah," said Bob. "They sent it to the State Crime Lab for analysis. Why?"

"I wanted to make sure before I grabbed another sample. I'll call the lab and see if they can rush the sample. Oh, before I forget. Was there anything on any of the cameras in the alley? I noticed several behind the buildings."

"Not really. One showed something, but it was fuzzy. We sent it to your tech guys to see if they could clean it up. The others were either not working or had a bad view. I will email you a copy of what we have, and you can look for yourself."

"Thanks, Bob."

Buck hit one of his speed dial numbers. Maxine Clinton answered right away.

"Buck Taylor. How's my favorite cop?"

"Hey, Max. Doing good. How're things at the crime lab?"

Dr. Maxine Clinton, Max to her friends, was the director of the State Crime Lab in Pueblo. She was a matronly woman in her early sixties, about five feet five with short gray hair. She probably thought she carried around an extra fifteen pounds she didn't need, but she was still a handsome woman.

Married for forty years, Max had four children, eleven grandchildren and six great-grandchildren. She lived in a 150-year-old farmhouse in Pueblo, where she liked to tend her garden and sit on her porch and drink iced tea. She was also a bourbon girl and could easily drink most people under the table. She was loud and outspoken, but she knew her job.

Max had received her PhD in Biology from the University of Colorado and worked as a biology professor for twenty years before joining CBI and accepting the challenge of running the lab, which under her leadership had become one of the top crime labs in the country. She was a hard taskmaster, but she had a belief system that didn't allow for defeat. Her goal was to give the crime investigator, no matter which department or municipality they worked for, all the information they would need to solve any crime. She held that as a sacred obligation to the victims. She was incredibly dedicated, and her team at the lab practically worshipped her.

Buck would be included in that group. Many times, during a complicated investigation, it had been Max and her team that lit the spark that led to a breakthrough. Max was one of Buck's favorite people, and she felt the same way about him.

"Couldn't be better," she said. They spent a few minutes catching up before Max asked how she could help him today.

"Aspen PD sent you a sample of some vomit they found at a crime scene. I wanted to see if you had any results yet."

Buck heard Max clicking away on her computer. "Here it is. We received the sample earlier today, and it is being processed. You're not on the notification list. What's your interest?"

"The victim is a good friend of mine. I'm in town to help if I can. Can you put a rush on this, Max? It's important."

Max didn't even hesitate. "I'll put this in for an overnight DNA test. I'll call you tomorrow when

I have the results. Is your friend okay?"

"Right now, he's in critical condition after a knifing. The vomit could be from the perp."

"No worries, Buck. We won't let you down."

She ended the call the way she always did. "You're a good man, Buck Taylor. God will watch over you. Stay safe."

Buck hadn't been to church since he received his confirmation, but he always appreciated Max's little blessing. It wasn't that he didn't believe in God. He wasn't sure what he really believed in. He didn't like organized religion, but he never held that against anyone. A lot of people had prayed for his wife during the five years she fought metastatic breast cancer, but in the end, Lucy still died. Although he had been mad at first, he soon realized that to be angry at God, he first had to believe in God, and he could never get there. He always felt there were forces in the world that he couldn't explain, and he always thanked the river spirits whenever he had a chance to do some fly-fishing. He didn't have a place for one God in his life. He never held Max's beliefs against her. He always figured that it couldn't hurt if she believed he was worthy.

He called Mac back to the Jeep, and they slid in and headed for Mac's hotel. Mac was once again quiet on the drive over.

CHAPTER TWENTY-FOUR

Alicia Hawkins was parked outside the bus station in Glenwood Springs. She wore a black wig and dark sunglasses and hid her face anytime someone drew near. She had been parked for a couple hours looking for that perfect person, her next victim, and she was running out of time. Three days in Aspen had not rewarded her with one opportunity, and she was getting concerned. She needed her fifteenth victim before she went after the bar owner. It was a promise to her grandfather that she meant to keep. Besides, she still hadn't put together a solid plan of how to take the bar owner. She was fit for her age, and the bouncer always seemed to be somewhere close by. She was working on a plan, but that would depend on how she felt about the two fanboys she had been communicating with since Key West.

Alicia was stunned by the number of fans she had on the internet. She assumed most people would be turned off by her activities, but there was a large group that seemed to worship her, and she was amazed to find that there was even a private Facebook page dedicated to her. What a crazy world. She was already more famous than her grandfather, and that both excited and repulsed her. She figured it was like those women who married convicted killers in prison, knowing they would never have a normal life.

Anyway, two of her fanboys, Josh and Louis, had taken a real interest in her work and had been reaching out lately. They wanted to get together with her and become her students. She had no idea if they were serious, but they were persistent, and the more she thought about it, the more it sounded like fun. Think of how famous she would be if she had an army of killers working with her—well, maybe not an army, but a couple enthusiastic followers trained in her methods could be a good thing.

She decided to reach out to them through the dark web and ask them to meet her in Aspen. They were due to arrive in a day or two, and she would see how they fit in. She was worried that they might be part of the FBI, but she had to take a chance. She would need help getting to the bar owner, and these two guys might be just what she needed. And if things didn't work out, well, maybe they could be victims seventeen and eighteen.

She checked the schedule she had picked up on her first visit to the bus station. The last bus from Denver had arrived, and she watched patiently as the passengers exited the bus. She wondered if any of the travelers would ever realize how close they had come to being the victim of a serial killer. The thought made her smile, and she visualized what she would do to each one of them as they walked away from the bus,

She was about to call it quits and head back to the cabin she was renting when she spotted a petite young girl standing at the curb, looking lost. She hiked up her coat against the chilly breeze and looked around like she was waiting for someone to come pick her up.

The bus pulled away from the station heading for the parking lot, and within minutes she was all alone on the sidewalk. Darkness had long ago settled over the Roaring Fork Valley, and with it came the possibility of snow and colder temperatures. It was early fall, but winter could occur at any time.

Alicia watched her for a few minutes to make sure she was alone, and then she slid out of her car, grabbed a rolling suitcase out of the trunk and skirted around the girl towards the entrance to the station. Once inside the revolving door, she turned around and headed back out the door, looking like any of the other passengers exiting the station. She walked past the young girl and stopped.

"Hi. You look lost. Can I help you?" she asked.

"That's okay," she said. "I just need to find a place to eat."

"Where are you heading? Perhaps I can give you a ride?" asked Alicia.

The girl nodded and shrugged her shoulders.

Alicia smiled at her. "Look. It's too late to find an open restaurant, and hotels here are expensive. I am heading home, and I've got lots of food and a warm place to stay. Why don't you join me? It's better than sleeping outside in the cold."

The girl looked at her suspiciously and pulled back. Alicia reached out her hand. "There's nothing to be afraid of. I'm the Reverend Monica Chase. My church is the First Presbyterian Congregation in Aspen, and I have a cozy cabin in the woods outside of town. Please. Let me help you."

The religious introduction must have struck a chord, and the young girl smiled and reached out her hand and shook Alicia's hand. "Karen," she said. "Karen Holcomb from Portland, Maine."

Alicia's smile was warm and comforting. "Well, Karen. It's a pleasure to meet you. We can talk more once you are fed and warm. My car is over there." She pointed towards the small green car, one of the few left in the lot. They headed for the car, Alicia pulling her roller suitcase and Karen swinging her backpack over her shoulders.

Alicia stowed the bags in the trunk and climbed in next to Karen, who was unzipping her coat now that she was inside a warm car. Alicia was worried that the warm car might make Karen question her decision. It didn't seem to occur to her that if Alicia was coming back from a bus trip, her car shouldn't be warm, but the question never came up. She just snuggled into the warmth and closed her eyes. Before they left the lot, Karen was asleep.

Alicia headed down Highway 82 towards Aspen. About a mile south of town, she turned down County Road 21, drove about a mile and turned down an unmarked dirt road and headed back into the trees. The house was a cozy little hunting cabin she'd found on one of the vacation rentals by owner sites on the internet. The owner was out of the country and was happy to rent it to a member of the clergy for a couple weeks of solitude and reflection.

She pulled into a small circular parking area and stopped the car. She softly tapped Karen on the arm, and the girl slowly opened her eyes. She saw Alicia's smiling face and smiled back.

"Come on. We need to walk back about a half mile to the house. Grab your backpack out of the trunk, and don't be afraid of the dark. I walk this trail every night after work, and I know it like the back of my hand."

Karen slid out of the car and pulled her backpack out of the trunk. She didn't question why Alicia didn't take her own rolling suitcase. She closed the trunk and followed the glow of Alicia's flashlight. The path wasn't difficult, and they soon crested a small rise and saw the lights of the cabin burning brightly in the distance.

Alicia unlocked the front door to the cabin and stepped out of the way so Karen could step in first. She closed the door and turned off the outside light. The cabin was large and open, and the lights gave the honey-colored wood a soft, warm glow. Alicia lit a fire in the gas fireplace and told Karen to make herself at home while she threw some dinner together. She walked into the kitchen, thinking that this was way too easy.

She cooked up some pasta and sauce and called Karen to dinner. She put candles on the table and took two bottles of wine from the closet down the hall. Everything was perfect, and Karen dug in like she hadn't eaten in days. They talked about life and food, and then the conversation turned to Karen.

Karen had walked out on an abusive boyfriend and hopped on the first bus out of town. Her parents had moved to Oregon a couple years back, and she figured she might head that way and surprise them. She had no intention of telling her ex-boyfriend where she was heading, and for now, she was going to play it by ear.

Alicia offered her another glass of wine and then excused herself and took the glasses over to the counter to fill them. They finished dinner, walked into the family room and sat on the carpet in front of the fireplace. The warmth was comforting, and it didn't take long before Karen got a glazed look in her eyes and started yawning. She leaned back against the couch and finished the last of her wine. The glass slipped from her hand, and Alicia caught it, and then the lights went out, and Karen fell into a deep sleep. The sleeping pills in the wine had done the job.

Alicia felt her excitement start to build as she half dragged, half carried Karen to the ground-floor bedroom. She hadn't bolted the shackles to the wall but had decided to strap Karen to the bed. That method had worked well with the cowboy in Oklahoma, and she hoped it would work as well this time. She stripped off Karen's clothes and looked over her petite body. Her skin was fair, her short brown hair shined in the candlelight and her breasts were small but perfect. Alicia strapped her hands and feet to the bed frame and walked out to the family room to turn off the rest of the lights and blow out the candles. She walked back into the bedroom, stripped off her own clothes and spent a few minutes getting herself aroused. Feeling good, she unrolled her bundle of knives and pulled out a thin four-inch scalpel. It was time to begin.

CHAPTER TWENTY-FIVE

Bax pulled her Jeep up to the gate, followed by Detective Boyd in his unmarked LCSD SUV. She glanced around and noticed there was no call box or gatehouse, and she wondered how she was supposed to let the people inside the gate know she was waiting. That question answered itself as the gate swung inwards. They pulled both vehicles through the gate and followed the dirt road for about a quarter mile before arriving at an enormous modern mountain home. It appeared to be one story, with lots of wood, stone and glass, and it covered a huge swath of ground. They parked in front of the massive entry doors and slid out of their vehicles. Bax grabbed her backpack off the seat, and Detective Boyd did the same.

The entry doors opened before they reached the top step, and a short, bald man wearing dark-rimmed glasses stepped through the door. She wondered if he was the butler or house boy until he reached out his hand.

"Officers, Martin Campbell. Mr. Fontaine's

head of security."

Bax and Detective Boyd both shook hands with him and introduced themselves, although Bax had no doubt that he probably had their pictures in his phone along with their profiles. He waved his hand towards the entry and stepped slightly aside so they could enter.

Bax stepped into the foyer and stopped and stared. The hall and attached great room were huge, with a massive brass-and-stone circular fireplace in the middle of the great room. Everywhere she looked, the views out the huge walls of windows were impressive. Martin Campbell asked them to follow him, and they walked through a chef's dream kitchen and down a flight of stairs to the security office. Bax stepped into the room and thought she had stepped into NASA or a television studio. One entire wall was covered with monitors, each showing an almost continuous path around the property. There were four technicians seated at separate consoles, and each person was busy working their keyboard or moving around a joystick.

"Mr. Fontaine asked us to review the past two days of tape and report on any unusual vehicles that passed our gates. We've found one vehicle from yesterday that fits that profile. Marcus, please pull up the tape we reviewed earlier."

Bax and Detective Boyd stepped over to Marcus's console, and he clicked a few keys and directed them to look at the screens to the right. He pushed a button, and what had been twelve separate camera views turned into one large picture. He rolled the camera forward as they all looked on.

At first, it was just traffic on the highway, but then a slow-moving vehicle came into view and appeared to almost stop as it drew even with the gate. The SUV's windows were tinted dark, and it was impossible to see who was in the car, except for the shadows of what appeared to be three people.

"The vehicle is a 2016 Ford Explorer. It appears to be either dark blue or black," said Martin Campbell.

Bax asked Marcus to freeze the picture, and she looked closer at the car. "How can you tell the make and model? There are no markings on the side of the vehicle," asked Bax.

Marcus clicked a couple more keys, and the side view of the vehicle was replaced with a head-on view. Bax was impressed.

Because the front windshield can't be tinted in Colorado, they had a perfect view of the driver and passenger. As Marcus pulled the camera view back, they also got a view of the license plate. The plates were from North Carolina, and Detective Boyd pulled out his iPad and started to type in the information.

"There is no need for that, Detective. We ran the vehicle through our vast database to get the make and model. We will forward the videos to you. We have also taken the liberty of running the plates through the North Carolina Department of Motor Vehicles, and we have included that information in the email to you and Agent Baxter as well."

Bax stepped back from the console. "Mr. Campbell, this is an amazing system you have here. May I ask? Does it cover the entire property, as well as the highway?"

"I'm sorry, Agent Baxter, that is proprietary information that I cannot divulge, but suffice it to say, there is very little that can happen on this property that we are not aware of. Mr. Fontaine is a very private person, and he can afford the very best."

"One last question. Do you have a digital assistant in the house?"

"No, Agent Baxter, Mr. Fontaine does not allow anyone in the household to have a digital assistant. He is concerned about privacy."

Detective Boyd looked up from his iPad. "Would it be possible for us to interview Mrs. Fontaine?"

"Mrs. Fontaine is waiting for you in her sitting

room. I will take you there now, if you will follow me."

The sitting room was as big as Bax's apartment in Grand Junction and was as impressive
as the rest of the house, with a large fireplace
flanked by a wall of windows. Mrs. Fontaine sat
on a leather couch that Bax figured probably
cost more than she made in a year. They introduced themselves to Mrs. Fontaine, and Martin
Campbell stepped out of the room and closed
the door. Mrs. Fontaine pointed to the two chairs
opposite the couch, and Bax and Detective Boyd
sat down and sank into the softest leather chairs
either one of them had ever sat in. The leather
was like butter.

Constance Fontaine was sitting cross-legged
on the couch with her bare feet tucked under her
legs. She wore jeans and a flannel shirt, and she
was stunning. The only thing amiss was that she
looked terribly hungover. She took a sip of water
from the bottle on the table next to her and
looked at her visitors.

"My husband asked me to speak with you, but
please be aware that I can't seem to remember
anything that happened after I left the bar. It's
like the whole evening disappeared. The doctor
at the hospital said I was drugged with a fast-acting sedative."

"Mrs. Fontaine," said Detective Boyd. "We believe that shortly after you left the bar, you stopped along the side of the highway. There are indications that there might have been a car parked on the side of the road and possibly another woman. We found a second print from a high heel shoe that is smaller than yours. Do you recall stopping to meet someone?"

Mrs. Fontaine looked deep in thought and, after a minute, rubbed her forehead with her fingers.

"I seem to still be hungover. Now that you mention it, I think I did stop to help someone. There was another woman. She was all alone, and the hood of her car was up. I remember walking back to her car, and then the lights went out until I woke up and found that poor security guard lying next to me. It was horrible." She started to cry and took another sip of water.

Bax handed her a tissue from the box on the desk. "Mrs. Fontaine, do you remember anything about the woman or the car? Anything that might help us?"

Constance Fontaine shook her head. "I'm so sorry. I wish I could remember more, but my head is empty. It's a terrible feeling."

Bax and Detective Boyd stood up to leave. It was obvious that they were not going to get anything more out of Constance Fontaine. They turned and headed towards the door.

"My husband didn't say much at the hospital, but I could tell from the tests the nurse ran. Was I raped while I was unconscious?"

Bax stepped back to the couch and looked into Constance Fontaine's eyes. "We believe you were, but we will know more once the tests come back. I'm so sorry."

Constance Fontaine nodded, and Bax turned, and they left the room. They could hear her crying behind the closed door.

Bax and Detective Boyd thanked Martin Campbell for his help and walked to their cars.

Bax said, "I will call the crime lab and put a rush on the samples. Can you make sure they get to the lab right away?"

"No problem, Bax. I will also run the video of the car through facial recognition and call a friend of mine in North Carolina to see if they can get a line on the owner of the SUV."

They shook hands, and each slid into their respective vehicles with a promise to call as soon as something popped. Bax pulled out her phone and called Max Clinton.

"Hey, Max," she said. "I need a favor."

"Hiya, Bax. How can I help?"

Bax told her about the possible rape and that this case might be tied to the other home invasion that she and Buck were working on, and could she rush the results? Max, as usual, was willing to do whatever she needed to do once the samples arrived. They talked for a minute about the cases and bounced some ideas around, and then Max told her that God would watch over her, and they hung up.

Her next call was to Buck to fill him in. Buck answered right away.

"Hey, Bax. How'd things go in Estes Park?"

"It's crazy, Buck. From what we can tell this same crew has committed five break-ins and stolen five expensive cars. In each case the MO was exactly the same, and then all of a sudden we have two cases, in less than a week, and neither one fits the MO. I feel it in my bones that this is the same crew. I can't figure out what changed."

Buck thought for a minute. "Tell me what's different about these last two cases."

"Well, the first thing that stands out is the increase in violence. In the case in Telluride, they beat the husband almost to death, and in this case in Estes, they killed a security guard and possibly raped the victim."

Buck wasn't aware of the rape and expressed his surprise. "Walk me through the Estes case step by step."

Bax spent the next fifteen minutes giving

Buck a quick synopsis of the events surrounding the stolen car. When she was finished, Buck was quiet for a minute.

"It sounds to me like this was a crime of opportunity. From what you described, it is possible they were staking the place out and couldn't figure out how to get through the security system. You said it was seriously sophisticated."

"That's what I was thinking too. They must have been looking for a way in when they encountered the car on the road, or someplace outside the compound. We know she was drinking in town with some friends. It's possible the crew spotted her in town and decided to take the chance and hit her after she left the bar."

"Was the deceased security guard on her security detail?"

"No. I think this was wrong place, wrong time. The security guard was driving into work and must have seen the car on the side of the road. Buck, whoever shot him was good. Real good. It was one shot, and he was down for the count. He was a good-sized guy, so I doubt the woman who belonged to the heel marks was the one who carried him into the woods."

"Okay. Until we get the DNA results back on the semen and we can track down the ownership of the SUV, let's work this with the theory that it is the same crew, and that something caused them to escalate their level of violence. Let's do this. See if someone in the office can run a motor vehicle computer check on the most expensive cars in Colorado. We are talking megabucks cars, so there can't be that many, and let's see if we can't anticipate their next move. The prices of the cars seem to be going up in value, so we might get lucky."

"You got it, Buck. By the way, how's PIS?"

"He's out of surgery, but he's not out of the woods yet. I'm going to spend a couple days here and see if I can help. Call me if you find out anything new."

Bax hung up and called the office to get one of the techs working on the computer search. She pulled out of the driveway and passed through the gate. She'd decided while she was talking to Buck that she would check out the bar and the surrounding shops and see if anyone remembered anything that might help. She headed into town.

CHAPTER TWENTY-SIX

The RV was parked in a small campground, a couple miles outside the Aspen city limits. Jessie, Earl and Toby were lounging on the couches listening to music or reading their posts online while Victoria Larsen worked the keys on her laptop, like a maestro playing a fine instrument. She was hard at work, trying to crack through the firewalls of their next victim's digital presence.

Victoria wasn't concerned that it was taking a little longer than she had planned. She was highly trained, and there were very few systems she couldn't crack. She didn't have any qualms about using the talents the government had taught her for evil instead of good. During her time with the CIA, she'd seen and done a lot of things she would consider as not necessarily good, and if the government could use her to do evil things, why not do them on her own and get paid a lot of money? Besides, it wasn't like she was stealing government secrets or passing false information to a political campaign. They were stealing cars from wealthy people who could well afford the loss.

Jessie stood up to stretch and walked over to the table Victoria was working at. They had been sitting around for two days, and they were getting bored. As far as she was concerned, the digital crap was a small part of what they did. She believed that most of their information came from watching the house and the people in it. Of course, the digital information did give them a foot in the door, and she knew it was a big help. She just hated to admit it.

Victoria leaned back in her chair and stretched, a big smile on her face. "Got it," she said. She leaned into her laptop and started clicking keys with lightning speed.

Jessie kicked Earl in the foot, and he took off his headphones and moved from the couch to the table. Toby still sat in the corner, playing a video game on his phone. They sat opposite Victoria and waited patiently while she ran through the digital systems she now had access to.

She pushed back from the laptop. "Okay, I have access to the security system and the digital assistant. I also have Bluetooth access to his entertainment system, which is extensive."

She clicked a couple more keys. "I transferred all the access to your laptops and phones. Go ahead and log into the system so I can authenticate you, then you can begin surveillance."

"Who's our victim?" asked Earl.

Victoria Larsen looked up. "James Murphy."

Earl looked at Jessie and then back to Victoria. "James Murphy, the actor? The guy who was in all those fast car movies?"

"One and the same," she said. "Murphy owns one of only three hundred Bugatti Chiron Sports in the world. The car is worth three point six million dollars, and from what I can tell, it is sitting in the garage of his house, which is about three miles from where we are sitting. What we need to determine is whether anyone is actually in the house. His security system is low-end compared to his entertainment system. I guess when you are the highest-paid actor in the world and you are only twenty-eight years old, your priorities are a little skewed."

Earl looked at Jessie. "Sounds like it's time to get our gear and find a place to set up on the house." He held up his phone for her to see. "I pulled up Google Earth, and his house is surrounded by forest on three sides, and the closest neighbor is across the street, a quarter mile away, front door to front door. Should be a piece of cake."

Jessie looked at the picture. "Looks right. Why don't you and Toby go scout a spot and take shifts, while I start to search for security codes and passwords."

Earl grabbed Toby as he passed by, and they headed for the rear of the RV to gear up. Jessie set her laptop up on the table opposite Victoria and logged into the system.

"Did you have to kill the security guard?" Victoria asked without looking up from her laptop. "I've been monitoring the local emergency service channel, and there is a lot of chatter. You stirred up a hornet's nest."

"We had no choice. He came out of nowhere. If Earl hadn't been gone so long, we might have been able to subdue him, but since I was alone with the victim's car, what was I supposed to do?"

"I can't answer that. I wasn't there, but ..."

"No, you weren't there. I did what I needed to do to survive, so what gives you the right to question my response? I don't see you risking your ass to steal these cars. All you do is sit back in your little digital world and listen to people's lives. We take all the risk."

Jessie stood up and walked back to the small side bedroom and slid the door closed. Victoria was concerned. They had pulled off some serious heists in the past couple weeks, and she'd known eventually it would take its toll on the team. She was glad this would be the last project for a while, and in less than a week, they would all be home in Montana for a much-deserved rest. She hoped Jessie could keep it together for a few more days. This heist was going to need their full attention.

She turned back around to her laptop and sent an email to their broker in California, letting him know that they should have information on the car in the next couple days and to make sure the buyer was ready to take delivery. The idea of a big payday helped clear a little of the concern she had for Jessie.

Earl and Toby, dressed in camo, walked out of the back of the RV. They looked like typical elk hunters except that neither one carried a weapon. The last thing they needed was to get caught in the woods with a firearm. Instead, they carried field glasses and cameras, and if anyone asked, they were taking photos for a wildlife magazine. They each gave Victoria a hug and headed for the SUV. They still had a little light left to find a place to camp so they could start their surveillance tonight. They couldn't wait for this last heist to be over. The previous two had taken a toll on them as well.

Victoria watched them leave and called up the tracker she had placed in Toby's backpack. She hadn't told their father about the tracker, but she felt more comfortable knowing where they were. She hadn't said anything to any of them, but she wondered why Earl had been gone so long in Estes Park. She knew Earl had a past, but she'd never gotten into the specifics with his father. Now she wondered if that was a mistake.

She set up the laptop to record everything that came through the various systems she'd discovered in the house, and now all she needed to do was wait until someone logged into the system from inside so she would have the passcodes she needed. She also logged back into the Larimer County Sheriff's Department server to see if there was any new information about the shooting of the security guard. She needed to keep apprised of what was going on with the investigation. The last thing any of them needed was a midnight raid on their RV by law enforcement.

She pushed the laptop aside and stepped over to the window. She hoped Earl and Toby had dressed warmly enough. The nights were getting colder, and soon it would snow. Hopefully, they would be back in Montana before that happened, for a much-needed rest.

CHAPTER TWENTY-SEVEN

B uck pulled up in front of the motel where Mac and his traveling companions were staying. He asked Mac if they would like to join him for dinner, and Mac said he would check with his buddies and be right back. He slid out of the car and limped to unit seven and used his key. A few minutes went by, and the door opened and out walked Mac, followed by two other elderly men.

Buck thought they were a sad sight. Mac with his cane, followed by a shorter, heavyset fireplug of a man with a full head of white hair who was using a walker. The third man appeared much younger than Mac or the other man, and he was shorter than Mac but taller than the fella with the walker, and he still had a military air about him. They slid into the Jeep, and Mac made the introductions.

"Agent Taylor," Mac said, pointing to the man with the walker. "This is Sergeant Devlin Kyle, and this taller fellow is Sergeant Willie Carlisle, both former SBS, now retired. Gentlemen, this is

Agent Buck Taylor."

They shook hands, and Buck asked them if steak was a good choice for dinner, and they all nodded. Buck pulled out of the space in front of unit seven, pulled onto Main Street and headed for The Ranch.

The Ranch was an excellent steakhouse in town, mostly a local joint, and didn't have the same kind of prices as some of the other restaurants in town. It had a Western feel with lots of wood and leather, and the owner was fond of showing off his hunting abilities by hanging a bunch of animal heads on the walls. It was a fun environment, and Buck hoped the travelers from Britain might enjoy a little mountain hospitality.

Buck let the travelers out at the front door and pulled through the parking lot to find a space in the back. By the time he got back to the entrance, his guests were being seated by the hostess. She smiled as Buck stepped up to the table, handed them all menus and then left them to their own devices. The waiter brought glasses of water and took their drink orders. Three beers and a glass of Coke.

Buck offered them some words of wisdom about the menu, and after receiving their drinks, they each ordered. Buck didn't let the conversation lag, and he used his interrogation skills to find out everything he could about PIS and his life before Aspen.

"So, you were in the SBS together? If I remember correctly, that's the Special Boat Service, correct?" asked Buck.

Willie was the first to respond. Buck noticed a bit of harshness in his accent, unlike the silky smoothness of PIS's accent. "That's correct. It's much like your Navy SEALs. We were trained to go anywhere, anytime, to handle whatever needed to be done."

"Was Pheasant your squad leader, since you mentioned you were all sergeants?"

Devlin took over. "He was a fresh-faced lieutenant when we were first assigned to his unit. Mac and Pheasant had been friends since grade school, and he was already assigned to Pheasant's squad when we came along."

"How is it that Pheasant and Mac ended up together?" Buck asked. "I would assume since they were friends, they wouldn't have been assigned to the same unit."

They all laughed, then Mac responded. "Pheasant got anything he asked for. With status comes perks."

They ordered another round of beers and dug into their meals. "What kind of status did Pheasant have?"

Devlin replied, "Not did have. I guess technically he still does have."

Buck looked confused until Devlin clarified his statement. "Pheasant is royalty." Buck watched as Mac signaled to cut him off, but he continued. "At the time we served together, Pheasant was tenth or eleventh in line for the throne."

Mac said, "I don't think we need to bore Agent Taylor with all this old history."

"That's okay, Mac. We know so little about him that it's fascinating to find out about some of his life before he got here."

"I don't think we should be speaking out of school. He must have had his reasons to keep people in the dark, and it's not our place to expose his past."

Devlin apologized for speaking out of turn and took another sip of his beer.

"I didn't mean to pry, Mac. I consider Pheasant to be a good friend, and we have been through a lot together. His life before Aspen is a mystery, and whatever you tell me here tonight will remain here."

Mac looked at Buck with serious eyes and held his gaze. Buck sensed that Mac was trying to get a feel for the kind of man he was. He must have believed Buck had only the best intentions, because he started to loosen up a little.

"Pheasant's father was the Royal Gamekeeper. He oversaw all the forests in Great Britain. He was also a duke, which put him fourth in line to the crown. That was where Pheasant developed his tracking skills. He and his sister spent hour upon hour in the woods with their dad, hunting and tracking. It became a family game, trying to hide from each other. I was a good tracker in the early days, but I couldn't hold a candle to Pheasant, or his sister for that matter. Those two would rather be in the woods than in school, and by the time we were ten, Pheasant was one of the best trackers in England, and not just for someone his age. He was one of the best at any age."

Mac took a big gulp of his beer and continued. "Pheasant decided early on that he wanted to be in the boat service, so against his father's wishes, we both joined up together. His dad, even though he disapproved, pulled some strings and got us into SBS training. Pheasant excelled and dragged me along with him. We graduated first and second in our class. Was about the hardest thing I ever did, but Pheasant breezed through it. He was able to pull some strings of his own and got us assigned together. We chose Devlin and Willie to fill out our squad."

"We served in a lot of places together before we were chosen as one of the first anti-terrorist groups, but we spent most of our time rescuing British citizens and diplomats from hot spots around the world. We were in some hairy places."

Devlin and Willie both nodded in agreement.

Buck hated to interrupt, but he wondered about something PIS had said when they were lying on the ground behind the blown-up cabin. "Did you guys ever serve in Vietnam? Pheasant made a comment when we were in the middle of an ambush, about methods the U.S. Marine mortar crews used on the enemy, and I was curious about the comment."

Willie continued. "Most of the files are still kept under lock and key, and we could be imprisoned for even talking about it, but the answer would be yes. We had several missions in both North and South Vietnam, along with our counterparts in the SAS. That was where we almost lost Pheasant."

CHAPTER TWENTY-EIGHT

*V*ietnam, 1969.

The war had already started to go badly for the Americans, and the British government chose not to publicly support their American friends with British military personnel. The British had already fought one war in Vietnam back in the forties, and they didn't want to get mired down in another one. When we arrived in the country, our mission was to cause confusion in the enemy ranks, and that included killing as many of their officers as we could find. We were also supposed to make our way to every little hamlet we could find and escort out any British citizens we found there, of which there were many.

We made a lot of trips from Vietnam to Cambodia to bring out British doctors, priests and journalists, and we also put a dent in the officer ranks of several of North Vietnam's army units. One general took a particular dislike towards us, and he made it his personal goal to track us down and destroy us. He almost succeeded.

We were in a nothing little village in the north,

not far from the Laotian border, interrogating the village elders about an NVA unit we were tracking, when we got word about a British emissary who had gotten stranded behind enemy lines when his chopper was shot down.

Pheasant told us to finish up with the elders, and he would head for the area of the downed chopper. It wasn't unusual for him to head out on his own and break trail, so he grabbed his gear and headed into the forest. We knew Mac would be able to track him, so we weren't concerned. Pheasant managed to get to the chopper a few hours ahead of the NVA. The pilots were both dead, and the emissary and his assistant were in bad shape. He was trying to render aid when an NVA unit showed up. He knew if he started a firefight that it would end badly for the civilians, so he tried to hide them in the woods. He walked right into an ambush. Now, Pheasant was a big prize, but the emissary and his assistant held no value to the general, so he had them both shot where they lay. Pheasant was taken captive.

It took us four days to track him down from where we found the bodies. It's still hard to talk about the things they did to Pheasant during the time he was held captive. When we got to the camp, it was abandoned. We found Pheasant tied to two crossed logs, and we thought he was dead. As we approached, he tried to raise his head, but he had lost a lot of blood.

His NVA interrogators had taken pleasure in beat-

ing him across his back with wet pieces of bamboo, and his back was torn to shreds. Then, the bastards decided to use him for target practice. We found out later that the general had had his men turn him around on the crossed logs and use a knife to cut an X where his heart should have been. The general stepped up, pulled his pistol and shot him right through the middle of the X. If Pheasant had been any other person, and not a person with a unique condition, he would have been dead. The general's shot was perfect, and he must have figured he would die soon, since he'd shot him in the heart, so they left him for dead and moved on.

By the time we got to him, he was all but gone. We cut him down and hightailed it for the border. Once across into Laos, we headed for a small hospital we knew about. It took us three days of tough travel to get there, but we were able to keep him alive.

The hospital was able to get him stable, we were able to get word to our command and they arranged for a chopper to evac us out. Our journey finally ended in a British hospital in India. Pheasant spent four months in rehab, and we were temporarily reassigned to another squad. By the time we got back to India, Pheasant was healed up, and he had fallen head over heels in love with a young British doctor. Her name was Charlene Quinn, and she had been at his side the entire time he was there. They were inseparable, and we figured that sooner or later, they would get married, and he would probably leave the service.

We were so very wrong.

CHAPTER TWENTY-NINE

Bax parked her state-issued Jeep Grand Cherokee on West Elkhorn Avenue, down the street from the bar Constance Fontaine and her girlfriends had patronized the night before. It was a chilly afternoon, and there wasn't a cloud visible in the Colorado bluebird sky. Bax stepped out of her Jeep and looked up and down the street.

"This is going to be hard without a description," she thought to herself as she grabbed her backpack and locked the Jeep. She wasn't expecting anything to come of this little excursion, but she knew that sometimes the answers came from the strangest places when investigating a crime. So, no matter what, she knew she had to try.

She started at the bar; she walked in and presented her credentials to the bartender. He introduced himself as Barry as he dried his hands on the bar towel. She pulled up the picture of Constance Fontaine on her phone and showed it to him. He looked at the picture.

"Sure. Mrs. F was in here last night. She's in here a lot with her girlfriends, and they are quite a group. Good looking, loud and really good for business."

"Did you notice anyone paying attention to the group of women?"

"It would be easier to tell you who wasn't paying attention to the group. They always attract attention."

"Anyone watching them but trying to do it without being noticed?"

Barry thought for a minute as he loaded the washed beer mugs into the chest freezer next to the tap. He waved over one of the waitresses. Vicky was tall, thin and attractive. Her dark hair was done up in a quick bun, and she was setting the condiments out on the tables. She walked over to the bar, and Bax introduced herself.

"I heard Mrs. F ran into some trouble last night. Is she okay?" asked Vicky.

"Do you all call her Mrs. F?"

"She prefers it," said Vicky. "She told us that 'Mrs. Fontaine' makes her feel like her mother-in-law. She's pretty hip for an older lady, and she's a great tipper."

"Vicky, was anyone paying any special attention to Mrs. F and her friends, maybe trying not to look obvious?"

Vicky looked serious for a moment. "There was this one table. When Mrs. F is here, she attracts a lot of attention, but the three people at the table near the back tried to make like they weren't even interested, but I got the feeling they were watching her anyway."

"Tell me why you got that feeling?"

"Nothing specific. It was like they kept glancing over towards her table, but like they didn't want anyone to notice. Kind of sideways glances. They were also here for quite a while after they finished their dinner."

"Can you describe these three?"

"Sure. The woman was a honey blonde. She was tall and pretty. Blue eyes and a small birthmark on her cheek. She had a real sweet Southern accent. She also seemed to be doing most of the talking. The one guy was a good size. Around six foot but built like a football player. He had dark curly hair, and you could tell he was interested in the women. I spotted him a couple times, checking them out. The other one was shorter and younger. He also had curly dark hair, and he had some acne on his cheeks. He was quiet the entire time they were here. I need to get ready for the rush. I hope that helps."

Bax thanked her and made some notes on her tablet. She would transfer all this information to the investigation file once she got back to her hotel. The descriptions weren't great, and the description of the woman differed from the picture they'd gotten from the surveillance camera at the Fontaine place, but it was a good start. She thanked Barry and headed out into the fading afternoon light. A light rain shower had passed through while she was in the bar, and the air felt a bit cooler, but the smell of wet pine trees always made her smile.

Bax stopped at all the stores and restaurants on either side of the bar but didn't get any additional information. The night before had been busy, and all the shops were filled with tourists. She was glad to see that the small city had been able to recover from the flood. Estes Park had been one of her favorite places to visit with her family when she was growing up. Her dad wrote a lot of magazine articles about the recreational activities in the area, and it was one of the first places he took her rock climbing. It also brought back memories of the flood.

The flood had started at six a.m. on July 15, 1982, during the height of the summer tourist season. Lawn Lake was a natural lake that sat at 11,000 feet in Rocky Mountain National Park. In the early 1900s, it had been dammed to increase its capacity and used for irrigation. The morning the dam failed, the wall of water rushed down the side of the mountain, scouring out a massive amount of dirt and debris as it went.

The water roared down the Roaring River valley, flowed into the Fall River—overwhelming the lower Cascade dam and rushed through the town of Estes Park. The flood ended when the water settled into Lake Estes at the eastern edge of town. The aftermath of the flood was devastating. Several lives were lost, and seventy-five percent of the commercial operations in town were destroyed.

The town had made an incredible recovery and continued to make improvements to attract more and more tourists. Bax remembered reading about the flood in *Life Magazine*. Her dad had come back a couple months after the flood so he could do an article for *Life* about the flood and the recovery efforts. She remembered looking at his photos many years later, and all she could see were piles of mud and debris. Now the street was wall-to-wall tourists.

Bax dodged a couple cars and decided to hit a few more shops along the opposite side of the street. For the next hour, she chatted with several shopkeepers. They all remembered seeing Mrs. Fontaine's car parked near the bar, and some of them remembered Mrs. Fontaine roaring down the street as she left the bar, but no one remembered seeing anyone watching the bar. She was about to call it a night when she reached the small ice cream parlor almost directly opposite the bar. She needed a break, so she walked in and ordered a chocolate ice cream cone. While she waited for the cone, she started a conversation with the woman behind the counter, who happened to be the owner. When Bax mentioned a curly-haired young man with acne on his face, the woman stopped and looked at her.

"I remember him, sweetie," she said. "He seemed a little odd to me, and for quite a while, he sat outside on the bench and watched the street. Even after he finished his ice cream, he sat there and watched. He was there a good couple of hours."

"Do you know when he left?" asked Bax.

"Not really. We got busy, and I almost forgot about him. When the rush was over, I looked to see if he was still there, but he was gone."

"Did he pay cash or use a card?"

The woman thought a minute. "I think he used a card. Let me get my box of receipts."

She walked into the back of the shop and disappeared. Bax couldn't believe she could get this lucky, and she hoped it was true, so she sat at one of the small round metal tables and finished her cone.

The owner walked back into the shop about five minutes later and handed Bax a small receipt. Bax noted the time on the receipt, which matched the period of time the woman had observed the young man.

"I think this is the one," she said. "I hope it helps."

She stepped away to help a family of four, and Bax took a picture of the receipt. She felt excited, but she needed to keep it in reserve. She still had a job to do. She called fellow CBI agent Paul Webber.

"Hey, Bax. What's up?"

"Hey, Paul. Do you have time to do me a favor?"

"Sure thing. Whatcha got?"

"I'm gonna send you a picture of a receipt. Can you see if you can get Visa to tell you the address and full name of the owner of the credit card?"

"Is this about the murder in Estes Park?"

"It could be. These guys may have finally made a mistake. I could have the break we need, right here in my hot little hand."

"No worries, Bax. Send it my way, and I will do what I can to track it down."

Bax thanked Paul, hung up and sat for a minute. She sent the picture of the receipt to Paul Webber, and then she dialed Buck. The call went to voice mail, so she left him a message and hung up. She suddenly realized how tired she was, and she decided to head for her hotel and call it a night.

CHAPTER THIRTY

Alicia Hawkins sat down on the edge of the bed, exhausted and satisfied. She looked at Karen's body lying there and was pleased with how well she'd done. She hadn't lost count this time, like usual, and she was able to keep Karen alive through seven hundred fifty-seven cuts. Looking at the body, she felt it was a new personal best. Her grandfather would be proud of her.

She lay down on the bloody sheets, smeared blood on her breasts and stomach and relived the experience until the thrill of the kill finally faded. She already had a good bit of blood on her, but the blood she smeared on herself now was still warm, and she wanted more. She wanted to remember this day for a long time.

Karen had woken up about halfway through the cutting, and the look in her eyes showed the utter fear she was feeling. Alicia couldn't believe how excited she got, but she kept to the pace she wanted to set, and it paid off in the end. This time, she made sure all the cuts were shallow, so as not to nick an artery.

She stood up and stepped away from the bed, turned and looked at Karen. This was a true masterpiece, and she couldn't wait until the FBI saw this victim. She smiled at the thought. She felt she had turned a corner and was well on her way to reaching the one thousand cuts her grandfather had tried to achieve.

She walked into the bathroom and ran a hot shower, which felt good on her sore muscles. It always amazed her how tired and sore she was after killing someone. It hardly seemed like work at all. She let the hot water wash over her body and tried to relax.

When she climbed out of the shower, she was clean and felt refreshed. She got dressed, grabbed her coat and her keys and headed for one of the fast-food restaurants in Glenwood Springs. She felt safer using the drive-through, and she put on her black wig and sunglasses.

She had a couple hours to kill before she met Josh and Louis. She wanted to meet them the first time in a public spot, so she'd chosen the Lowe's parking lot. She figured with all the men coming and going, if something went wrong, she could always scream and figured someone would come to her rescue.

She sat in the parking lot, eating her burger and fries and watching the people coming and going. She could just as easily pick one of these poor saps for her sixteenth victim and not have to worry about the bar owner. It would be so much easier. She'd already seen several young women who would fit the bill nicely. She spotted a couple young men that might be an interesting challenge, especially since she was feeling more confident since the kill in Oklahoma. She was looking forward to trying again.

The problem was, she'd made that promise to her grandfather that she would complete his legacy by killing his sixteenth victim, the one that got away. She intended to live up to that promise, but she was going to have to move quickly. The anniversary of her grandfather's death was rapidly approaching.

She was sitting there daydreaming when an old Chevy van pulled up alongside her. She almost couldn't believe her eyes. The van was white, which wasn't too bad since most workers used white vans. The problem was all the demon art that was painted on the side facing her, and the words born to kill in huge letters. She looked around to see if anyone was watching them. She felt more conspicuous than she had in months, and she cringed, hoping she hadn't made a colossal mistake inviting these two neophytes into her world.

Josh and Louis climbed out of the van, approached the driver's side and introduced themselves. Josh was white, stood about five feet five, was overweight with shoulder-length hair and dressed like he had fallen into a used clothes bin. Louis was a fair-skinned black kid with spiky hair and a feeble attempt at growing a beard. He too was dressed in clothes that most poor people would throw away. They stood smiling at her like two goofs, and she signaled for them to get into the car.

Josh gushed all over her as she shook his clammy hand. She looked at his lily-white hands and wondered if this kid had ever done a hard day's work in his short life.

"God, Alicia. What a thrill to finally meet you in the flesh." Josh giggled like a schoolgirl. "We have been dreaming of this day for weeks. We're so glad to be here."

Josh almost couldn't contain himself in the back seat. "When do we start? I can't wait to claim my first victim."

Alicia looked startled. "Look, fellas. If we are going to do this together, we need to set a couple ground rules. First, never ever mention a victim in public. If you want to survive more than one victim, you need to be invisible. And speaking of invisible. What the fuck is the deal with the van? You look like a traveling billboard for a creep mobile."

They both looked ashamed, and they got

quiet. "Sorry, Miss Alicia," said Louis. "We were so excited to come here, we never thought about the van. Our friends think it's cool. We didn't mean anything by it."

Alicia felt like she had kicked a puppy. "Okay, guys. Let's forget about the van for now. Tell me about yourselves. Where you're from and why you think you are cut out to do this kind of work. Pardon the pun."

They both laughed, and that eased the tension. Louis told her he was from West Virginia, and that his father was a drunk. His mom had died in childbirth, and he had been raised by his grandmother in Florida. He'd learned early on how to hunt, and he always got a thrill cutting out the guts of the small animals he killed.

Josh had had an equally sad life, and he was also from Florida. They had been friends since kindergarten. He told her they'd started to follow her career, and her kills, and they knew they had to meet her. He told her they would work harder than anyone she ever knew, and all they wanted was a chance to prove themselves.

Alicia asked them some questions about their families and their habits, and after they were done talking, she told them to meet her later that night on the street in front of the Jackpot Bar in Aspen. She told them to park the van on the next block and walk back to her car. She shook their hands, and they slid out of her car. She had a lot to think about now that she had met them. She felt good about their enthusiasm, but she didn't have a sense of how they would act when the time came to kill a human being.

Alicia headed back to Aspen. She needed some sleep, and to do some internet research on her two new friends. She wasn't convinced that they weren't FBI, but they were so odd that she had trouble seeing them as anything but a couple young weirdos. She was about to enter a critical period in her serial killer career, and she hoped these two wouldn't be her downfall.

CHAPTER THIRTY-ONE

Buck picked up the check, and they stepped out into the cool night air. Mac invited Buck to join them for a drink, but Buck refused. He wanted to get back to the hospital in case PIS woke up, so he bid his new friends good night and walked to his car. The night had been filled with new and interesting revelations, and Buck needed some time to process the things Mac and his crew had told him.

PIS was royalty. Buck would have never guessed that. He knew PIS must have had a good upbringing, and from the way he carried himself, he obviously went to some excellent schools, but royalty? That was hard for Buck to fathom. He had never met royalty before, but the more he thought about it, the more he felt he could see PIS in that role. The other thing that was hard to believe was that someone who looked like PIS —tall, thin and wiry—could have been an elite soldier, what today is called a Tier 1 operator. Buck had met SEALs and Delta Force guys while he had been stationed at various bases during his time in the army. Most of them looked like

Mac and his friends—stout, solid, muscular men, hardened by their experiences and training. PIS was none of those things. Buck knew he had some mad skills. He had seen them in action, but he didn't look like a special operator.

PIS was quiet, respectful and looked more like an accountant. Yet PIS had proven his value on more occasions than Buck could count. He also thought back to the conversation he'd had with PIS about someone setting up a scholarship fund for ranger Susan Corey's son and how PIS had blown off the fact that someone had done that. Now, he wondered once again if PIS was the one who set it up. The problem now was that none of this made any sense. If he was wealthy, why did he live in the woods?

At that point, the investigator in Buck kicked in, and he wondered if maybe PIS did have a place he went home to every night, which was why no one was ever able to track him. After all, he always had clean clothes on, and he never smelled like most of the homeless Buck had encountered. He might even have someone taking care of him. Buck thought if he was royalty, maybe he had an entire team of servants.

Buck pulled into the parking lot of the hospital, stopped the Jeep and slid out. He shook off the ideas about PIS that had been rolling around in his head and walked through the front doors.

One nurse was working at the counter at the entrance to the ICU, and she nodded as Buck walked in.

"Evening, Agent Taylor. Did you have a nice dinner?"

"Hi, Ramona, how's our patient tonight?"

"No real change, sir. The doctor came by about half an hour ago, and PIS is still sleeping."

"Thanks, Ramona, I'm going to head in there and stick around for a little while."

Ramona nodded, and Buck walked down the hall. He opened the door to PIS's room and stood in the doorway. PIS was sleeping soundly, but it was all the medical machinery that mesmerized Buck. One time, when Lucy had had a reaction to a new chemo drug, Buck had taken her to the hospital. She'd spent a couple days in intensive care, and Buck remembered the sounds of all the machinery and the blinking lights that never stopped. He shook off that memory and walked into the room. The sights, sounds and smells were all too familiar, and he almost turned around and walked out, but he knew he needed to support his friend.

Buck sat in the chair next to the bed, pulled out his phone and checked his messages. He checked the voice mail from Bax and smiled. Bax was making progress on the car theft case, and for a moment, he felt bad. He should be helping her, but he knew she understood that he needed to be right where he was. The message indicating that she had tracked down a receipt from one of the possible car thieves was great news. He checked his watch and decided it was too late to call her now, even though he knew she was probably wide awake and still working.

The second voice mail was from Hank Clancy. He wanted him to know that the task force had lost track of Alicia Hawkins. They still believed she was heading to Colorado, so they were now working out of an office in the Denver Field Office. He also found out that Buck and Bax had sent out a warning to all the papers and news outlets in the state, and he was hoping they hadn't scared her off. They were still trying to figure out if there was something significant about her coming to Colorado and why she would take the risk.

Buck deleted the message and was about to put his phone away when it buzzed with an incoming call. He checked the number and smiled.

"Hey, kiddo. How ya doing?" he said.

"Doing all right, Dad. I got your message when we came in from the fire line, and I wanted to call you right away. I saw the picture of the serial killer girl. You really think she'd come after us?"

"Not sure, Cassie, but I wanted to make sure you had the information and were on alert. I didn't want to scare you, but we all thought it was the best thing we could do."

"Do you have any idea where she is?"

"We think she's heading for Colorado, but we can't figure out why. She has to know we would be all over her if she showed up here, so we're trying to work through it."

"Okay, Dad. I showed the rest of the team her picture, and my guys will watch out for me, so don't worry about me. Listen, Dad, I had a message from Aunt Beth. She said she left you several messages, but you won't call her back. She thinks you're avoiding her, and she said it was important. What's going on?"

"I've been busy lately. I'll get around to calling her soon, but not right now."

Cassie interrupted. "She said Grandpa's sick, and he wants to see you."

"Yeah, he's sick, all right. Look, Cass, they chose to go live in Arizona with Beth because she can take care of them. She's the doctor in the family, and she knew I wanted nothing to do with either of them, so I really couldn't care less that he's sick."

"Dad, I don't know what happened between you and Grandma and Grandpa, but whatever happened, it was a long time ago, and since you refuse to talk about, we can't help you. I know

Grandma would like to see you."

"Beth can deal with them, that's the way she wanted it."

"You're punishing Grandma for something that Grandpa did, and it's not fair. Mom changed. I don't know why you won't."

Buck stared at the phone. He had no idea what she was talking about. He hadn't seen either of his parents since Lucy had gotten sick.

"What do you mean, your mom changed? Since when?"

"Dad, we're not stupid. We know when Grandpa was sitting around the gas station with all his old cronies, he used to call us kids his 'little beaner babies,' and then laugh about it. Yes, he was a racist. He never liked the fact you married a Latina, and we know he said he was too busy to go to your wedding, but we are proud of our Hispanic heritage, and he is still our grandfather, so we accepted him as he was."

Buck was speechless. He didn't realize the kids knew about his history with his father. The man was a racist, and he was also a drunk, and when he got drunk, he said a lot of stupid shit, most of which Buck could live with by avoiding him. What bothered him was that his mother never did or said anything about it. Lucy always tried to smooth things over when his father got out of hand, but Buck would never forgive the old man for what he'd said when he found out Lucy was dying. He could look past the "beaner baby" stuff, but when his father told Lucy that her cancer was God punishing her for marrying outside her race, Buck had had enough, and he and his father almost came to blows before Buck threw both his parents out of his house. Neither of them bothered to show up for Lucy's funeral, and he would never forget that.

His father was always putting down Lucy's father in front of his friends even though he was one of the hardest-working people Buck had ever met. What was so crazy was that Fernando Torres's ancestors had been in this country a hell of a lot longer than Buck's family. Fernando's ancestors had settled in the country as part of a land grant issued by the Spanish king in the late 1600s. Lucy's family had a rich and proud history, and he was glad that his children were a part of that heritage.

"Grandma flew in a few weeks before Mom died, and they had a long talk. We didn't tell you because Mom thought you'd put a stop to it. David arranged it, and she stayed at his house. Grandma apologized to Mom for everything bad Grandpa had said about her, and they buried the hatchet. She came in again after Mom died, and she and Grandma Rose spent hours down at the dock where we spread Mom's ashes, and they just talked. According to David, they walked back to his house arm in arm. You were out of town on a case and we thought it was the perfect time. I know this may be hard to believe, and we didn't mean to do it behind your back, but we all thought it was important. You never told us what Grandpa said to Mom, and we know it was pretty bad, but if Mom could make it all okay, maybe you can too."

Buck sat and stared at the phone. He didn't know whether to be aggravated or be relieved that it was all out in the open. He found it hard to believe that Lucy would keep that kind of secret from him. He'd had no idea they had spoken. He didn't know what to say, so he told Cassie he would call her back, and he disconnected the call. He put his phone away and stared out the window. He looked at PIS and all those tubes and wires he was connected to, and he wondered if a man avoided his family for all those years, what the toll on that person would be. He closed his eyes and leaned his head against the back of the chair. With everything he had learned about PIS and now everything he had learned about his own family, he was going to need some time to make sense of it all.

CHAPTER THIRTY-TWO

Alicia Hawkins was sitting in her car across the street from the Jackpot Bar, running the plan through her mind one more time. She knew what she needed Josh and Louis to do; she hoped they could pull it off. Her internet search had found little information about the two. They had a Facebook page and a Twitter account, but other than that, there was almost nothing of value on the web. She was going to have to go with her instincts alone. She needed them to pull this off, and she only had a few days to make it happen.

She spotted them coming around the corner, and she waited as they slid into the car, one in front and one in back. Once settled, they looked out the windows.

"What are we looking at?" Josh asked.

"You see the Jackpot Bar across the street? That is where my next victim is coming from, and I need you to help me abduct her. She may be an older woman, but I am worried she is going to be formidable."

"Who is she?" asked Louis, now staring out the back window.

"She owns the bar, and every time I've seen her, she is with this huge bouncer."

"Why did you choose her?" asked Josh.

"I didn't choose her, my grandfather did."

They looked at her like she had lost her mind. They had read all the stories in the newspaper and online about her grandfather's exploits as a serial killer, and they knew he was dead, so they were unsure how her grandfather could have chosen this woman.

"My grandfather chose her when she was a young woman and was on the way to his tunnel when he ran off the road and almost died in the crash. The woman in the car with him, who no one knew existed until I discovered her, was supposed to be his sixteenth victim." She wrapped her hand around the jade horse hanging around her neck.

"Two days from now is the first anniversary of my grandfather's death, and as a tribute to him, I am going to kill his sixteenth victim, who will also be my sixteenth victim."

The two young men almost couldn't contain themselves; they were so excited. They were thrilled to be part of such a moving tribute, and they were excited to be a part of history. This was so great that people would be talking about it for years to come. They could almost see their names in the history books, next to Alicia Hawkins's name as well as all the now-famous serial killers in history. This was a stroke of genius, and they pledged then and there not to let her down.

Alicia slowly walked them through the plan, as she saw it, and asked them for their input. She was putting a lot of faith in these two unknown characters, but she wanted to see what they thought of the possibility of the plan's success.

After listening to her plan, they agreed that it was possible. The variable would be the bouncer. If they could get past the bouncer, then getting the bar owner shouldn't be a problem. They walked through the details once more, and then Josh and Louis slid out of Alicia's car and headed for the bar. They wanted to get a good look at the bouncer and the owner.

The bar was packed and noisy as usual with young people, and the band on the small stage in the corner was playing covers of current hits by various artists. It was so loud that they could barely hear themselves talk. They paid their ten dollars each at the door and noted the muscles on the bouncer. He was one big dude. They smiled as they walked past him and found two seats that had just been vacated at the bar.

Due to the busyness, there were three bartenders behind the bar tonight, but it was easy to pick out the owner. Alicia had been right on point with her description, and they had a hard time believing this woman was somewhere in her late sixties, early seventies. She was drop-dead gorgeous, and the sleeveless top she was wearing showed a lot of cleavage and a well-toned, muscular body. They sat for a minute staring at her, until they realized the male bartender was standing in front of them, waiting for their order.

They each ordered a bottle of Coors and looked around the bar. They had never drank Coors, but they'd heard it was made in Colorado, and they wanted to look like they fit in with the rest of the crowd. For the next thirty minutes, they sat, listened to the music and worked out the details of the abduction. Their conclusion was that if they had to, they would kill the bouncer. After all, they were going to be serial killers; what did it matter if their first victim was the bouncer or some old lady?

They finished their beers and headed for the door, once again noting how big the bouncer was as they walked past him and out the door. Alicia was still parked across the street, and they slid into the car and gave a nod.

"Piece of cake," said Josh.

Louis didn't look as sure as Josh did, but they

were buddies, so he went along. Alicia told them to plan it all out like they had discussed and get ready. They needed to deliver the woman to Alicia's cabin in the woods in two days.

Alicia pulled away from the curb, and they followed her in their van to the cabin. They clocked the drive from the bar to the cabin parking area at ten minutes. They climbed out of their vehicles, and Alicia led them down the darkened path to the cabin, which shone like a beacon in the night. Josh and Louis noted the steepness of the trail in one spot because they wanted to make sure they didn't slip carrying the woman. They didn't care about hurting her; she was going to die anyway. They were more concerned about hurting themselves and not being able to help Alicia with the kill.

Alicia led them into the cabin and led them downstairs to the bedroom. She wanted to gauge their reactions when they saw Karen, dead and still tied to the bed. They both stopped in the doorway and stared. Josh walked towards the end of the bed and got closer for a good look. He looked up at Alicia with admiration in his eyes.

"Incredible, look at all those cuts," he said. He circled the bed and looked at the body from several angles. He asked Alicia if he could touch the body, and Alicia handed him a pair of blue nitrile gloves. Her DNA was already on record, but she wanted to make sure their DNA wasn't found on the body. This was her kill, and she wanted all the credit. She glanced over at Louis, who was still standing in the doorway. She thought he was paler than when she'd first met them.

"Come closer, Louis. If you are going to be a part of this, you need to find out if you have the stomach for it."

Louis took a few hesitant steps into the room and looked at the bloodstained sheets. Other than in books, he had never seen a dead body before. Josh laughed and told him to stop being a pussy and come closer. This was going to be their legacy someday. Louis took another tentative step, swallowed hard to keep the bile from getting into his throat and ran from the room and out the front door, where he proceeded to vomit in the shrubs next to the door. When Josh reached him, he was on his knees, wiping his mouth.

"Sorry, man. I've never seen a dead body. God, there's so much blood. Sorry, man."

Josh patted him on his back and grabbed his arm to help him up. "Hey, don't worry about it. You'll get used to it, but in the meantime, you can help with grabbing the victims. I'll do all the cutting."

Louis smiled. He knew Josh would have his back, and that made him feel better. He turned around to walk back into the house and saw

Alicia looking at him from the front door. He thought he should apologize, but Alicia turned and walked back into the cabin. A cold chill ran up his spine, and it made him uneasy. He shook it off and walked into the warm cabin and closed the door.

Josh came in a few minutes later, carrying two sleeping bags and two AR-15 rifles. He had a pistol clipped to his belt. Alicia looked at the weapons, said nothing and headed for the bedroom, carrying a large black plastic trash bag. While Louis set up their gear in the living room, Alicia asked Josh to help her move the body from the bed. She needed to sleep, and she wanted to put some clean sheets on the bed.

Josh helped her pick up Karen and carry her to the walk-in closet next to the bathroom. They dumped her in the middle of the floor, stripped the stiff sheets off the bed and placed them in the bag. They flipped over the mattress, and Alicia put the new sheets on the bed while Josh carried the trash bag to the mudroom off the kitchen. Once done, Alicia said good night and closed the door. Josh grabbed Louis's car keys, and they headed back to their van. They planned to sit on the bar for a while and hopefully follow the bar owner back to her house. They were now in the research portion of the abduction, so they sat outside the bar and waited.

Alicia stood by the bedroom window and

watched Josh and Louis head into the woods. She was feeling okay about Josh, but she was having serious doubts about Louis, and she started to formulate a plan. A plan that would make Louis her seventeenth victim.

CHAPTER THIRTY-THREE

Bax had just sat down to breakfast when her phone rang. She looked at the number and answered. "Hey, Paul. What's up?"

Paul Webber had been doing research on expensive cars registered in Colorado. "Hey, Bax. I sent you a couple cars that might be candidates, but after speaking with some of the owners, I think I've narrowed it down to one that makes sense. Most of the owners I spoke with have either moved their cars out of state for the winter or have them locked away in a secure automotive storage facility. I spoke with one of those facilities in Denver, and if the owner is even half truthful, these places are like Fort Knox. I doubt our thieves would try to hit one of those facilities, but I have passed on the information, and the guy I spoke with is going to add more security, both physical and technological."

"Great, Paul. So, what does that leave us?"

"Out of twenty-seven mega-dollar cars we were able to find, we have spoken to all but one owner. The owner is that actor from all those fast car movies, and according to his agent, he is working on a film in Italy, and the car is locked in his garage in Aspen, along with a half dozen other cars."

"What makes you think this might be the car?"

"The car is a red Bugatti Chiron Sport. It is one of only three hundred made in 2019, and according to the registration, it was purchased four months ago for three point six million dollars."

Bax let out a long whistle. "You have to be kidding. Someone paid *that* much money for a car? People must be nuts."

"I guess if you can afford it, and this guy certainly can. He made fifty million dollars for his last movie, he likes fast cars and this is one of the fastest, most expensive cars in the world. That's like the perfect storm for a car guy. You wouldn't spend that much on a car if you had it?"

Bax laughed. "I'd need to talk to my accountant first. Paul, can you text me his address? Is there a security person or anyone I need to talk with?"

"Yes, and get this. The only security on the car is the locked garage and a video camera, which is there only because the insurance company required it. Right now, the only people on the property are the handyman, who's in his sixties, and a housekeeper, who is not much younger.

You want some help?"

"Yeah. Why don't you meet me in Aspen? Buck is in Aspen already, but he is tied up between PIS and the Alicia Hawkins case. I'll give him a call and fill him in. Great information, Paul. Thanks."

Bax hung up, took a sip of her coffee and was about to put a fork full of scrambled eggs in her mouth when her phone rang again. She checked the number and hit the answer button.

"Hi, Max. You're up early. What's up?"

"Hi, Bax. I wanted to catch you before you started your day. We got the DNA results from the Fontaine woman's rape kit, and the perp is in the system."

Bax set her fork back down on the plate. "Local?"

"No. The information was put in the system in Mount Airy, North Carolina. I requested a copy of the arrest report, and it's rather unimpressive. It appears that a high-school prank got a little out of hand, and an underage girl was groped. Her father pressed charges. The problem was, the kid who was arrested was eighteen, so they charged him as an adult and made him register as a sex offender. The sex offender designation required him to have a DNA sample on file. Bad for him, lucky for us."

"That's a pretty harsh sentence for a prank,

Max. I wonder if there was more to it than that?"

"I can't tell without requesting a copy of the court ruling, but my guess would be that you're right. But anyway. His name is Earl Richard Jefferson, twenty-six, six feet four and two hundred forty pounds. I knew you were on the road, so I sent everything we have over to Paul Webber, so he can do a deep dive into Mr. Jefferson."

"Max, you're awesome. I'll touch base with Paul on my way to Aspen. Thanks, Max."

Bax hung up and asked the waitress if she could pop her eggs and bacon in the microwave for a few seconds to warm them up, and the waitress said she'd take care of it. When she returned a few minutes later, she had a plate full of fresh scrambled eggs and crispy bacon, and she refilled Bax's coffee cup. She smiled at Bax and left the check on the table. Bax finished her meal, put a twenty-dollar bill on the table and headed for her car.

She threw her backpack on the front seat, pulled out her phone and dialed Buck. Even though it was early, she knew Buck would be awake. Buck answered and, with a whisper, said, "Hey, Bax. What's up?"

Bax filled him in on the DNA match and the information she had gotten from Max Clinton. She also told him about the information Paul had been able to gather on the expensive cars. Buck was silent for a minute, and she heard a door quietly close behind him.

"Sorry, Bax. I didn't want to disturb PIS."

Before he could continue, Bax asked him how PIS was doing. Buck took a few minutes to fill her in on PIS's condition and gave her some of the highlights from his conversation at dinner with Max, Devlin and Willie.

"Royalty, huh? I always wondered if he was more than he appeared." She hesitated for a minute. "Knowing how private PIS is, do you think he'll want to see his former teammates?"

"I have been wondering about that myself. As far as I know, PIS has never told anyone about his past life, and I still don't know what made him disappear all those years ago, but I'm wondering if them coming here to find him might have been a bad idea. I sat here all night, hoping he might wake up so I could tell him before they show up for another visit. The doctor is due in about an hour, and I might know more then. So, fill me in."

"I'm leaving Estes Park. I should be in Aspen in a couple hours."

She told him about the call from Paul and the car he'd located in Aspen, and she gave him a quick rundown on the DNA results.

"The information on Earl Jefferson works with the North Carolina license plate we are running down, from the video at the Fontaine house." She also told him about the young guy who had been on what appeared to be a stakeout across from the bar in Estes Park. She planned to have one of the techs from Denver travel to Estes and create a composite sketch of the kid on the bench.

"Great work, Bax. As soon as you can get an address for this guy Earl or a hit on the plate, call the state police in North Carolina and see if they have an investigator who can check out the house. We need to know if Jefferson is in town and who might be with him. Give me a call when you get to Aspen, and we can swing by and look at this Bugatti together."

"Buck, anything new on Alicia Hawkins?"

"No. I was going to call Hank Clancy in a little while and see if they were making any progress. Any luck with the information you put online?"

"I haven't had a chance to check. I'll call Paul and see if someone in the office can run a check on the social media and VRBO sites. I'll see you in a couple hours."

Bax pulled out of the parking lot and headed towards Aspen. As she left town, she dialed Detective Boyd and filled him in on everything that had happened since she'd left him the night before. He thanked her for the information and said he would run an internet search for Earl

Jefferson. She told him to call when he had anything, and she would do the same.

Bax called Paul Webber and asked him to also do a background search on Earl Jefferson. It wasn't that she didn't trust Detective Boyd, but CBI had access to a lot of resources that the detective didn't, and she wanted to cover all the bases. She hung up after talking with Paul and concentrated on the road. Hopefully, by the time she reached Aspen, she would have more to report to Buck.

CHAPTER THIRTY-FOUR

Buck stepped back into PIS's room, grabbed his backpack and was about to run out for some breakfast when his phone rang. He looked at the number and answered.

"Hey, Bob. What's up?"

Bob Brady sounded distraught. "Hey, Buck, sorry to call so early, but we've had a little disturbance in Wagner Park this morning, and I could use your help."

"What kind of disturbance, Bob?"

"My officers are holding your three friends. Get here as soon as you can."

Buck looked confused, then it hit him, and he wondered what kind of trouble Mac and his team had gotten themselves into. He left the hospital, climbed into his Jeep and headed for the park.

He turned onto South Monarch Street, parked behind an Aspen Police Department SUV and an Aspen Fire Department ambulance and walked towards the crowd gathered near one of the wooden picnic tables.

Mac, Devlin and Willie, with the cane and walker sitting next to them, were handcuffed and sitting on the bench next to the table. Willie was being treated for a cut on his forehead, and Mac was holding a towel against his bloody nose. They looked up as Buck approached. An EMT was also working on some cuts and scrapes on a homeless man sitting on the ground.

Bob Brady turned and walked towards Buck, who raised his hands in a "What the hell happened?" gesture.

Bob Brady started laughing. "Your three new friends are some characters. They attacked a. homeless vet in the park. That's him sitting on the ground, and they refuse to speak to anyone but you."

Buck looked at the table and was confused. "How is that possible? Two of them can barely walk."

Bob laughed again and walked towards the bench. His officers stepped away as they approached and were trying, with great difficulty, to not laugh themselves.

Buck stepped up to the trio. "Mac, what's going on? The chief says you attacked a homeless vet."

Mac looked up at Buck and nodded. "He's the fella who stabbed Pheasant."

"I did not," yelled the vet sitting on the ground.

"Mac, why don't you start at the top," said Buck.

"We stopped in that Irish pub for a drink after we left you. You know, the one Pheasant was drinking at the night he was stabbed. We were talking to people in the bar, and someone mentioned that they had seen that fella there"— he pointed to the vet— "get into a fight earlier in the day with Pheasant, and Pheasant had him pinned to the ground. When several other people mentioned it, we decided we should have a little talk with the fella, so we went looking for him. We talked with some homeless folks, and they told us where to find him and to be careful because he was crazy. We found him sleeping under this table, and we politely asked him to come out and talk to us."

"I assume, since we're all sitting here and you're in handcuffs, that he refused to speak with you?"

"Aye. He spoke with us in a foul manner, so we decided to teach him a lesson. The rest is why we are here in handcuffs."

"Mac, you guys aren't that young anymore. You could have been hurt."

"Nonsense," said Willie. "A few more minutes and we'd have had him."

Buck was not amused. "Why do you think he hurt Pheasant?"

"We don't know why, but they were seen rolling around in the grass, and Pheasant had to restrain him. Heard there was a lot of foul language."

"He also had a knife," said Devlin.

Buck looked surprised, and he looked, questioning, towards Bob Brady. Bob handed him a sealed evidence bag containing a military-issued Ka-Bar knife. Buck examined it through the plastic.

"Might be some blood on it," said Bob Brady.

Buck looked over to the vet. "Mind if I talk to him?"

Bob Brady nodded, and Buck stepped over to the vet. The EMT wrapped up what he was doing, and the officer guarding him stepped aside. Buck knelt next to him.

"What's your name, soldier?"

The vet looked Buck up and down. "I didn't hurt PIS, he's my friend."

"That's fine, but what's your name?"

"People call me Stick. Real name's Paul Stickley."

"Where'd you serve, Stick?"

"All over. Afghanistan, Iraq. Was with the 101st Airborne. Captain." He asked Buck to reach into his upper jacket pocket. Buck did and pulled out a silver star medal. Buck asked him if the medal was his, and he nodded. Buck put it back in his pocket.

"Okay, Stick. You want to tell me what happened?"

"Those crazy old coots attacked me. I was sleepin' under the bench when they grabbed me and started pounding on me. Big guy hit me with his cane, and the guy with the walker set it on my chest and held me down. I didn't do nothin'."

"They say you stabbed PIS. Is that true?"

"PIS is my friend. He helps me when I need help. I wouldn't hurt him."

"They found a knife in your things. Looks like it has some blood on it."

"I use that for cutting up meat. Had a rabbit two nights ago and skinned it with the knife. Never stabbed PIS with it."

"Stick, tell me what happened the other day when you got in a fight with PIS?"

Stick looked around like he was unsure what to say. Buck leaned in closer and looked at him. Buck had learned over the years that silence makes people uncomfortable, and he'd turned it into an interrogation technique that had worked well for him. His patience was legendary.

Stick watched Buck for a few minutes without saying a word. He finally gave up.

"PIS saved my life. We weren't fighting. I got some bad dope and was ODing. PIS was trying to give me the Narcan, but I couldn't stop thrashing. He finally laid down on top of me. The Narcan brought me around. There was no fight."

"Thanks, Stick." Buck stood up, and a young homeless woman standing off to the side said, "It's true, Officer. I was there. We had been partying all night and got some bad junk. Stick would be dead if PIS hadn't come along."

Buck thanked her and walked back to Bob Brady, who had overheard the whole thing. "I think this was a misunderstanding. My suggestion would be to let them all go. Let's give him back his knife. I doubt he wants to file charges against PIS's friends."

Bob Brady agreed and had his officers remove the handcuffs from everyone. Buck walked back over to Stick. He spoke quietly with him for a minute, so no one could hear, then he reached into his pocket, pulled out a twenty-dollar bill and handed it to Stick. They shook hands, and Stick and the homeless woman walked away.

Buck walked back to the trio of Brits as the

EMTs and police officers cleared the crowd that had gathered. He asked Mac if they had eaten breakfast yet and told them to head for his Jeep and that he would be along in a second. He walked back to Bob Brady.

"They are lucky Stick didn't kick their asses. He's got a pretty good build under that coat. You want to grab some breakfast with us? Might be interesting."

Bob Brady headed back to his SUV, and Buck walked back to his Jeep. He wondered how much more trouble these three were going to be before PIS woke up.

CHAPTER THIRTY-FIVE

The restaurant was crowded, but the hostess was able to find them a table in the back corner. They all sat down and ordered drinks. Coffee all around and a Coke for Buck. The waitress took their breakfast orders and walked away.

"What the hell were you guys thinking?" asked Buck.

Willie was the first to respond. "We thought we had him dead to rights. Several people in the bar said they saw the incident and described it as a fight. How were we to know?"

Bob Brady looked up from his coffee. "You should have come to either Buck or me. That's our job. You can't take the law into your own hands, even if PIS is your friend."

They all looked contrite, and the conversation turned to PIS's condition and progress on the case. Of which there hadn't been much. Buck decided to take the conversation in a different direction.

"You guys told me about how Pheasant got the scars on his back, and about the doctor he fell in love with. He carries around an old cigar tin with a small china teacup, a plate and a tea ball in it. At the bottom is a black-and-white picture of a pretty young woman. Is that a picture of the doctor who treated him after he was injured in Nam? When I asked him about it one night, he told me that some things were better left unsaid."

A sad silence seemed to come over the trio, and they looked at one another. It was as if no one wanted to tell the story of the tea set. It was apparent to Buck and Bob Brady that there was something important about that picture. Devlin took a sip of his coffee and set the cup down. He looked at the others, who nodded, and he looked at Buck.

"That tea set brings up some bad memories. We got called up to evacuate some British citizens from a small hospital in Uganda. We had been stationed in Africa for a couple months, and this had become part of our routine. Sometimes we did three or four evacuations in a week. The fighting in Uganda at the time was brutal, and we went wherever we were needed. We choppered into an area near the hospital and made our way through the jungle. Before we got to the hospital, we knew something was wrong. It was eerily quiet. Even the birds and animals were silent."

"We moved silently into the hospital grounds, and the scene was something none of us will ever forget. There were bodies scattered everywhere. Many were missing limbs or heads, and many of the women and girls had been raped before being butchered."

He stopped for a minute and took a sip of coffee. The eggs that had arrived a few minutes before were getting cold, but Buck and Bob Brady were focused on Devlin.

"Pheasant had no idea until we walked into the hospital that Dr. Quinn was even in the country. The last they'd spoken, she was working in a hospital in London. Somehow, her letter to Pheasant arrived after we left the base. The hospital's doctor had taken ill, and she had been asked by the hospital in London if she would be willing to fill in for a couple weeks. She had only arrived at the hospital two days before we got there."

"We found the ill doctor on the floor as we entered the hospital. He had been disemboweled and shot repeatedly. There were two patients in the two operating rooms that had been hacked to death, and then we found Dr. Quinn. She had been tied down to a hospital bed, stripped and raped by god knows how many men and boys. When they finished with her, they slit her throat. It was horrible."

There was silence at the table as everyone listened to the story. Willie wiped the tears from his eyes and continued. "Pheasant walked in before we could stop him, and he stood there and didn't say a word. He seemed numb. While we took care of burying the bodies, Pheasant was in her room, which had been ransacked like everything else. Among the debris, he found one cup and one saucer from a tea set he had bought her while we were on leave in London. The rest of the set was destroyed. Hidden in a niche in the wall, he found the small teapot and the tea ball."

"When we got back to him, he was sitting amongst the ruins with the cup and saucer and odd things he had found, including the picture. We found an old tin box, put the items in it for him and led him outside."

"Mac had been speaking with a couple young women who had managed to escape into the forest. The carnage had been caused by a local warlord who called himself General Mutombo. He wasn't any kind of recognized general, just a thug who had a few dozen men and boys he had recruited to help him. According to the women, it was the general himself who had killed the two doctors."

"We radioed in our situation, and since it was dark, we were told to wait until morning for evac. Sometime during the night, Pheasant disappeared into the jungle. By the time we noticed he was gone, he had about a five-hour head start. Mac was able to track him, and half a day later, we caught up with him, or I guess I should say, we found the destruction he had left in his wake."

"We reached the rebel camp late in the afternoon, and what we found was unimaginable. There were bodies everywhere, and like at the hospital, many were hacked to death, many were shot, and there wasn't a soul left alive. We found the general tied to a tree. He had been castrated, and his throat had been slit, almost taking his head off. In the middle of the camp, we found Pheasant's uniform and his weapons. We never saw him again after that. Mac tried to find his trail, but Pheasant was too good, and we never found a trail to follow. We didn't know if he was dead or alive. All we knew was that he had killed a lot of people that day."

"We left the camp as we found it, took Pheasant's uniform and weapons and made it back to the hospital, where we were evac'd back to base. The SBS sent several teams back to the area to search for Pheasant, but after a week, they called off the search. The SBS interrogated us about Pheasant's disappearance and about what we had found at the hospital. I don't know if they ever found the general's encampment, but no one ever mentioned it to us. He was officially listed as missing in action, and we moved on with our careers."

They ate their breakfasts in silence, and Buck could see that even to this day, it was hard for these men to talk about what had happened that day. If he were to try to understand, he would have a hard time picturing PIS as a stone-cold killer. Buck, more than anyone, had come to respect PIS over the years, and he tried to imagine PIS living with the nightmare of finding his girlfriend brutalized and the aftermath of what he did out of revenge. Buck wasn't sure, under those circumstances, if he would have reacted any differently. His family was his whole world, yet he figured he'd spent too many years as a cop and would have a hard time setting that aside to seek revenge. But then who knows how anyone would react in that situation?

He did know one thing. He now had a better understanding of why PIS had chosen to stay out of society and avoid living a normal life. He was even more worried that the presence of Mac and his buddies, after all these years and with all the emotions associated with that tragic day, might not be a good thing for PIS. He had no idea how PIS would react to them being in Aspen, but he wondered if he should suggest that they leave now and not wait around until PIS woke up.

Finished with breakfast and emotionally drained, Mac asked Buck if he would drive them back to their hotel. Buck picked up the check off the table, paid the bill and left a nice tip for the waitress. He said goodbye to Bob Brady and headed for his Jeep. They drove back to the hotel in silence. Buck told the trio that he would call them when Pheasant woke up, and he would pick them up if PIS wanted to see them. He let them out in front of the hotel, pulled onto Main Street and headed back towards the hospital. He was almost to the parking lot when his phone rang.

Buck answered the phone, and Max Clinton greeted him the way she always did. She then told him that the DNA results from the vomit in the alley where PIS had been stabbed were back from the lab. Buck listened, thanked her, hit his flashers and spun the car around in the street. He speed-dialed Bob Brady, told him to meet him back at Wagner Park and hit the gas.

CHAPTER THIRTY-SIX

Earl and Toby dropped their backpacks next to the RV and stepped through the door. They looked tired and cold. Victoria Larsen and Jessie were sitting at the table looking at pictures on Victoria's laptop. They both looked up as Earl and Toby walked in.

"We have everything we need from watching the house. There is no one home but a housekeeper and a maintenance guy. This should be a piece of cake."

Jessie nodded and asked them to look at the screen. "We got the same impression. Haven't seen anyone who looks like a movie star or anyone other than the folks you saw." Victoria had been monitoring the security cameras and digital assistants for the past couple days.

Victoria continued. "Your dad will be here tomorrow night. We've spent enough time in this town, so let's plan on going for the car as soon as he arrives. We've set up a rendezvous point at a turnout heading up Independence Pass."

She pulled up a local map on her laptop and

pointed to a turnout near an old abandoned mining camp. During the day, it was a local tourist trap, but at night no one went there. She highlighted the route they would follow once they had secured the car, and Jessie studied the map and memorized every street, including a couple backup routes, just in case something went wrong.

Earl and Toby slipped off their camo gear and crashed on their beds. They needed a couple hours of sleep, and then they would start making their final plans. The hardest part would be getting into the gated property, but they had no doubt that Victoria had already devised a plan to circumvent the security systems at the front gate. They were looking forward to a couple months off at the ranch in Montana.

In the meantime, Jessie and Victoria were going back through the camera feeds from the house to make sure they hadn't missed anything. They were all tired, and with this being their last job for a while, they didn't want any loose ends or mistakes.

After reviewing three days' worth of videos taken off the digital assistants and the security cameras, Jessie was feeling more and more confident that they were ready to make the grab. The older couple taking care of the house had developed a standard routine they followed to the letter every day, and it concluded with a couple hours of television-watching in the evening, checking all the doors and setting the perimeter alarms and retiring to their room in time for the nightly news.

Jessie had narrowed down the timeline before they went off to bed. Victoria had all the alarm codes, so gaining access to the house after the alarms were set would not be a problem. The only unknown was a ten-minute window when the maintenance guy was out of the picture. Since it happened every night, Victoria was convinced it was a dead spot in the alarm coverage. She had backtracked the entire system several times, but she couldn't say where the guy was going or what he was doing. She had located all the alarm zones, and she knew it had nothing to do with the system, but she was at a loss as to what he was doing during the ten minutes he was missing from view.

She chalked her concern up to a little paranoia and made sure that when she and Jessie set the schedule, they avoided that ten-minute window. By the end of the night, they had a plan that got them in and out in less than three minutes, and they were pleased. Victoria ran the plan through the simulator program she had on her laptop, and each time the results were the same. The successful removal of the car from the premises. She also had finished capturing all the police and sheriff's department frequencies, and they were now plugged into her laptop, so she could monitor everything that was happening with local law enforcement. By the time they slipped into bed, everything was running on autopilot. They each fell asleep dreaming about what they were going to do with all the money that was sitting in their online bank account.

The last thing Victoria did before calling it a night was check in with her broker. The deal was already set, and the money had been transferred to his bank. Once the broker received word that the car was enroute, he would transfer the money to Victoria's account. This would be their biggest payday yet, and she was very proud of her adopted family.

CHAPTER THIRTY-SEVEN

J osh and Louis thought they were ready. They had spent the last two days watching the bar owner, and they were confident that they knew the best time to grab her. Luckily for them, the bouncer did not go home with her after they closed the bar. Like a good soldier, he made sure she was safely in her car before he headed to his own house. They followed the same routine every night.

Once she got home, the bar owner would park her car in the garage that was separated from the house by about fifteen feet. She would open the back door to her house, walk in, shut off her alarm system and then come back and close the back door. This was the only mistake they saw her make, and this was where they would grab her. They would need to be close to the door when she got home, so they decided to split up. Josh would stake out the backyard of her house, while Louis would keep watch at the bar. Once she was in her car, assuming there was no sudden change of plans, Louis would race the half mile to her house and be ready for Josh's call.

There was a blind spot on the side of her garage between the garage and some trees where they could hide without being seen from the street. From that spot next to the garage, they were also hidden from her neighbors. They felt good about their plan.

The sun was clearing the mountains by the time they headed back to Alicia's place in the woods. They were passing by a park when they noticed a lot of police activity. They pulled to the curb and watched for a minute, hoping this didn't have anything to do with them. The police had a couple old geezers handcuffed and sitting at a wooden picnic table. They also had some homeless guy sitting on the ground a few feet away. He was also handcuffed.

They watched as an older fellow walked up and talked to one of the cops, who they figured was the chief of police, from all the stars on his collar. The older guy then walked over and spoke to the homeless guy on the ground. Josh recognized the older guy right away. That was that state cop, Buck Taylor. Alicia had told them to be on the lookout for him and let her know if they spotted him. They didn't know that much about his role in all of Alicia's plans, but she seemed spooked whenever she mentioned this guy. She also seemed pissed.

Having seen enough, they decided that whatever was going on in the park had nothing to do with them, so they pulled back onto the street and headed for Alicia's. They wanted to run their snatch-and-grab plan by Alicia to make sure they hadn't missed anything. They also wanted to get some sleep so they would be ready when it was time to grab the bar owner.

Alicia wasn't pleased when they told her that they had seen Buck Taylor in the park with a bunch of cops. She had them describe everything they saw, then she sat back quietly and contemplated her next move. It would be so incredible to hit Buck Taylor. Revenge would be so sweet, but she couldn't jeopardize her commitment to her grandfather. This was her tribute to him, and nothing would stand in her way. She also wondered why Buck Taylor was still in town. It had been several days since she had killed his homeless friend, and she'd figured he would probably help with the investigation, but by now they should have had their suspect in custody, and he should be moving on. She wondered if that was what all the police activity was in the park. Maybe they'd gotten the DNA results back and were attempting to arrest the homeless vet. She wished she could get in her car and drive over to the park to watch, but she was too close to take that chance.

If the opportunity presented itself after she was done fulfilling her tribute, maybe she would take on Buck Taylor.

Alicia walked through the plan for the abduction with Josh and Louis one more time as they fine-tuned it. Feeling good about what was to come, she changed the subject. She was still concerned that the FBI was already in Aspen looking for her, and she had a plan to cover her ass.

"I want you two to find a couple good spots along the trail to the cabin, and I want you to set up an ambush. Once we have the bar owner, I am going to need time, and I am worried that the police and FBI response might be faster than I expected."

Josh looked disappointed. He had hoped they could be there while Alicia did her work, and they could learn more about her techniques. He had studied everything written online about her, but getting the chance to see it all up close and personal, well, that was what he had been hoping for.

"Do you really think that could happen? How would they even find you?" asked Josh.

"Look, Josh. I know you want to see how this is done, but this kill is important to me. I promise you that once we are out of here and headed for California, there will be plenty of opportunities to teach you the proper way to use a scalpel and keep your victim alive. You will have my undivided attention, okay?"

Louis tapped Josh on the arm. He was relieved

that they were not going to be in the room while Alicia sliced up her next victim, but he tried not to show his relief.

"We promised to help Alicia with whatever she needed. Besides, it might be fun to kill a couple FBI agents, and who knows, maybe that Buck Taylor guy will be with them and we can kill him too."

Josh smiled, and he and Louis high-fived.

"Don't you worry, Alicia," said Josh. "We will make sure no one gets anywhere near this cabin."

They grabbed their coats and headed for the front door. Once they were gone, Alicia sat down at the kitchen table and sipped her cup of tea. She hated the waiting, especially after she'd already picked out her next victim, and more than anything, she hated to have to rely on people she didn't know she could trust. Everything depended on these two guys. She hoped they could deliver. The plan was sound, and she felt reasonably confident that it would work, but there was always that element that couldn't be accounted for. She finished her tea and cleaned the cup.

Alicia Hawkins sat by the fireplace and cried. It was the first time she had cried in a long time, and she wasn't sure what had brought this on. She had been thinking about her grandfather and how much she missed him. In a short time, she had been able to achieve everything he had achieved, and because of the internet, she was world-famous, which he had never achieved. Maybe it was all finally catching up to her. She was tired of hiding and never being able to sleep more than a couple nights in any one location. She also missed her family more than she realized. She knew her grandmother and her parents were concerned about her, but she couldn't stop now. This kill was important on so many levels.

She got hold of her emotions and started to move into killing mode. It wouldn't be long before she would have her next kill. She walked to the other bedroom, opened the closet door and looked at the plastic tarp that contained the bloated body of her last kill. She smiled a wicked smile and closed the door. She would be ready when the boys came back with the bar owner, and if the FBI or Buck Taylor tried to stop her, there would be hell to pay.

CHAPTER THIRTY-EIGHT

Buck pulled to the curb, slid out of his Jeep and headed to the small congregation of homeless people milling around the picnic table in the corner of the park. He spotted Bob Brady and two of his officers coming from the other side of the park. They reached the table at about the same time, and the conversation among the homeless stopped as they moved into the crowd. Stick was sitting at one corner of the table, sipping a beer.

"Stick," said Buck. "We need to talk to you."

Stick put his beer down on the table and looked around like he was trying to find a way out. One of the police officers reached him, grabbed his arms and pushed him down on the table. The crowd around them started to get noisy, especially when they handcuffed him.

"What the fuck is going on?" yelled Stick. "I answered all your questions. What more do you want?"

Bob Brady pushed through the crowd. "Stick, you're under arrest for stabbing PIS." While

Stick stood there looking bewildered, Bob read him his Miranda rights, and the two police officers escorted him towards the waiting patrol car. Buck and Bob Brady headed for their own vehicles.

Back at the police station, Stick was put in a holding cell while Buck and Bob Brady reviewed the DNA report that was now on the screen of Buck's laptop.

"DNA came back as a perfect match," said Buck. "The lab was able to get access to his military file, which contained a copy of his DNA."

"Yeah, I get that," said Bob Brady. "But how do you explain it? His alibi was confirmed by the girl in the park, and no one there raised any doubt about his story."

"I can't explain it, so let's go talk to him and see if we can figure this out."

The officer who had put the cuffs on Stick walked back to the holding cell and led Stick to a small interview room. Buck and Bob Brady deposited their guns in a wall safe outside the room, and the officer buzzed them in.

Stick was sweating and looked more afraid than anyone Buck could remember. He looked at Buck with pleading eyes.

"I didn't hurt no one. You got to let me out of here, I can't stand small spaces." His entire body shook.

"Okay, Stick. But we have a problem. You see, we gathered some evidence in the alley where PIS was stabbed, and your DNA was a perfect match. Can you help us understand how that's possible?"

Stick stopped shaking. "I told you about PIS saving me."

"That's right, you did, but that was in the park earlier. We think you caught up with PIS in the alley later and stabbed him. Maybe it was dark, and you didn't realize it was PIS, or maybe you had a beef with him from earlier."

"I didn't hurt PIS. He's my friend, and he saved my life."

"Why don't you tell us what really happened in the alley?"

"I never go into the alley. Ask anyone. I stay in the park."

"Stick, where do you get food, if you don't go into the alley?"

Stick turned pale, knowing that he was caught in a lie. All the homeless frequented the alleys, since there were no restaurants or trash dumpsters near the park. The closest place to find food was in the alley.

Stick put his head in his hands and closed his eyes. "Talk to anyone. PIS was my friend.

I wouldn't hurt him." He lifted his head and looked at Buck with tear-filled eyes.

Buck looked at the DNA report on his laptop. "Stick, you said that PIS gave you Narcan that night when those British fellows said you and PIS had a fight. Do you remember that night?"

Stick nodded his head. "I got some bad dope, like the girl in the park said. PIS gave me the Narcan, or I would have died."

"Did you get sick from the dope? Maybe vomit?"

"No. I hadn't eaten anything since the day before. Nothing in my stomach to throw up. Why?"

"When was the last time you were in the alley? And remember, we can check the security cameras and see when you were there."

Stick thought for a minute, not sure what was going on. "I hadn't been down that end of the alley in a couple days. The restaurants are all at the other end, not by the bookstore. So most of us never go down that end. There's never anything good to eat."

"Stick, we found your vomit in the area where PIS was stabbed. Can you explain that?"

Stick's expression said it all: confusion, bewilderment and something else that Buck noticed. For the first time since they'd brought him in, Buck could see a question looming in Stick's mind. Was it possible he'd stabbed PIS and didn't remember doing it?

Stick buried his face in his hands and cried. Buck and Bob Brady decided to give him a minute to think about it, so Buck picked up his laptop and they stood up. The officer on duty outside the interrogation room buzzed the door, and Bob Brady pulled open the door. Buck was about to close the door behind him when he heard Stick say something that stopped him in his tracks.

"The girl with the purple stripe in her hair can tell you when I got sick."

Buck stepped back into the room and stood by the table. "Stick, what did you say?"

Stick looked up and wiped his runny nose on his sleeve. "I just remembered. I got sick from some bad food a couple days ago, and a girl with a purple stripe in her hair helped me out, so I wouldn't drown in my own puke. If you can find her, she will tell you I didn't get sick in the alley."

"What else do you remember about this girl you say helped you?"

By this time, Bob Brady had stepped back into the room and was looking at Buck.

"Not much," said Stick. "She rolled me over so I could puke easier, and she found me a blanket and covered me up. That's all I remember."

"Buck," said Bob Brady. "What are you thinking?"

Buck led Bob Brady out of the interrogation room and sat on the edge of a desk, his mind racing as he considered the possibilities.

"This is going to sound far-fetched, but try this. Stick gets sick, and this girl helps him, then scoops up his vomit and leaves it in the alley after she stabs PIS."

"Okay, that's a little bizarre, but why?"

"To throw us off the track. I think Alicia Hawkins is in Aspen."

"Buck, that's a hell of a jump. We're gonna need a lot more than the drug-induced memories of a homeless guy. Besides, why hurt PIS? If I remember right, he didn't have anything to do with the serial killer case."

"That I can't answer, but I know someone who might. I'm heading back to the hospital to see if PIS is awake. Let's keep Stick on ice for a while till I can figure this out."

Buck grabbed his backpack off the desk, slid his gun back into his holster and headed for the door. He needed answers, and he needed them fast.

CHAPTER THIRTY-NINE

Buck pulled into the hospital parking lot, grabbed his backpack and raced for the front door. He took the elevator up to the ICU and stopped short when he got to PIS's room. The room was empty. He walked back to the nurse's station, where he found out that PIS was awake and had been moved to a regular room. He took the elevator up to the third floor and found PIS's room.

PIS was indeed wide awake and talking with the male nurse assigned to his room. He stepped into the room.

"Ah, Agent Taylor, a pleasure to see you, sir."

"PIS, are you okay? You had us all pretty worried."

"A minor inconvenience. I shall be up and about in no time."

The nurse left the room, and PIS's jovial expression turned serious. "I believe you have an enemy about, Agent Taylor."

Buck had tried for years to get PIS to call him

Buck but to no avail. No matter the circumstances, PIS continued to call him Agent Taylor, even in private.

"What are you talking about, and how much do you remember about the attack?"

"I remember it all very clearly. My attacker was a young woman, that was what caught me off guard. I thought she was having a drug reaction, so my focus was on helping her. I never saw the knife until it was too late. I must be getting old. That would have never happened in my youth."

"What does that have to do with me having an enemy?"

"After she stabbed me, she whispered in my ear, 'When you see Buck Taylor in hell, tell him Alicia says hello.'"

"Are you sure she said, 'Alicia says hello'?"

"No doubt. If it helps any, I did notice that she had a purple stripe in her hair. If I remember correctly, that sounds like your serial killer to me. What I don't understand is how she connected me to you."

Buck sat back in the chair and thought for a minute. PIS may have been homeless, but he had a good grasp of things going on in the world around him, so it didn't surprise him at all that PIS knew about Alicia Hawkins. A lot had gone on in Aspen during that week a year ago, but what confused him was that PIS hadn't had anything to do with Alicia Hawkins, so why target him?

A crazy thought occurred to him. They had all been concerned about the possibility of Alicia Hawkins targeting one of Buck's children. It never occurred to him that she might target his friends. PIS was old and homeless and looked weak and frail; he would be an excellent target if she felt she couldn't get to Buck. But how had she connected them?

"Agent Taylor. From what I understand about this young woman, she is evil. She is back in Aspen for a reason, and you are a part of it. If you find her, you need to finish this. She does not deserve the benefit of the doubt. You must take her out."

Buck stared at PIS, and he could see the intensity in his gray eyes. What made PIS's words even darker was knowing what he knew now about PIS's past. He had no doubt that PIS would have no qualms about taking Alicia's life, but Buck was a cop. He had a different moral code that had served him well. Deep down inside, he knew PIS was probably right, but Buck was still about justice and not revenge.

"PIS, I'm a cop. When the time comes, I will arrest Alicia Hawkins, and she will be tried and convicted. If the state or the federal government wants to execute her for her crimes, that's up to a judge and jury to decide. I will not play judge, jury and executioner."

PIS looked at Buck and smiled. "I understand how you feel, Agent Taylor. I once had those kinds of values, but that was long ago. I know, in the end, you will do the right thing."

"PIS, talking about long ago. Some friends of yours from the past are in Aspen and would like to see you."

PIS cut him off. "I know they are here, Agent Taylor. I will deal with them in my own way, but I have left orders with the nurses that they are not to be allowed in my room."

Buck wasn't surprised by PIS's comment. He had wondered how their arrival would sit with the secretive Brit. Buck dropped the subject and pulled out his phone. He hit a speed dial button and waited.

Hank Clancy answered. "Hey, Buck. What's up?"

"Hey, Hank. I have good reason to believe that Alicia Hawkins is in Aspen."

"What makes you think that? It's like she's fallen off the radar. Why Aspen?"

"I don't know the why, but a friend of mine was stabbed a couple days ago, and he just woke up. He said the person who stabbed him was a young woman with a purple streak in her hair, and she left him a message for me."

"Is this friend someone she would have known about or been able to find out about?"

"I'm still working on that, Hank, but it would not have been easy to connect us. I'm not sure how she found him, but I believe she did."

"Okay, Buck. You keep your guard up. I'm gonna roll the task force, and we will get there as soon as we can. Stay safe."

Hank hung up, and Buck looked at PIS. He was about to say something when Bax walked into his room.

"Agent Baxter, how wonderful to see you again."

Bax nodded at Buck and walked over to the bed and gave PIS a slight hug. She didn't know PIS as well as Buck did, but they had worked together on a couple cases with Buck, and like everyone else, she had a deep fondness for the strange man.

"PIS, you don't look too worse for wear. How are you feeling?"

"Not bad. Nothing a few days in this luxury resort won't cure. I'll be back on my feet in no time at all."

Bax now turned her attention towards Buck.

"Paul Webber is on his way and should be here in a couple hours. We are going to contact the owner of that expensive car that lives here in Aspen, or at least his caretakers, and see if they have noticed anything out of the ordinary."

She noticed the dark expression on Buck's face. "Did I interrupt something?"

Buck told her about the call he'd made to Hank Clancy and about their belief that PIS had been attacked by Alicia Hawkins. She looked stunned.

"Why would she come back to Aspen, Buck, and how would she even know about PIS?"

"That I can't answer, but maybe we can do a little research and see if there is anything important happening here in Aspen that might have brought her home. As far as how she found out about PIS, I have no idea."

Bax pulled her laptop out of her backpack and fired it up. "I have some time until Paul arrives. Let me do a little data mining and see what I can find."

Buck looked over and saw that PIS had his eyes closed and was breathing softly. He wasn't sure what to think anymore. Sleeping like he was, PIS looked almost angelic, but Buck knew there was a side to PIS that no one else knew about. He hoped that knowledge wouldn't impact their relationship going forward.

Buck picked up his phone from the table and called Bob Brady. "Bob, PIS is awake, and he confirmed Stick's story. He was stabbed by a woman with purple hair. I just got off the phone with Hank Clancy, and he is mobilizing his task force. You need to be prepared for a sudden influx of federal agents in your town. Go ahead and release Stick. Also, can you have your guys check and see if there are any missing person reports in the area?"

"No worries. What are you going to be doing?"

"I'm going to talk to her family and see if any of them have heard from her."

CHAPTER FORTY

Mac, Devlin and Willie climbed out of the Lyft car they had ordered and headed towards the hospital entrance. They were hoping PIS was finally awake, and they would be able to visit with him for a while. Mac had mentioned at breakfast this morning that they should probably think about heading back to Washington, DC, to rejoin their travel group. No doubt, the tour guides must be wondering what happened to them, since they disappeared without telling anyone where they were going. He was surprised that no one had alerted the authorities to their disappearance.

They were crossing the hospital driveway when a Cadillac SUV pulled to the curb in front of them, and the driver stepped out of the car and held open the back door.

"Gentlemen. Someone wishes to have a word."

Mac looked at the others, and they all nodded. The driver's accent was British, but it was somewhat Americanized, possibly a Midwestern twang. They stepped over to the door and slid inside, taking their cane and walker with them. They were not sure who they were about to meet, and they were all on high alert. The driver closed the door, slid into his seat and drove away from the hospital.

Mac tried to ask the driver a couple questions, but the only response he received was silence. They also noticed that the windows were so darkly tinted that they could barely see out of them. They drove a few miles outside of town and turned down a dirt road, which eventually opened into a large field with an incredible view of the mountains. The driver pulled to a stop next to another SUV, and the driver of that vehicle slid out, walked over and slid into the front passenger seat of the SUV they were in.

"Good afternoon, gentlemen. It is nice to see you again."

The man doing the speaking seemed familiar in some way, but they couldn't be sure. He was tall, with short gray hair and a gray Van Dyke beard. He was impeccably dressed, and his accent was as smooth as silk.

It was Willie who made the connection and spoke up. "Stanford, is that you?"

"Yes, Mr. Willie. It is."

They stared at one another in disbelief. A member of the Stanford family had been employed by the Iverson-Smythe family at all times since the 1300s. The Stanford family had always served as majordomos to the duke and ran the family estates. Their histories were so intertwined, it was hard to tell where one started and the other left off. To say the trio was stunned would have been an understatement. The idea that a Stanford was in the United States and still working for Pheasant's family boggled the mind, especially since they assumed Pheasant had ceased all contact with his family when he disappeared. That was obviously not the case.

"I can see you are a bit confused by all this, but trust me when I tell you that I am not here today to clear up any of your questions. I come with a request from Pheasant. He appreciates the fact that you were able to locate him, even if by accident, and that you felt compelled to come all this way to track him down. However, he would prefer that things remain as they are. He does not wish to see you at this time. Towards that end, we feel it is best if you either return to your tour group or return to England without further attempts to visit him in the hospital."

Mac was the first to speak up. "I don't understand. We've come all this way to visit a friend we thought was dead, and all you can say is go home? I'll be damned if I'll do that without at least an explanation."

Devlin and Willie started to agree, and Stanford held up his hand. "Gentlemen, I know how you must feel, but it is for your own good that we make this request. There will be no further discussion of the matter. I'm sorry. Tomorrow afternoon, a jet will arrive at the Aspen airport. The pilot is prepared to take you wherever you would like to go. If you want to rejoin your tour in Washington or if you would like to fly directly back to England, just let the pilot know." He pointed to the driver. "Gerald will pick you up once the plane arrives and take you to the airport. You will not need any flight documents, just yourselves and your bags. Please enjoy your last night in Aspen. Gerald will make arrangements for you to have dinner in one of Aspen's finest restaurants. I know this is very difficult to understand, but please know that we appreciate your discretion. Safe travels."

With that, Stanford slid out of the car, closed the door, climbed into the other SUV and drove away. The trio were too stunned to speak. They had no idea what they had gotten themselves into or what Pheasant was involved in, but whatever it was, they had been clearly told that their being in Aspen was bringing undue attention to Pheasant, and that attention was not appreciated. Was it possible that after all these years, Pheasant was still involved with the government? He was definitely not a soldier anymore, at least not in the classic sense, but what the hell had happened during the last thirty years, and why was he in Aspen?

Gerald dropped them off outside their hotel and told them he would pick them up at seven for dinner. He pulled away from the curb, and they just stood there and looked at one another. Over the years, they had found themselves in some unusual situations, but this was strange.

Devlin and Willie headed to their rooms, but Mac stayed outside to have a smoke. He finished his cigarette, pulled out his phone and clicked on the Lyft app. He entered the hospital as his destination and waited for the driver. He had been friends with Pheasant for too long to just walk away.

CHAPTER FORTY-ONE

Buck pulled up to the little Victorian house on West Hallam Street, turned off the engine and sat for a minute looking at the house. The last time he had been here, the Hawkins family's lives were turned upside down. Not only had they found out that their father and grandfather, Thomas, had been a serial killer starting back in the fifties and sixties, and that his wife had been having an affair with the local sheriff following the accident that left her husband a quadriplegic. The worst of all was finding out that Alicia—daughter, granddaughter and college student—was following in her grandfather's footsteps. Buck was amazed that after all they had been through, the family had been able to stay together.

He was about to step out of the car when the front door opened, and Judith Hawkins stepped out onto the front porch and stood against the rail looking at him. Judith was the matriarch of the family. She looked older now than she'd looked on the day she found out her husband had murdered fifteen women, but she still stood tall.

Buck could only imagine how the last year of her life must have gone, with the whole town talking about her husband and now her granddaughter. She lived in a world of monsters, but she still held her head up high.

Buck walked up the steps to the porch and shook her frail, translucent hand. She shivered at the touch.

"Mrs. Hawkins, it's nice to see you again."

"Agent Taylor, it's nice to see you as well. Is there some news of my granddaughter?"

"We're not sure, ma'am. We've heard rumors that she may be back in the area, and we were wondering if she had tried to contact you or anyone in the family?"

Mrs. Hawkins sat down on the swing, and Buck sat down next to her. She pulled her shawl tighter around her shoulders. Buck could see the sadness that still filled her eyes. The last time they'd sat on this very swing and spoken, Mrs. Hawkins had asked Buck to please find her granddaughter.

"I doubt she would try to contact us, Agent Taylor, and it's odd that she would come back here, where she is so widely known. Are you certain of your information?"

"No, ma'am, this is all just speculation at this point. The FBI has been tracking her, and they lost her somewhere in Oklahoma. We were hoping she had tried to contact you folks."

"Do you really think we would tell you if she had?"

The voice coming from behind the screen door belonged to Thomas Jr. Buck looked up as he pushed open the screen door and stood next to his mother.

"Haven't you people caused us enough grief for one lifetime? My mother barely leaves the house anymore. She can't go to church or the supermarket without someone calling her names and spewing vile filth in her direction. We are prisoners in our own house. The whole town hates us, and you have the nerve to show up on our doorstep to see if we have heard from that monster. I want you off my porch and out of our lives."

"Thomas, enough." Mrs. Hawkins still wielded power over her son, and he shut up and stepped closer to the screen door. If looks could kill, Buck would be fighting for his life right now.

Mrs. Hawkins said, "Agent Taylor did not create this problem. This is your father's doing, and he didn't force your daughter to become a monster, just like him, that was her choice. Agent Taylor has treated us with nothing but respect, and no matter what our circumstances, we will not treat him with anything less. I am sorry, Agent Taylor. With the first anniversary of Thomas's death fast approaching, we are all a little emotional."

"Ma'am, if I may ask, when did your husband pass away?"

"It will be one year tomorrow. We had him cremated, and we scattered his ashes at a location that was special to him. We were afraid that if vandals found out we had buried him, they might destroy his grave either out of spite or looking for ghoulish souvenirs. Tomorrow will be the first time we have been back to that location since then."

Buck hadn't noticed it before, but the little bug that ran around in his brain when something started to make sense about a case felt like it was doing an Irish jig on his skull. Could it be that simple? Could she be coming back to visit the site where they'd scattered her grandfather's ashes?

"Ma'am, does Alicia know where you scattered your husband's ashes? Does she know about this special location?"

Mrs. Hawkins sat silently and thought for a minute. If she made any connection, it did not show on her face.

"I don't believe she did know about that place. Even my children didn't know it until I told them about it. It was a place only Thomas and I knew about, and I don't believe it was ever discussed. Why do you ask?"

"I'm just trying to figure out if there is a special reason she might come back to Aspen now. Why she would take the risk?"

"You're barking up the wrong tree, Agent Taylor," said Thomas Jr. "My daughter is far away from here, and if she ever did show up, we might find out that I have the same tendencies my father had, and I might save you the trouble of arresting her."

"Thomas, enough of that talk. She is still your daughter and my granddaughter, and she may have done some terrible things, but I will not have you talking that way in my house."

Thomas Jr. pushed through the screen door and let it slam behind him. Mrs. Hawkins shivered and pulled her shawl up around her neck.

"I hope you find my granddaughter, Agent Taylor, before someone who doesn't care about her finds her first. It was nice to see you again."

Mrs. Hawkins stood up from the porch swing, shook Buck's hand and stepped into her house. Buck stood for a minute playing the conversation back in his head. The presence of the little bug in his brain told him that what they had discussed was important. He just needed to figure out why.

Buck walked back to his car, pulled out his phone and dialed Bax, who answered on the first ring.

"Hey, Buck, I just left you a text. Paul and I are heading to speak to the folks about the car, but I found something interesting. I couldn't find any newsworthy event happening this week in Aspen that might attract Alicia Hawkins, but I think I figured out how she found out about PIS. Look at the text, and I'll call you when we finish here."

"Okay, Bax. Stay safe."

Buck hung up, slid into his Jeep and headed back to the hospital. He wanted to talk with PIS a little more about the attack. He had a muddy picture in his brain, and he needed to clear up a few things to bring it into focus.

CHAPTER FORTY-TWO

Bax pulled up to the massive weathered steel gate and pushed the button on the communication tower. She held up her CBI ID card so the camera could see it and waited.

"May I help you, Officer?" The female voice was clear and distinctive, without the hint of an accent.

"CBI Agents Baxter and Webber. We would like to speak with Mr. James Murphy, please."

There was silence for a minute, and then the gate started to swing open. Bax was amazed. The gate looked old and covered with rust, yet it swung open with hardly a sound. She pulled through the gate and followed the long driveway past several fenced fields containing a variety of horses. Bax had grown up around horses, and she could see that these weren't thoroughbreds but working horses, and they looked well cared for.

She parked her Jeep in front of a log-and-stone house that looked more like a Western apartment building than a private residence and seemed ideally suited for its location against the backdrop of Aspen Mountain in the distance. They grabbed their backpacks and walked towards the two massive wooden front doors.

The door on the right opened silently as they approached, and an older gentleman wearing a beat-up cowboy hat, jeans and a flannel shirt stepped out onto the porch.

"If I could see your IDs again, folks. Can't ever be too careful," he said. Bax noticed that he had a touch of an accent, but it sounded more East Coast than Western. He put on a pair of reading glasses and carefully compared the photos to their faces. He handed them back their IDs.

"Thanks, folks. Sheriff said you two were okay, but I like to be sure. Come on in."

He stepped to the side and let Bax and Paul pass through the door into a room that Bax could only describe as huge and warm. There was wood everywhere, except for the massive stone fireplace that sat in the middle of one wall. All the furniture was rustic wood and leather, and the fire burning in the grate gave the room a soft glow.

"Sir, you checked us out from the time we pulled up to your gate until we walked up to the door?"

The older man turned and faced Bax. "Yes, ma'am. We have an arrangement with the sheriff's office. We had a bit of a stalker problem a while back, and, well, we support the sheriff's office in their volunteer programs, and they, in turn, help us keep track of who's coming and going. It's a good relationship."

"Did the sheriff tell you why we are here?" asked Paul.

An elderly woman stepped out of a doorway next to the fireplace. "He just told me it was important," she said. She walked over and held out her hand for a handshake, which Paul noticed was strong and firm. "I'm Mary Winslow, and that good-lookin' cowboy is my husband, Roy. It's nice to meet you both."

They shook hands all around, and then Mary invited them into the kitchen, where she had a fresh pot of coffee brewing and an apple pie cooling. Bax stopped them before they entered the kitchen and leaned in close.

"Is there a spot in the house not covered by the security cameras or the digital assistants?" she asked softly.

Roy looked at his wife and nodded, and she headed down the hall past the kitchen to a single door in the back of the house. They stepped through the door and found themselves in a small office space. Mary closed the door.

Roy said, "This is our space. I hate all that electronic gadgetry, so I had them leave a space for just us, to get away from it all."

The room was comfortable, and it contained a small desk, a couch and a large TV mounted to the wall.

"If I may ask, Agent Baxter. This seems a little mysterious. What's going on?"

"We believe a team of car thieves might be targeting Mr. Murphy's Bugatti. They have stolen several very expensive cars in several states, and they have been working in Colorado for the past couple weeks. Mr. Murphy's car is one of the most expensive cars registered in the state, so we are trying to be proactive."

Roy looked disgusted. "I told Jimmy not to buy that damn car. Told him it would be nothing but trouble. But why the secrecy?"

Paul took over. "We think the team is hacking into home security systems and digital assistance devices and using them to study the houses and the residents' movements. That's why we wanted to speak out of earshot of anything internet-connected. Have you noticed anyone around or noticed anything odd concerning your internet or your security system?"

"I can't say I have, but then I try to avoid the internet thing as much as possible," said Mary.

"Are you folks here alone, right now? I read that James Murphy is in Europe, filming a movie."

"Yeah," said Roy. "We take care of the place while our grandson makes movie magic."

Bax and Paul looked at each other. "You're his grandparents?" Bax asked.

"Yes," said Mary. "I'm sorry. I thought you knew. We've been taking care of him for years, since his mom, our daughter, died. Breast cancer. When he hit it big, he bought this place and moved us out here from Indiana. We love the solitude and the beauty, and Roy loves the horses. We also have a couple day workers who help around the ranch. It's a good life." She hesitated. "Are these car thieves dangerous?"

"I don't want to scare you," said Bax. "They have injured several people and possibly killed one man."

Mary and Roy looked at each other nervously.

"What do you need from us?" asked Roy.

Paul pulled out his laptop and sat down at the desk. "I'd like to have you call your security company and ask them to give me access to your account. I want to see if anyone has tried to get access without your knowledge. While I'm doing that, I want to put your security cameras into a loop so Agent Baxter can go to the garage and put a tracker on the car."

"We would also like to put you folks up in a

hotel for a couple days. Will the horses be okay without you for a bit?" asked Bax.

"Yeah. That's not a problem," said Roy. "I'll let the boys know. They come by in the morning to feed and water them, but they're usually gone by noon."

Bax handed Roy her phone. She didn't want him calling from his cell or the house landline, just in case they had been compromised. He dialed the security company, spoke to someone for a few minutes and then handed the phone to Paul. Paul talked to the person on the other end and started clicking keys. After a few minutes, he looked up at Bax.

"We put the camera system into a loop. Go ahead and put the tracker on the car," he said.

Bax and Roy left the office, and Paul continued working on his laptop while talking to the technician on the other end. By the time Bax and Roy got back, he was finishing up with the tech. He hung up and sat back in the chair.

"The system was definitely hacked. The tech I was working with can see the intrusion, but they can't figure out how their system was breached. To say they were stunned would be an understatement. Bax, this was some world-class hacking. Whoever broke in has some mad skills. I will remove the loop once we leave, then Mary and Roy can go on with their lives until they are ready to leave."

"Awesome," said Bax. "I called the director from the garage, and he is making arrangements to put the Winslows up in a hotel in town. Can you monitor the cameras and the system remotely?"

Paul nodded. He had access to the entire system, and they would know as soon as someone entered the house.

Bax called Pitkin County Sheriff Earl Winters and arranged to meet with him and his SWAT team at their office. Since they had a tracker on the car, her plan was pretty simple. Let the bad guys grab the car and then have several SWAT units spread out around town and see where it went.

She was helping Mary pack a couple bags when her phone rang. She didn't recognize the number.

"Baxter."

"Hi, Agent Baxter. This is Detective Sergeant Leroy Johnson with the North Carolina State Police. My commander asked me to call you about that individual you wanted us to check out. Do you have a minute?"

"Good afternoon, Sergeant. Please, go ahead."

The sergeant explained that he'd stopped by the last known address of Earl Richard Jefferson, and he found the house empty. The neighbors said the family had loaded up their RV and moved out about two months ago. He also said he did a search for other family members. He found a Jessie and a Toby Jefferson listed at the same address, as well as Frank Jefferson and a Victoria Larsen. He also found a civil marriage certificate showing that Frank and Victoria had been married about three years ago.

"One other thing of note. Frank Jefferson was investigated several years ago for auto theft. The case was dismissed for lack of evidence. That was in 2008, and he's been clean ever since. He has a commercial driver's license, and I was able to find a semi registered in his name. I'm emailing you everything I've got. Hope this helps."

Bax thanked the sergeant for his help and hung up. She was excited. The semi was a huge lead. She needed to call Buck and the CBI director, but first, she needed to set up a surveillance net with the sheriff. She called the CBI office in Grand Junction, reached the cyber unit and asked them to start doing a deep dive into the Jeffersons and Victoria Larsen. She asked them if it was possible to check the most recent travels of the semi registered to Frank Jefferson. The cyber tech told her that it might be possible to follow them by checking state weigh stations and ports of entry, starting in Colorado, and then checking the neighboring states to see if they could get a travel direction. He told Bax he would get the team right on it and would call her back if they found anything.

CHAPTER FORTY-THREE

Buck found PIS sitting up talking with one of the nurses. The nurse left the room when Buck walked in. PIS looked much better than he had the day before. This Brit constantly amazed Buck with his stamina and ability to heal. A year ago, PIS had checked himself out of the hospital just a couple days after having surgery to remove a five-inch-long chunk of wood from his right shoulder.

"Good morning, Agent Taylor. Any luck with locating your young serial killer?"

Buck filled him in on his conversation with Alicia Hawkins's grandmother. He also asked him to walk through the night in the alley when he'd gotten stabbed.

PIS, slowly and deliberately, retold the events of that evening. He knew Buck was keying in on everything he said, looking for even the smallest detail. He had worked with Buck enough to know that nothing was to be left out of the narrative, no matter how minor.

PIS stopped his narration and looked up at

Buck. "I suppose the doctor filled you in on my unique condition, which is the very reason I am not now lying on a slab, instead of resting comfortably in this bed?"

"He told me. Said you most likely have a twin somewhere who is perfectly normal. He also told me it looked like someone had marked your heart a long time ago and shot you. I'll bet that's an interesting story."

Buck didn't want PIS to know that his friends had spilled the beans on some of PIS's adventures. He hated lying to him, but he figured it was more of an omission than a lie. PIS was a very private person, and Buck figured that if he wanted to tell him about his past life, he would.

PIS just brushed the comment off with a wave of his hand. "Possibly a tale for another day. Right now, we need to concentrate on your serial killer."

Buck pulled out his phone and opened the text that Bax had sent him. He read her summary and then looked at the photo she'd attached. Buck hadn't seen this picture before, but he assumed this must be the same picture that Mac had referenced. It was a picture of Buck and Sheriff Winters standing near the search and rescue truck, and standing just off to one side was PIS. The note under the photo indicated that the homeless man in the background had aided the search teams looking for the missing ranger. Buck showed PIS the picture.

"Well, Agent Taylor, I believe that is one mystery solved. Your young serial killer was born and raised around here. She would have known who I was. She probably did her research and figured out that you and I had worked together on several cases. She probably assumed we were friends."

"I still don't get what she hoped to achieve by attacking you instead of coming after me."

Buck was about to say something else when the little bug in his brain smacked the side of his skull. It was something her grandmother had said. Buck hadn't kept track of when Alicia's grandfather died, but Mrs. Hawkins said that he would be dead one year tomorrow. Buck sat back in his chair. PIS looked at him.

"I've seen that look before, Agent Taylor. I believe you are on to something important."

"I think I am, PIS. According to her grandmother, her grandfather died one year ago tomorrow. Now think about this. Her grandfather killed fifteen women before his accident. He was planning to kill his sixteenth victim the night of the crash. When Alicia left Oklahoma a couple weeks back, the FBI listed that kill as her fourteenth. A lot of death in just a year. Suppose she wanted to make a big statement to mark her grandfather's passing. Suppose she wanted to mark the first anniversary of her grandfather's death by killing her sixteenth victim. The victim he never got to kill."

PIS looked serious. "That would be quite a tribute to her grandfather, but that would also mean that somewhere out there is another body. By your reasoning, number fifteen is probably already dead. If you are correct, you need to stop her today."

"Fuck, Buck. That's a hell of a theory."

Hank Clancy stood in the doorway with two of his task force agents. He looked exhausted. He also was not wearing his typical government-issue uniform, as Buck liked to call it. Instead, he had on jeans, Western boots and a leather jacket. He ran his hands through his hair.

"Your friend is right. If this is some grand scheme to honor her grandfather, then we are already too late to save some poor soul from her wrath, but that still doesn't answer why she tried to kill your friend here. It's almost like she was inviting you to be a witness to her depravity."

Buck introduced Hank to PIS, and they shook hands. They exchanged some pleasantries, and then Buck cut them off.

"How could she know I would show up? Nothing in the article indicated that PIS and I had anything more than a working relationship. There was no guarantee that I would get here, and she did her damnedest to cover her tracks. I don't think she was focused on me being here. I think she found a way she thought might hurt me. No offense, but if you had seen PIS around town, he looks thin and frail. I think he was an easier target in her mind than me."

"Okay. For now, let's put that aside," said Hank. "The question is, how do we find her before someone else dies?"

Buck pulled out his phone and speed-dialed a number. Bax answered. "Hey, Buck. What's up?"

"Hey, Bax. Did you ever get any responses to the information you posted on the vacation rentals by owner sites?"

"As a matter of fact, we didn't. I didn't check today, because of the car theft thing, but let me pull up my email and see if anyone responded."

Bax came back a minute later. "Nothing, Buck. Sorry."

"That's okay, Bax. Any idea of how many VRBOs are in the Aspen Valley?"

"Couple hundred, I would guess. Why?"

"I've got an idea. Let me talk to Hank and get back to you. How'd it go with the car owner?"

"I've got a tracker on the car, and we have access to their security cameras. We are putting the two people who live there up in a hotel, and I'm just walking into a meeting with Sheriff Winters to set up a surveillance net."

"Nice work. Keep me posted."

Buck hung up his phone, and it rang again. Buck recognized the number and answered. "Yes, sir."

"Buck sounds like we've got a lot of activity going on in Aspen. Can you give me a quick rundown?" asked Director Jackson.

Buck filled him in on the car theft ring, and then they spent a few minutes discussing Alicia Hawkins and Buck's latest theory. The director listened without comment until Buck was finished.

"Do you think your friend PIS was a substitute for you, and this was a revenge thing? That seems like a stretch, since you had nothing to do with her grandfather dying. If I remember right, he was already dying when you finally found the connection."

"Correct, sir. I think it was a spur-of-the-moment response when she saw the picture on the internet. I think in her twisted mind, at that moment, she blamed me for her not being able to go to his funeral or say goodbye. I think PIS was an easy target, but right now, none of that matters. We need to figure out how to find her."

"Buck, based on your report from Oklahoma, she rented an out-of-the-way cabin. Do you think she did the same thing in Aspen?"

"We were just discussing that. Bax has not had any response from any rental owners about renting to a single woman, which didn't surprise me."

"Buck, can the FBI help with this?"

"Yes, sir. Hank is here with me now. We just spoke with Bax and were moving on to the next step. I will call you back as soon as we have an idea."

Hank was just finishing up a call when Buck disconnected his phone. "Hank, can your computer folks pull up a list of all VRBOs available in this market?"

"Great minds, Buck. That's what I was doing while you were on the phone with your director. I asked them to pull up every rental and start calling the owners. The SWAT team will land at the airport in about two hours. If we have any sort of list, we can have them start physically checking rentals."

"That's going to take a lot of time. I wish there was something we could do in the meantime to narrow down the list."

PIS had nodded off again, so Buck and Hank stepped out into the hallway. Buck's phone rang, and he looked at the number and answered.

"Hey, Bob. What's up?"

Buck listened for a minute, asked a couple questions and hung up.

"That was Bob Brady. His dispatch just got a call about a possible missing person. He doesn't think it's related to Alicia Hawkins because she doesn't match the profile. This woman owns a bar in town, and she is in her seventies. He is on his way to check it out, and I told him I would meet him there. You coming?"

Hank nodded, and they headed for the door.

CHAPTER FORTY-FOUR

J osh and Louis couldn't have hoped for a better situation. Maggie Stevens, the bar owner, lived in a small house that sat back off the road and was partially hidden from the street and her neighbors' houses. Her driveway was hidden by trees on one side, and Josh was able to unscrew the lone driveway light hanging off the front of the garage, placing the garage and the back door into total darkness. The sky was cloudy, and the moon was hidden, making the night feel darker. All things considered; Josh felt good about the set up.

He set his backpack down in the spot he'd picked out behind her trash cans along the side of the garage. He pulled out the taser, checked to make sure it was fully charged and laid it on the ground. He had asked a friend of his, back in Florida, to purchase the taser so there was no record of it in his name. He then checked to make sure his semiautomatic pistol was loaded. He had a round in the chamber, and the safety was on. He stuck the gun into his belt. Next, he pulled out a length of rope and a couple large wire ties that he had picked up at a local hardware store. He snugged his coat up against the mountain breeze and sat down next to the cans to wait.

He was concerned that Louis was getting cold feet and that he might not be able to pull off the initial attack to subdue Maggie Stevens, so he'd changed the plan at the last minute, and he sent Louis in the van to keep an eye on the bar and alert him when she was leaving. He wasn't sure if Alicia Hawkins had noticed Louis's hesitation about this whole serial killer thing.

He had decided the night before that if Louis screwed up any part of the abduction, he might have to make Louis his first victim. He didn't want to think that way. He liked Louis, but he was concerned that Alicia Hawkins might feel the same way and decide to do away with them both. He liked Alicia, but he sensed she could be unpredictable, so he would now have to keep an eye on them both.

Louis had parked the van a block from the bar and had a perfect view of the front door. He wasn't sure what he was supposed to do next. He had seen plenty of stakeouts on television cop shows, but those shows never really dealt with the boredom that comes with just sitting in the same place for an extended period of time. He noticed that the bar was busier than the first night he and Josh had staked it out. He realized he needed to pee, and he was getting colder. He knew Josh would not like it if he ran the van so he could use the heater. Josh had told him the fastest way to get spotted was smoke from the tailpipe.

He finally gave in to his baser urges and decided he would go into the bar and use the restroom. As crowded as it was, he figured no one would notice him, so he slid out of the van and headed for the front entrance.

The noise, when he opened the door, was deafening. The local band was playing a mix of heavy metal and country, and it hurt his ears. He nodded to the bouncer and stepped towards the crowd.

"Hey, you," said the bouncer.

Louis froze. He wasn't sure what he had done wrong. After all, he had just walked in. What could he have possibly done to attract the bouncer's attention? He turned slowly and faced the bouncer. He could feel his stomach gurgle, and he was afraid he was going to vomit right there in front of the bouncer. He swallowed hard.

"Yes, sir?"

The bouncer pointed towards the sign on the wall. Louis looked at the sign and realized his mistake. There was a twenty-dollar cover charge, and he needed to show his ID. He breathed a sigh of relief as he pulled out his driver's license and a twenty-dollar bill from his wallet. The bouncer put the twenty in a drawer, compared his face to the picture on the license and handed him back his ID. Louis nodded and headed for the restroom and then to the bar, where a tall cowboy-looking dude was just getting up. He slid onto the stool and waited for the bartender.

Louis turned around on the stool and got lost watching the people until someone tapped him on his shoulder, and he almost jumped out of the seat. He spun back around as if he had been caught doing something wrong and stared right into the face of Maggie Stevens. His heart almost jumped out of his chest. She was speaking to him, but he could barely hear her over the band.

"What'll it be?" she asked a second time.

Louis leaned into the bar. "Coors, please," he said, louder than he'd expected it to come out. She nodded and walked away, grabbing a mug from behind the bar. Louis watched her walk away, and he caught himself staring. This woman was beautiful. Alicia said she was in her seventies, but she looked like she was in her forties. He watched her tight ass as she walked down the bar, and she had nice firm breasts. He suddenly had serious doubts about killing this woman. She turned and headed back in his direction, and he diverted his eyes. He was afraid his thoughts would give him away. She set the beer on the bar, and he pulled a ten out of his wallet and handed it to her.

He took a long drink from his glass and closed his eyes for a second. What was he doing here? Not just here in the bar, but here in Aspen? Josh was his best friend, but maybe he shouldn't have let him talk him into this. He knew deep down inside that he was no serial killer. He'd never hurt anything in his life, especially people. What would his grandmother say if she found out about this?

The problem now was he was in too deep. He should have called the cops when Alicia showed them her most recent kill. "She's nuts," he thought to himself. He'd found no joy in seeing that dead body, only sadness, but he was doing this for Josh. His hands started to shake, and he tried to control his thoughts. He watched the bartender, and several times she looked back, and he diverted his eyes. His mind was racing. This was a bad idea, coming in here like this, so he finished his drink and headed for the door. He hoped his quick departure didn't raise any suspicions.

Outside the bar, he stopped on the sidewalk and tried to calm down. He took a deep breath and leaned over with his hands on his knees. After what seemed like an eternity, he stood up and walked back to the van. He thought about maybe just driving away and leaving Josh here. He was scared, but he'd made a promise to Josh, and he would never go back on a promise. But this was it. Once they were done with this job, he was going to head off on his own. He had no idea where, but it didn't matter. He was just going to get out of town.

Sitting in the cold van gave him time to calm his nerves and thoughts. He almost fell asleep but woke suddenly when he heard a noise outside the bar. He looked over and spotted the bouncer and the bar owner locking the front door. They said good night, and he watched the owner walk into the small lot next to the bar and slide into her car. He pulled out his phone and sent Josh a text.

SHE'S LEAVING NOW.

Louis started the van and pulled away from the curb. He didn't need to follow her because he knew where she was heading. He drove the three blocks and pulled to the curb a couple houses down from hers. He watched her car turn into her driveway and disappear behind the row of trees. He slid out of the van, looked around the empty street and walked towards her driveway. He stopped at the end of the driveway and waited.

Maggie Stevens pulled into her garage, slid

out of the car and closed the garage door. She stopped for a minute and looked at the burned-out bulb over the garage door. She looked around slowly and then headed for the back door. Using her key, she unlocked the back door and stepped into the kitchen, leaving the back door open behind her. Josh had positioned himself just outside the back door, and he watched as she hit the buttons on the alarm panel. She turned, and Josh was in her face. He fired the taser, and the two leads shot out and stuck in her chest. Josh was stunned to see confetti fly out along with the two electric barbs. He had no idea where the confetti had come from. The owner never made a sound, and she hit the floor hard. Josh jumped on top of her, pulled the syringe out of his pocket, stuck the needle into her shoulder and pushed the plunger. Maggie Stevens lay quietly on the floor, and Josh sat on the floor next to her body and tried to calm down. He set the syringe down on the floor next to the body. Everything had gone like clockwork.

Louis had stood at the back door in the shadows and watched as Josh stabbed her with the syringe Alicia had given them. Without a word, and just like they'd planned, he raced back to the van, started it and, with the lights off, backed down the street and pulled into her driveway. He jumped out, ran around the van and slid open the side door, then ran inside and helped Josh carry Maggie Stevens out to the van. Once Maggie was in the back of the van, Louis ran back into the house and started picking up the tiny pieces of confetti. He didn't know what they were for, or why they'd shot out of the taser, but he didn't think it was a good idea to leave them lying around. He gathered up every piece he could find in the dark and ran back to the van, stuffing the papers in his pocket.

While Louis was picking up the confetti, Josh jumped into the back seat with the body, grabbed the large wire ties and bound her hands and feet. Louis slid the side door closed, jumped into the driver's seat and pulled out of the driveway. Halfway down the block, he turned on the headlights, and walking across the street, directly in front of him, was a man in a green army jacket. Louis jammed on the brakes and turned the wheel hard to the left, just missing the guy. He almost had a heart attack, and Josh, who was tying up Maggie Stevens, flew forward and slammed into the back of the front seat.

"What the fuck, Louis," yelled Josh as he picked himself off the floor, rubbing the side of his head.

Louis's hands were shaking as he stepped on the gas and careened around the corner. "Fuckin' guy came out of nowhere."

Louis stomped down hard on the accelerator.

The last thing he saw, through the side mirror, was the guy in the green coat yelling and waving his arms and then giving him the middle finger.

Louis headed for the cabin, keeping one eye on the speedometer and one eye on his side mirrors, hoping the guy didn't call the cops. The last thing he needed was to get stopped by a cop for speeding, or for almost running over that guy. His adrenaline was pumping, and his entire body tingled. He felt like he wanted to throw up. His mind cleared, and the reality and the gravity of what they had just done burned deep into his brain. He shuddered as he thought that he had just helped sign this woman's death warrant. He wondered again what his grandmother would think.

CHAPTER FORTY-FIVE

Bax and Paul Webber walked through the front door of the Pitkin County Sheriff's Office, checked in with the desk officer and were buzzed through the security door. They walked back to the conference room and shook hands with Sheriff Winters and Sergeant Jamie Winters, the sheriff's daughter and lead SWAT officer. Sergeant Winters had six SWAT officers with her, and they all grabbed chairs around the table.

"Bax, Paul. It's good to see you again. How can we help?"

"Thanks, Sheriff. Here's what we know so far. This team has stolen at least five extremely expensive cars in Colorado that we are aware of. They have also beaten a man almost to death, raped a woman during one of the thefts and killed a security guard. They only target the highest-valued cars, and you have one of those cars here in Aspen."

"Murphy's car?" asked one of the SWAT officers. "Always thought that car would end up being trouble."

"Correct," said Bax. "We know that the security cameras at the Murphy property have been hacked. We assume the hackers have also been monitoring the location through the family's digital assistants. We are confident that they are going to go after the car, but we have no idea when."

Paul took over. "We have placed a tracker on the car, we are monitoring the cameras and we have made arrangements for Mr. and Mrs. Winslow to spend a few nights in a hotel in town."

Bax pulled up a street map of Aspen on her laptop, connected to the projector on the table and put the map on the wall behind the table. "Here's our thoughts." Using a laser pointer, she started pointing to spots on the map. "We would like to position several teams at these locations. Once we know the car is moving, we can move in and make the arrest."

Sergeant Winters said, "The reports we read seemed to leave out how they are moving the car. Do we know if these cars are still in the state, or are they someplace else?"

"Excellent question," said Bax. "We spoke with the state police in North Carolina, where our DNA suspect is from, and we might have a better idea of how they are moving the cars. The father of our suspects is an over-the-road truck driver. We think they meet up, soon after the grab, put the car in a trailer and the dad drives it someplace. We have been told that California is the most likely shipping port for these high-end cars."

Paul passed out photos and information sheets on the five suspects, and everyone was reading intently. One of the SWAT officers—Kramer, according to the name tag on his uniform—spoke up.

"If I could make a suggestion? There are not many places in the valley where a tractor-trailer could sit and not arouse suspicion. We are also looking for an RV. What if we have our patrol units start driving through all the RV parks between here and Carbondale? We're between seasons, so their occupancy should be low. If the RV is here, we should know in a couple hours. Then we can sit on the RV, and that cuts our surveillance needs down by half. Then we could position ourselves on both sides of the highway leaving Woody Creek and wait for the car to move."

Woody Creek, Colorado, population 263 as of the 2010 census, is a small town located along Highway 82, north of Aspen. It makes up for its small size by being home to many celebrities, authors, musicians, politicians and actors. This was the location that James Murphy, actor, entrepreneur and philanthropist, had chosen to build his magnificent ranch house.

"I agree," said Jamie Winters. "There are only two ways out of Woody Creek. If they head south, they are going right through the middle of Aspen. That car is going to stick out like a sore thumb. Either way, they have to get on Highway 82 before they can do anything. I would like to put one of my units at the entrance to Aspen, and then we can put our three other units and you guys north of town, and we wait."

"In the meantime," said Sheriff Winters. "I'll have my patrol units start looking for a parked semi and the RV. I'll call Bob Brady and see if he can have a couple of his officers check the RV sites in town."

They spent the next few minutes going over the plan and the placement of the units. Bax reminded everyone how dangerous these people were and to be careful.

Sheriff Winters stepped back into the room. "We may not get much help from the Aspen PD. Seems they have a missing woman, and they are trying to figure out if it's related to Alicia Hawkins. Bax, Buck is on his way to the missing woman's house and asked if you and Paul could meet him there." He handed her a slip of paper with an address on it.

Bax and Paul thanked the team for their help and agreed to meet back in the office at eight p.m. to strategize one more time and set up their teams. They shook hands all around and headed for the door.

Bax pulled out of the parking lot and headed down Main Street. The address the sheriff had provided was only a couple blocks from the Sheriff's Office, and Bax pulled to the curb in front of a small wood-framed house tucked back a little off the street. She spotted Buck's car as well as several black government SUVs. She slid out of the car, grabbed her backpack and waited for Paul, who pulled in behind her. They headed for the congregation of law enforcement officers standing in the driveway.

Buck made the introductions for those who did not know Bax or Paul Webber, and he filled them in on what they knew.

"First, we're not sure this is connected to Alicia Hawkins. According to the woman next door, she spotted the back door open when she let her dog out. She has a limited view of the house from her yard, barely enough to see the door. She thought it was odd that the door was open. She knows the owner of the house gets home late. She owns a bar in town. The first thing Aspen PD did was check with the bar as soon as they got the call, but she has not shown up at the bar yet today."

Bob Brady continued. "The thing that makes

us believe it is not connected is that the missing woman is seventy-two years old and is not homeless. According to the bouncer at the bar, she is also one tough lady and can handle herself in most situations. She definitely does not fit the pattern."

"What's the woman's name?" asked Paul.

"Her name is Maggie Stevens, she owns the . . ."

"Jackpot Bar," said Paul.

Everyone looked at Paul, and Bax broke the silence. "Paul?"

"Buck, this is definitely related to Alicia Hawkins."

Paul started to explain when Buck got a strange look on his face. "Shit. I completely forgot."

Now everyone turned and looked at Buck.

Paul spoke up. "Maggie Stevens was supposed to be Thomas Hawkins's sixteenth victim. She was in the car with him the night he crashed. She spent months in the hospital and had almost no recollection of that night. I spoke to her during the investigation because the most recent victim had been seen in her bar the night she disappeared. A subsequent interview, and information we gathered on the accident, led us to believe she was on her way to being the sixteenth victim. She also identified a small jade necklace that Alicia Hawkins wore that looked like something she remembered having before the accident."

Paul pulled out his laptop, opened it and started clicking keys. He was in the process of pulling up the investigation file—the murder book, as it used to be called. With CBI going totally digital, he had immediate access to all the files for every investigation CBI had been involved in for the past ten years, with more files being added every day.

"This all makes sense," said Buck. "We were wondering why she would come back to Aspen, and now it all works. She wants to honor her grandfather on the anniversary of his death, and what better way to do it than to kill the woman who was supposed to be his sixteenth victim, and will now be hers. That also means we have a fifteenth victim out there somewhere. We need to find Alicia Hawkins and fast. The clock is ticking."

A sense of urgency flooded the group standing in the driveway. Hank pulled out his phone and started calling the task force, and Bax was on the phone calling the forensics team in Grand Junction. She told them she needed them there as soon as possible. Paul was pulling up more notes from the interviews with Maggie Stevens to see if he could find anything that could help.

Buck walked away from the group and stood looking out into the street. Bob Brady walked up and stood alongside him. "We all miss shit, Buck. We've all had a lot on our plates."

"It's not that, Bob. I should have remembered Paul interviewed her, and that's got me pissed off. We could have put her under surveillance. That's important, but the reality is we didn't lose any time today. What's bugging me is the way it was done. Alicia Hawkins is not a strong woman. Her victims have always been young, petite women, except for the young man in Oklahoma, and even he wasn't a big guy. These were people she could control. This looks like a blitz attack. This woman owned a bar and has for years. From everything you know about her, and what her employees told us, she is no-nonsense and hard as nails. Definitely not the type Alicia Hawkins would go after. What I can't figure out is how Alicia Hawkins pulled this off."

Buck caught Bax's attention and waved her over. "How'd things go with the sheriff?"

"Good. Jamie Winters has her team spreading out looking for the RV and possibly a semi. Tonight, we will position ourselves around the area and wait for the car to move. We will have to play it a little loose until we see where the car is heading. In the meantime, it's a waiting game. What do you need?"

"Hank has the FBI folks checking VRBO rentals in the area. I know his computer people are good, but I trust you guys. I know you said you didn't hear back from any of the owners for the ads you placed, but do you think you and Paul can dig into the internet world and figure out a way to speed up the process? We need to find her lair."

"We'll give it our best shot."

Buck nodded, and Bax headed over to Paul, pulling out her laptop as she went. Buck knew he could count on his people, above all else. If anyone could find Alicia Hawkins, it would be Bax and Paul Webber.

CHAPTER FORTY-SIX

B uck walked into PIS's hospital room and found the Brit sleeping. He sat down in the visitor's chair and watched him for a moment. PIS stirred and opened his eyes. He looked at Buck.

"Good afternoon, Agent Taylor. It's nice to see you."

He looked at Buck and saw something in his eyes that he rarely saw.

"Something is troubling you, my friend."

Buck filled PIS in on the events of the day. He told him about the missing bar owner, and how he had missed the signs of what Alicia intended, and it was probably going to cost this woman her life. Buck didn't usually deal in self-pity, but he was feeling bad. His job had almost cost PIS his life, and now it was going to cost this woman her life. He felt helpless, which was also an affliction that rarely hit him.

PIS raised the head end of the hospital bed and got a serious look in his eyes. "That is ridiculous, Agent Taylor. I was stabbed because I let my guard down. She may have been trying in some strange way to hurt you, but I am the only person who could have prevented the stabbing, and I failed. As far as the bartender is concerned, fate gave her many years of good life that could have ended the day of the accident. Once again, you had nothing to do with that. There is no way you could have known that that evil bitch would decide to celebrate a perverted life by finishing its final act. No one could have known that."

Buck had never heard PIS talk like this, and it hit a nerve. He was being foolish, and he needed to get his head on straight.

"You must change your focus," said PIS. "You need to focus on finding and ending this evil creature before she can hurt anyone else."

Buck looked at PIS and could see something in PIS's eyes he'd never seen before. PIS looked malevolent, and it took Buck a second to gather himself. He wondered if what he was seeing was really there, or a reaction to the story Mac and his friends had told him. He shook off the thought.

"I will find her and arrest her, PIS. That's what I do. She is entitled to her day in court. I can't just execute her. I couldn't live with myself. I would be no better than she is if I did that." Buck caught himself, but it was too late.

PIS looked at him and smiled. "They told you, didn't they?"

"I'm sorry, PIS. They were regaling me with tales of your time together, and it came out."

"That was a long time ago, Agent Taylor. That person died in the jungle. What I say to you now is logical. She has killed fourteen or fifteen people. She is evil and needs to be stopped. Prison is too good for someone like her, but I also know you, Agent Taylor, and I know you will do the right thing. You are a man of conscience, which is why I value your friendship. Please disregard the ramblings of an old man."

Buck smiled. This was the PIS he knew. He stood looking out the hospital window. "Where are you, Alicia Hawkins?"

PIS had fallen back to sleep, so Buck pulled out his phone and called Hank Clancy. Hank answered right away.

"Hey, Buck."

"Hank, any luck with the VRBO search?"

"Nothing yet. There are over a thousand VRBOs in this area. We've eliminated a bunch, but we have a ways to go. In the meantime, I have every member of the task force out, looking for anything that might help."

"Thanks, Hank. Call me if you get anything."

Buck hung up and dialed another number.

"Hey, Buck. I was about to call you," said Bax.

"You had some luck with the VRBO search?" said Buck.

"Not yet. Paul's still working that angle, but here is something new to think about. The forensic team from Grand Junction is at Maggie Stevens's house. Someone discharged a taser. The team found several taser ID tags in the kitchen. Not as many as there should be, which means someone tried to clean them up but missed a few."

Buck stopped abruptly, his mind running in a bunch of different directions. "Alicia Hawkins never used a taser before, at least there's no evidence on any of the bodies to indicate that."

"Maybe she used it this time because she knew Maggie Stevens was going to be a challenge to take down," said Bax.

Buck thought for a minute. "There's another explanation. Alicia Hawkins had help."

"Fuck, Buck. Up until now, everything we know about Alicia Hawkins tells us she works alone. That's a seriously scary thought that she could have someone working with her. Shit. That would change everything."

"Keep working with Paul on the VRBO stuff. I am going to run back to Maggie's house and see if they found anything else. Let me know if you find anything, or when you head out to meet the sheriff's team."

Buck hung up his phone and sat down in the visitor's chair. The idea of Alicia Hawkins having a helper was something that had never crossed his or anyone else's mind. His mind was filled with questions. Most importantly: How would she have met or recruited this person? Buck picked up his backpack and left the room. The little bug in his head had gone into overdrive.

CHAPTER FORTY-SEVEN

Victoria Larsen went through the camera feeds from the Murphy house. She spotted the two people who drove up in the Jeep and followed them as they entered the house. She didn't know who they were, but she was running the license plate through the Colorado motor vehicle registry. She grew concerned when she lost them for a few minutes after they met with the two residents of the property.

She knew what James Murphy looked like. She had seen all his movies, so she knew he wasn't in the house. It's possible these were friends of the two older people; she had been watching for days now.

She ran through all the cameras and was surprised to see a suitcase by the front door. She hadn't seen it there earlier. The old couple opened the door, and the man picked up the suitcase and carried it out to a waiting SUV. He put the suitcase in the back while the woman set the alarm, locked the door and slid into the passenger seat. The man climbed in the driver's side, started the car and pulled out. Victoria followed them with the exterior cameras until they drove through the gate and left the property. Victoria's radar was on high alert.

Jessie slid into the chair across from her and saw the concern in her face. "What's going on, Victoria?"

"I'm not sure," answered Victoria. "The old couple in the Murphy house just drove away, and they had a suitcase with them."

"Well, that's great news," said Jessie. "If they're gone, they won't get in the way when we go for the car."

"Maybe. Or maybe not. They had a couple visitors earlier, and I lost them for a little bit. There must be a spot in the house that doesn't have security coverage."

"Are you getting anything from the sheriff or the Aspen police?"

"Nothing about us. I picked up a lot of activity this morning from the police. Something about a missing woman."

"Look," said Jessie. "Maybe it's our lucky day. Let's take the car tonight, as planned, and get the hell out of here. I feel like we've been here too long already."

"You might be right, but I have this feeling that ..."

"Look, Victoria. Your feelings aside, sometimes we need to move when the timing is right. This is going to be our biggest score, and it will set us up for a long time. Let's move on it and go. Dad will be in the area in a couple hours, and by midnight we could be cleared out of here and on the road. You keep monitoring the police and sheriff and watching the cameras. If nothing happens by nine p.m., then Toby can drop us off, as planned. It will take us an hour to get from the drop point to the house, through the woods. That will give you another hour to abort if something doesn't look or feel right. If all looks good, we move. Okay?"

Victoria looked at her. "Okay. Go tell your brothers to get ready. Ten p.m. will be our drop-dead time. I'll let your father know."

Jessie hurried off to tell her brothers and to start to get their gear together. The hike from the drop point to the house was not rugged or steep, just long. They had walked it twice before and knew that an hour was a good estimate. They'd found a great spot to the west of the house that gave them a view of the entire property and the surrounding area. They would have no trouble seeing anyone who might be watching the house. With the old folks gone for the night, this was the perfect opportunity. They'd made a lot of money over the past couple weeks, but this would be the capper. This would set them up for years, and she couldn't wait to be off the road.

She found Earl and Toby sitting outside the RV at a picnic table playing video games. She laughed when she saw the game. They loved those car theft games, which she found weird, mostly because she knew how utterly unrealistic they were, but they enjoyed blowing stuff up, so she never stopped them from playing. It helped them relax, and it also kept them from being underfoot.

CHAPTER FORTY-EIGHT

S tick walked through the front entrance of the hospital and, after stopping at the front desk, was directed to PIS's room. He noticed how the volunteer at the front desk pulled back when he stepped up to the counter, and he noticed the security guard move a little closer. As he stepped into the elevator, he saw the security guard key the microphone he had attached to his pocket. He understood that his appearance made people uncomfortable, but maybe if he wore his silver star on his jacket, they might treat him with a little respect. After all, he was a war hero who'd gotten addicted to painkillers because of the injuries he'd suffered in battle. No matter how he looked, people should respect that.

He stepped off the elevator, and a second security guard walked up.

"Can I help you, sir?"

Stick stopped and looked at the security guard. He could feel his agitation building as he balled his fists. Sometimes he did that as a defense mechanism, and sometimes he did it to keep the pressure, building inside, under control. He wasn't sure which it was today.

"I'm here to visit a friend, sir."

"What friend?" asked the security guard.

He was about to respond when he heard a familiar voice. "Hey, Stick. What brings you to the hospital? You okay?"

Stick looked past the security guard and tried to remember the man's name. Then it clicked. He was the cop from the park. The one who'd given him twenty dollars so he could get some food.

"Here to visit PIS, sir."

Buck stepped up to the security guard. "Is there a problem here, Officer?"

The guard looked at Buck and noticed the badge clipped to his belt and the intensity in his eyes.

"Just trying to help this fella find his friend, sir."

The guard smiled through crooked teeth, and Buck thought to himself that if he wasn't in the hospital, he would have broken this guy's nose.

Buck turned to Stick and pointed down the hall. "Fourth door on the left. PIS will be glad to see you."

Stick stepped away from Buck and the security guard and headed for PIS's room. Buck pushed the down button for the elevator and leaned in a little closer to the guard.

"That man won a silver star for saving his entire unit from being killed. He is a war hero, and if you can't respect him, then at least stay away from him."

The elevator door opened, and Buck turned to leave, then turned back suddenly. "If I ever hear that you disrespected him again, I will come back and find you, and you won't like it." The security guard's smile disappeared.

Buck stepped into the elevator and headed for the parking lot. He was running out of time, and he hoped the forensic team at Maggie Stevens's house had found something helpful.

Stick walked into PIS's room and stood in the doorway. It looked like PIS was sound asleep, and he didn't want to disturb him, but he also didn't want to leave and face the security guard again. He had just decided to leave when PIS rolled over in the bed and smiled.

"Stick, how wonderful to see you, my friend. Come in, come in." PIS raised the head end of the bed as Stick walked over to the side of the bed. Stick reached out his hand, and PIS took it in his.

"I wanted to come by to thank you for getting me out of jail. The cops didn't want to believe I didn't stab you. You know I would never do anything like that." A tear ran down his cheek.

"I know you wouldn't, Stick. I'm glad I was able to help. Are you doing okay?"

"Yeah. That cop who just left gave me money for some food. I had a good meal, and I bought some food for some of the others too."

"That cop is a good man. If you ever need help, you let me know, and I will make sure Buck is there for you. Okay?"

Stick smiled and nodded. "Okay, PIS."

"So, what's going on in the alley, Stick? I heard Maggie from the Jackpot Bar is missing. What's the word on the street? You hear anything?"

Stick thought for a minute. "I heard some talk that she might have been grabbed by the girl who stabbed you. I don't think so. Maggie is a hard woman."

"Have you seen anyone hanging out around the bar that you didn't know?"

Stick looked deep in thought. "Just the death van that almost ran me over last night."

PIS looked at Stick and leaned forward in the bed. "What death van?"

"One of those vans like we had when I was younger. Has some weird pictures of demons and shit painted on the side. Saw it a couple times parked on the street down from the bar. Never saw who was in it."

"Good, Stick, very good. You said it almost ran you over last night. Tell me about it."

"I walked to the alley after dark to see who was around and find something to eat. Passed the van parked a block or so away from the bar. I fell asleep in the alley by the Chinese restaurant, got cold and woke up really late. I was heading back to the park when this van came down the street with its lights off. They turned the lights on just as I was crossing the street. Like to scare the shit out of me. Guy turned the wheel hard and blew around the corner."

"Okay, Stick. I need you to think really hard. What street did this happen on?"

"I don't remember. It was late, all the bars were closed, but it might have been three or four streets from the park, near the small church on the corner."

PIS pictured the street map of downtown Aspen in his mind. Three or four streets from the park, near a small church. He was having trouble picturing a church on any of the corners, then it hit him. It wasn't a church any longer. It was a private home, but it still had the sign out front because it was a historic building. That church was on the corner of Maggie Stevens's street.

"Stick, did you see the driver?"

"Caught a glimpse. Black kid, short hair."

PIS thought back to when he'd first been moved from the ICU to his room. He reached for the nurse's button and pushed it. He was trying to remember the conversation the two nurses were having when he first woke up in the room.

Jennifer, the friendly day nurse, walked in and asked him what he needed. She looked at Stick but changed her focus back to PIS.

"Good afternoon, Nurse Jenny. I was wondering if Mark or Nathan are on duty today?"

"Mark is working on two. Why?"

"Would you be a dear and give him a call? I need to ask him something unrelated to the hospital, but it is vitally important."

"Sure. I'll give him a call. Don't go anywhere." She laughed as she stepped out of the room.

PIS and Stick talked about the gang from the park for a few minutes, and then Mark McCloud stepped into the room.

"Hey, PIS. You doing okay?"

"Yes, thank you. Doing fine, Mark. I was wondering if you could help me out? When they brought me up to the room the other day, you and Nurse Nathan were discussing tattoos." Mark's left arm was covered in tattoos, and his right was partially covered.

Mark stood next to the bed and thought for a minute. "Oh, yeah. I remember. I saw some awesome art on an old van, and I was showing Nathan a couple pictures to see if he thought they might make good tattoos. Why?"

"Do you still have the pictures?"

"Yeah, they're on my phone." Mark pulled his phone out of his pocket and opened his gallery. He flipped through some pictures and handed his phone to PIS, who flipped through a couple pictures and then asked Stick to take a look.

Stick looked carefully at the pictures and nodded. "That looks like the same van."

PIS handed the phone back to PIS. "Mark, where did you see this van?"

"It was in the parking area at the end of East Lupine Drive. There's a hiking trail there we like to take sometimes." He looked at PIS.

"Isn't there a private home back in there too?"

"Yeah, about a half mile back. The parking area is like two small circles. One side is for the trail, and the other side is private. The van was on the private side. What's going on, PIS?"

"My friend Stick here said a van with lots of pictures on it almost hit him, and I was curious, since I did not remember seeing a van like you both described around town. Thank you, Mark. You have been most helpful."

Mark left the room, and PIS told Stick that he was getting tired and wanted to take a nap. They shook hands, and Stick left the room.

Stick spotted the same security guard standing by the nurse's desk, talking to a couple nurses. He had been hoping to get out of the hospital without another confrontation. The security guard stood up tall as he approached. He stepped over to the elevator and pushed the down button. Stick moved, hesitantly, into the elevator.

"You have a nice day, sir, and thank you for your service," said the security guard. The elevator door closed, and Stick smiled. It had been a long time since anyone thanked him for his service.

CHAPTER FORTY-NINE

Buck pulled to the curb outside Maggie Stevens's house. The CBI forensic van sat in the driveway, and several Tyvek-clad techs moved back and forth from the van to the house. Hank Clancy stood to one side of the back door, watching the techs working inside the kitchen.

Buck walked up to the back door. "Hank, anything new?"

"Hey, Buck. We found more taser ID tags under the kitchen table. Alicia must not have turned on the lights when she was cleaning up. I have one of my agents running down the ID number. With any luck, we will ID the person who purchased it for her."

"Any luck with the VRBO search?"

"We came up pretty much empty. Way too many variables, plus we can't get hold of a lot of the owners. Finding their contact information isn't easy since most of their reservations are handled electronically. I still have people working on it, but I am not holding out much hope. I think the ID tags might get us closer."

Buck thought about the approach they had been taking. The little bug in his brain was nagging at him, and he wasn't sure why. All he knew was that they were running out of time.

"Agent Taylor," one of the forensic techs called.

Buck and Hank Clancy walked to the door. The tech was holding an evidence bag containing a syringe they'd found in the kitchen. "We found this syringe alongside the toe kick of the kitchen cabinet. We pulled off some partial prints that we know belong to Alicia Hawkins. She doesn't even try to hide them anymore, but we found a second partial print that is not hers. We are running it through AFIS now."

The tech walked away, and Buck looked at Hank. The bug in his brain stopped jumping up and down.

"I think she had help."

"Seriously?"

"Yeah. Think about it. We agree that it would be hard for her to take down Maggie Stevens alone. Yet there's no sign of a struggle in the house. She would have struggled to get Maggie's limp body into a car, and now we have a fingerprint from an unknown person."

Hank's mind was trying to wrap itself around

the possibility of Alicia having help. "Do you think it could be another family member?"

"It's certainly possible, but I doubt it. I think she found an acolyte. Maybe someone who wants to be like her. Do you have a couple analysts we can pull off the VRBO search?"

"What'd ya have in mind?"

"I know there are websites devoted to Alicia Hawkins. Bax told me she has quite a following, which personally I find sick, but how about we have a couple analysts go through every site that mentions her name, including on the dark web, and see if anyone jumps out at us?"

Hank pulled out his phone, dialed a number and explained to the person on the other end what they were looking for. He hung up.

"I pulled everyone off the VRBO search and put them on this. Fuck, Buck. This will add a whole new wrinkle to finding her."

Buck's phone rang, and he looked at the number and slid the red button to the left. He knew he was going to have to deal with this sooner rather than later, but right now, he had a more pressing issue.

Buck called the director and filled him in on the possibility that Alicia Hawkins had an accomplice. He explained what the FBI analysts were working on and told him about the second fingerprint on the syringe.

"Okay, Buck. You need anything, call me."

He hung up and put his phone away. He was thinking about their next move when his phone rang again. He looked at the number and answered.

"Hey, Max."

"Hi, Buck. How's my favorite cop?" Buck never got tired of that greeting from Max Clinton, and he knew she only called if she had something that would help.

"Doing okay, Max. What's up?"

"We have an eighty percent match on the partial print the team found on the syringe."

Hank's phone rang, and he stepped away to answer it.

"You got a name?" said Buck.

"You bet. Print belongs to Joshua Kirby. He is listed as a juvenile offender. We are trying to get his file unsealed. Our estimate would be that he is in his mid-twenties right now. We also launched a search for his contact info. I will call you back as soon as we have it."

"Max, that's awesome."

Max ended the call the way she always did. "You're a good man, Buck Taylor. God will watch over you."

Buck turned just as Hank Clancy hung up his phone. Hank looked excited. "We've got a possible match on the partial from the syringe."

"Joshua Kirby," said Buck.

Hank's smile disappeared. "How the hell?" he said.

"Max Clinton called. They are trying to track down his juvy record."

Hank looked pleased. "Hah. I already have it, and I have agents enroute to his last known address in Florida. I also asked the analysts to focus on his name for the internet search."

Buck smiled. He didn't mind if Hank and the FBI won one once in a while, so he'd let him have this little victory.

Hank's phone rang again, and he answered. He pulled a small pad from his pocket and wrote something down. He hung up the phone.

"Kirby was arrested when he was sixteen for assault. He was sentenced to two years in juvy. He's been clean ever since. Now, this might be interesting. He was arrested with another kid, one Louis Thompson. There was a phone number for Louis in his file, and the number still worked. My agents spoke with his grandmother. She says Louis and Kirby left a week or so ago to meet a friend. She couldn't remember where they said they were going, or even if they did.

She said Louis has been following Kirby around since kindergarten. She never liked that kid. Thought he was a bad influence on Louis. She said they were driving in Louis's van. It's old and has lots of demonic paintings on the sides. We're going through Florida Motor Vehicles to get his plates."

Buck knew they were on the right track. The little bug in his brain was silent. Now, all they needed to do was find the van. The problem was it was late, and in a couple hours, it would be the anniversary of Alicia Hawkins's grandfather's death. He had no idea if Maggie Stevens was still alive, but if she was, she wouldn't be for long.

CHAPTER FIFTY

Alicia Hawkins stood at the end of the bed and looked at Maggie Stevens. She admired the shape the woman was in. Too bad she was going to have to mess that up, but that was life ... or death.

She injected Maggie again to keep her unconscious. The last thing she needed was Maggie waking up before she had a chance to strip her clothes off and get started. She didn't care if Maggie woke up after she started. She enjoyed watching the faces as they realized she was slicing them up. The fear in their eyes made her heart beat faster.

Josh and Louis were standing in the living room and had kept watch over Maggie while Alicia slept. Tonight was going to be a long night, and she needed to be well rested. She made sure to let them know before she sacked out that Maggie was off-limits. They were not to touch her. Alicia could see the lust in Josh's eyes. She knew if she left him to his own devices, he would have his way with the unconscious woman. This woman was special. She was a sacrifice in her grandfather's honor.

She had been watching Louis most of the day, and she was not sure what she was reading in his eyes. Ever since they'd carried her body up the trail from the van, Louis had been unusually quiet, yet she thought she could see his mind working, and she didn't like what she saw. She made sure both guys stayed in the cabin while they waited. She wasn't sure if she could trust Louis.

They ate dinner in silence, but she could see they were both getting restless. After dinner, she asked them to inspect the perimeter of the property and make sure they didn't have any unwanted guests. They still seemed disappointed that they would not be able to watch her slice up Maggie Stevens. Josh had been hoping that since they'd done such a good job kidnapping her, Alicia would have a change of heart and let them observe, or maybe even help a little, but that was not to be. He finally resolved himself to the fact that Alicia was not going to change her mind.

At the appointed hour, Alicia asked them to take up their positions along the trail so they could ambush anyone coming up to the cabin. Once she started, she didn't want to be disturbed. Reluctantly, they grabbed their assault rifles, checked to make sure they each had three additional magazines, grabbed their camouflage coats and hats and headed out the front door.

Alicia looked at her watch. She knew it was too early to start slicing on Maggie, but she wanted the time alone to reflect on her grandfather's legacy and how far she had come in such a short period of time. When her grandfather had first suggested that she would be the one to follow in his footsteps, she was appalled by the idea. She had never killed anything in her young life, and she didn't believe that she could actually do it. Boy, had she proven herself—and everyone else—wrong. Not only had she done it, but she did it in front of the entire world, and she managed to stay two steps ahead of the FBI while she was doing it.

She spent the next couple hours listening to music on her phone. She used the smooth jazz to calm her soul and her mind. She needed to be completely in the moment. This one was too important. She opened her eyes and looked at her watch. The time was fast approaching, so she got up from the couch, turned off the music and headed into the bedroom.

Maggie Stevens was still unconscious, and Alicia walked over next to the bed, leaned down and checked her pulse, which was strong, and her breathing, which was smooth and regular. She undid the buttons on her blouse and slipped it off her shoulders. She had to use a pair of scissors to cut the sleeves, so she could get it over the ropes binding her to the bed. She cut off her bra and admired the woman.

Her pants were next, and Alicia had to cut those and her panties off due to the bindings. Lying naked on the bed, she was quite a specimen. Alicia had no idea what Maggie had looked like on the day her grandfather was supposed to kill her, but she felt sad that he'd missed out on such a beautiful creature.

Alicia stepped into the bathroom and removed her own clothes. She walked back out to the bedroom and sat on the edge of the bed, next to Maggie. She ran her left hand over Maggie's body, stopping periodically while she pleasured herself, to the point of being in a frenzy. Having finally exploded, she lay down for a minute next to the body and rested. She was spent but exhilarated.

She kept her eye on the clock on her phone as she lay there and watched the numbers slowly clicking towards midnight. The time had come.

Alicia sat up, walked over to the dresser and opened her leather sheath, which contained her collection of knives and scalpels. She ran her hands over the instruments of destruction, looking for the perfect blade. She wished the FBI hadn't confiscated her grandfather's knives. If she could have used one of his knives, that would have been perfect. Her hand slowed and stopped over a small scalpel with a three-inch blade. She held the blade up to the light and admired the way it sparkled. This was the one.

She turned and walked back to the bed and stood watching Maggie Stevens breathe. She knew in a matter of hours that that would end, and it made her smile. She said a silent prayer to her grandfather and stepped to the side of the bed. Alicia Hawkins was about to begin.

CHAPTER FIFTY-ONE

Victoria Larsen ran one more check on the cameras and security system at the house. There was no indication that anything was amiss. She sat back and looked at Jessie.

"It's all clear. You should probably get going. I will do one more check once you are at the edge of the property, and if it's all good, you can go. There is nothing on any of the local police frequencies."

She handed Jessie a slip of paper with the coordinates for the location where her dad would be. Jessie plugged them into her handheld GPS and set the paper back on the table.

"See you soon," said Jessie, and she turned and walked out the front door of the RV. She slid into the front seat of her SUV and told Toby, who was driving, to head out. They pulled out of the RV park and headed north on Highway 82. After about a ten-minute drive, they turned onto an unnamed county road, drove a half mile and Toby pulled to a stop. Jessie programmed the coordinates for their dad's truck into the car's navigation system, pocketed the GPS and she and Earl slid out of the car, grabbing their backpacks. No additional words were needed, since they had followed this same procedure for several months, in several states, and it always worked flawlessly.

Toby pulled forward as Jessie and Earl ran into the woods, the darkness so complete that within seconds they were invisible. Toby headed for a little restaurant near the RV park, stopped the car and stepped inside. He would wait in the restaurant until he got the call from Victoria that everything was a go, and then he would head for the rendezvous point.

Jessie and Earl made good time, and they arrived at their hiding spot at the edge of the property with ten minutes to spare. Slightly out of breath, they sat down and waited for Victoria to run her last security sweep.

The call came fifteen minutes after their arrival. Victoria gave them the all clear, and they grabbed their gear and raced towards the back of the house. They ran up onto a large deck and waited at the back door to the kitchen. The house had electronic security locks on all the doors, and within seconds of their arrival, they heard the latch retract, and they opened the door and went inside.

The house was as quiet as a church, and they waited a minute in the kitchen to make sure no one was hiding in the house.

Satisfied that they were alone, they headed for the master bedroom. On one of her sweeps, Victoria had spotted a code for a possible wall safe connected to the system. Jessie and Earl entered the room and started looking everywhere for a safe. They finally found it behind a bookcase. Jessie pulled out an electronic meter, connected two leads to the safe and texted Victoria that they were ready. Several lights on the front of the meter started flashing, and then all the lights turned green. Jessie pulled the leads and put the meter away, turned the handle and opened the safe. She was shocked at what she found.

Inside the safe were several bundles of hundred-dollar bills and a dozen Rolex watches. She had no idea how much money they were looking at, but it would make a nice little addition to their bank account. She slid everything into a black bag, and they headed for the garage. Earl found the keys to all the cars hanging on a hook in the kitchen closet. He grabbed the Bugatti key, and they headed for the door to the garage. The Bugatti was parked in the center bay of a five-bay garage. Jessie stood for a second and admired the car, then signaled Earl to open the door, which he did with a push of the button on the master garage door panel. The door slid up, and he stepped to the side and waited.

Jessie fired up the engine and was mesmerized at the sound of power and the luxury of her surroundings. The car was a lot quieter than they had been expecting. She put the car in gear and pulled out of the garage. Earl hit the button to close the door and raced towards the car, being careful not to trigger the reversing mechanism on the door. They watched until the door closed, then they each stripped off their camo gear and put it into their backpacks, replacing it with dark nylon windbreakers.

Feeling confident, they jumped into the car, and Jessie headed down the driveway to the main gate. They watched as the camera on the back of the gate tracked their approach, and then silently, the gate swung open. Jessie pulled forward, checked to make sure there were no other cars on the road and then headed for Highway 82.

CHAPTER FIFTY-TWO

For a man who had made patience an art form, Buck hated to wait, especially when he knew he was running out of time. He was trying to figure out what his next step should be when Hank's phone rang. He answered, made some notes in his little notebook and hung up. They were sitting in Bob Brady's office, so the next step was easy.

"I've got the plate number from Florida," he said. He handed Bob the slip of paper with the number on it. "My guys in Florida have the name of the guy who bought the taser, and they are on their way to his address right now." Bob Brady picked up his desk phone and called dispatch.

"Connie, it's Bob. I have the plate number for that van you put out over the airwaves earlier." He read her the number, and Buck copied it down into his own notebook. "Go ahead and update the BOLO and send it statewide."

Buck grabbed his backpack off an unused desk and headed for the front door, followed by Hank Clancy and Bob Brady. While they'd waited for the call from Hank's analyst, they had broken the town up into sections and assigned every available patrol unit and reserve officer they could gather up, along with all the FBI agents they had available, to specific patrol areas. They blanketed the town, hoping to find the van. Buck and the others headed to their assigned areas. He didn't think it would be that hard to spot a van that looked like this one, but he was wrong.

After a couple hours, frustration was building as time ran short. They needed a break. He pulled over to the curb and sat for a minute. They had to be missing something. Truth was, they weren't missing anything except, perhaps, more bodies. There were too many side roads and forest service roads that led to cabins. This was like looking for a needle in a haystack, only the haystack was a huge valley. Buck rubbed his eyes. If only they had more time.

He was about to pull away from the side of the road when his phone rang. He answered right away.

"Bob, anything?"

"We're not sure. We received an anonymous call on the nine-one-one line. The caller refused to identify himself and didn't stay on long enough for us to get a trace; he gave the dispatcher an address and hung up."

"Doesn't tell us much, other than an address.

We don't even know if it pertains to Alicia Hawkins or not. It could also be a diversion," said Buck.

He looked at his watch. It was almost midnight, and they were out of time. He didn't want to get overly excited, but they needed to do something.

"Bob, I think we need to check it out. Give me the address and call everyone in. I am going to check it out and see if the van is at the address. If it is, we're going to have to devise a plan on the fly."

"Okay, Buck, but wait for backup." He gave Buck the address and called Hank and had dispatch recall all the patrols.

Buck plugged the address into his nav system and headed out. If he didn't miss any turns in the pitch-black night, he should be to the address in five minutes. Luck was on his side. He pulled to the end of the street, and there were directions to two parking areas: one public, one private. He parked his car in the public lot, grabbed his night-vision goggles out of his backpack and headed towards the private parking area, and there, sitting in the middle of the driveway, was the van, next to an old green sedan.

Buck approached the van from the passenger side with his pistol drawn and shined his flashlight into the passenger window. There was nothing visible except for some soda bottles and fast-food wrappers.

He walked back to his car, pulled out his phone and called Bob Brady.

"Is it there?" said Bob.

"Yeah. Let's get the FBI SWAT team here, ASAP, and tell them no lights. There is a trail leading to the cabin, but I can't see the cabin, so I have no idea how close we are. We need total silence. Keep everyone else away. We'll bring them in when we need them."

Buck hung up and opened the Jeep's back hatch. He slipped on his ballistic vest, clipped a backup pistol in a thigh holster to his leg and unlocked the gun case that was welded to the floor of the cargo area.

He pulled out his AR-15 and put four spare clips in the holders attached to his vest. He slipped on his navy-blue CBI jacket and put on his CBI cap. He closed the hatch, locked it and walked towards the road.

It didn't take but a minute for the first government-issued black SUV to arrive, followed by several more. Bob Brady and Hank Clancy slid out of the first SUV and walked up to Buck. Next to arrive was the FBI SWAT commander, who pulled out a topographic map and placed it on the hood of the car.

"We may have a bigger problem," said Hank Clancy. "We got word that Joshua Kirby's father owned several guns registered in his name, including two AR-15s. We could be walking into a trap."

"This is the path to the cabin. It looks to be about a quarter to a half mile," whispered the SWAT commander. "I think our best bet is to avoid the path and proceed through the woods. I would like you, Agent Clancy and Chief Brady, to remain behind us until we can secure the location. We are going in blind, and I am a little uncomfortable with that, but we have no choice."

The SWAT team agents were checking their weapons and communications gear, while Buck and the others reviewed what little bit of plan they had.

"I wish we knew more about the two guys and what their motivation is. Do they want to be like her, or are they here for protection and to help her abduct her victims? I would hate to think these guys want to go out in a blaze of glory and take a bunch of law enforcement people with them."

"I'm with you, Agent Taylor. We need to proceed with caution, but we need to go if we're going," said the SWAT commander.

Everyone looked at Hank Clancy, and Hank nodded. "Let's go."

The SWAT agents fanned out and entered the woods about ten feet apart. The plan was as simple as it gets. Move forward until you run into opposition or until you get to the cabin.

Buck, Hank and Bob Brady entered the woods about fifty feet behind the SWAT team. They moved cautiously from tree to tree and stayed as quiet as possible. Buck estimated that they were roughly halfway to the cabin when he heard one of the SWAT agents call the commander.

"SWAT seven to one. We have a body."

Everyone stopped moving.

"Six and four. Move up on seven and secure the area. Is it another female victim?" asked the commander. Everyone was aware that somewhere out there was Alicia Hawkins's fifteenth victim.

"No, sir. This is a male. He's dressed in camo and was holding an AR-15. His throat was slit."

Buck looked at Hank. "What the fuck?"

"Got me, Buck. Looks like someone saved us from getting into a shoot-out."

"Yeah," said Bob Brady. "But that still leaves at least one other armed person out there, that we know of."

Hank keyed his mic. "We may still have another armed person in the woods. Stay alert. Commander, head to the cabin. We will head for seven's location."

"Roger."

Hank, Buck and Bob Brady headed for the body while the rest of the SWAT team headed for the cabin. Their sense of urgency grew by the minute.

Buck walked through the trees to where SWAT seven was standing next to the body. He pulled a pair of nitrile gloves out of his pocket and put them on. The other two SWAT agents were on high alert, keeping lookout around them. He knelt next to the body. From the limited description they had of both Josh and Louis, Buck could tell that this was not Louis. This person was a white male. Buck looked at the wound in the neck.

"Whoever killed this kid knew what they were doing. The knife slid in here." He pointed to the start of the slice under the right ear. "Then sliced from right to left, through the windpipe. The kid would have never had a chance to scream. The slice is clean. Knife was incredibly sharp."

He stood up and removed his gloves. "Hank, let's keep these guys here, and as soon as we get to the cabin, I'll call the forensic team I had at Maggie Stevens's house."

Hank nodded, as did the three SWAT agents.

"Agent Clancy, SWAT one. We are at the cabin. Definitely someone home, but all the curtains are drawn, so we have no visual. We are preparing to breach."

Hank looked at Buck and Bob Brady, and they both nodded. He hated sending the team in blind, especially in a hostage situation, but they needed to move.

"Breach," said Hank.

Up ahead, they heard wood splintering and then several flashbangs go off. They heard muffled shouts, and then silence. Hank's radio crackled.

"Agent Clancy, SWAT one. Cabin secure. You are going to want to see this."

CHAPTER FIFTY-THREE

Bax was starting to nod off. It felt like they had been sitting in her Jeep for hours waiting for something to happen. Maybe they were wrong. Maybe, at this very moment, the car thieves were zeroing in on another car, someplace else. Maybe her gut was wrong.

She was starting to feel sorry for herself when Paul Webber looked up from his laptop screen.

"The security system just shut off."

Bax stopped feeling sorry for herself, started the Jeep and sent out a mass text to the sheriff's SWAT team.

ALARMS OFF. WE ARE IN PLAY.

Paul pulled up the interior security camera feeds and spotted two shadows entering the kitchen through the back door. He watched them as they paused for a minute and then followed them into the master bedroom, where he saw them deactivate the electronic locks on a wall safe behind a bookcase and remove what looked like cash and several watches.

Since their faces were covered, Paul couldn't get a good picture of them, but he was recording the entire event anyway. He now switched cameras and spotted them in the garage as they pulled the car out and then removed their camo outerwear and put on windbreakers. He got two excellent face shots as they were turning to make sure the garage door closed behind them.

Paul then switched to the app for the tracker Bax had placed on the car, and they started following the blip. The car passed through the main gate and turned left, exactly as they had expected. The car followed the street in a circular path and turned left onto Highway 82. Bax was surprised. They were heading towards Aspen.

Bax kept her lights off as she sent another text.

TURNED TOWARDS ASPEN.

She stayed in the parking lot of the convenience store with her lights off until she spotted the headlights for the Bugatti. As it passed by the store, she slowly pulled onto the highway behind them. Thanks to the tracker, she didn't have to keep them in sight. The tracker seemed to be working perfectly.

Paul followed the car with the tracking app as it drove through Aspen and continued down the highway towards Independence Pass, the back way out of Aspen before the road was closed for the winter. The highway was a little more open here, so Bax backed off even more. She watched as the car pulled off the side of the road into a chain-up area.

Up ahead, they spotted a large semi sitting in the chain-up area at the bottom of the pass. She crept slowly forward and stopped. Paul, using a night-vision scope attached to a video camera, filmed the whole thing.

The trailer was open, with what looked like boxes suspended in the air around the opening. There was a long ramp connected to the trailer, and they watched as the car pulled into the parking area and drove straight up the ramp and into the truck. There didn't appear to be a moment's hesitation by the driver. The two car thieves jumped down off the back of the trailer, and the old guy pushed what looked like some kind of controller, and the suspended boxes started sliding back into the trailer.

"Are you getting this?" asked Bax.

Paul nodded. "Amazing. No wonder no one has been able to catch these guys. They have this down to a science."

They watched, and within ten minutes, the truck was reloaded, and they were shutting the doors. The driver gave them each a hug, climbed in and fired up the big diesel. As they watched, another car that had passed them earlier came back down the pass and pulled into the chain-up area. The two thieves from the house climbed into the car, with the woman moving into the driver's seat, and they headed back towards town. The tractor-trailer pulled out of the area and slowly started up Independence Pass.

Bax sent another text as she swung the car around to follow the SUV.

EXCHANGE COMPLETE. STOP TRUCK AT TOP OF PASS.

Bax closed the distance to the SUV as they drove through Aspen. Paul sent a text to the team with the license plate number and called the sheriff to let him know what was happening. They were hoping the SUV would lead them back to the RV, so they could wrap up everyone at the same time.

Two members of the sheriff's SWAT team blew past Bax, coming from the other direction, as they headed for the top of the pass. The pass was steep on the Aspen side of the mountain, and they knew it would take the truck a while to get there. As a precaution, they had a couple state troopers and a couple Lake County deputies stationed in a parking area at the top of the pass.

Bax followed the SUV as close as she could, and as they passed through an area between

Woody Creek and Basalt known as Wingo, the SUV pulled into the Wingo Junction RV Park, drove around the loop and parked in front of an old RV with Colorado plates.

Bax pulled to a stop out of sight and sent a text to the teams following them. WINGO JUNCTION RV PARK.

Paul ran the tags, and within a minute, he received the notice that the plates were stolen. "No wonder we couldn't find the RV. We were looking for North Carolina plates."

Bax watched as the group from the SUV ran into the RV. Sergeant Winters pulled in behind her, followed by two other SWAT team members. She walked up to Bax's Jeep.

"Sergeant. What do you think?"

Sergeant Winters looked at the RV and called over a member of her team. "Brian. Go back around the loop and pull in quietly and cut off their back retreat. Amy, take Gus and work your way to the back of the RV." Gus the dog wagged his tail. This was what he lived for. "I don't want them running. Bax and I will pull our cars up to the RV from this side and box them in. Wait till they step out of the RV and hit them with your lights. Be ready for anything."

Bax and Paul were wearing body armor, and Paul pulled an assault rifle from the back seat and started moving, in the shadows, towards the

RV. Bax and Sergeant Winters slowly rolled their cars along the loop road and parked in front of the RV, blocking any possible escape path.

Bax spotted Paul off to the side of the RV and watched as Brian pulled his car across the road, blocking the back of the RV. They all got out of their cars and positioned themselves behind the cars and waited.

They didn't have to wait long until the door to the RV flew open, and the three people bolted for the SUV, carrying backpacks. The lights from the patrol cars came on and blinded them, forcing them to stop and try to see what was going on. Bax was on her radio.

"Police. Freeze. We have you surrounded," she said as the radio blared her message.

There was stunned silence as the three thieves stopped and banged into one another, not sure which way to move. Jessie dropped her backpack and reached towards her hip. Paul was the first to respond as she raised her pistol, and the sound was deafening in the still night air. The bullet hit Jessie in the shoulder, and she went down hard. Before anyone else tried something dumb, the SWAT team, along with Bax and Paul, were all over them.

Two of the SWAT officers threw a flashbang into the open RV door and then charged inside. They came out a minute later with a stunned

Victoria Larsen in handcuffs. Within seconds everyone was on the ground in cuffs, and Sergeant Winters was reading them their rights off the Miranda warning card. By this time, several more Pitkin county deputies had arrived, along with Sheriff Winters, who reported that the truck was stopped at the top of the pass without incident. He shook Bax's and Paul's hands and then made the rounds, checking on his deputies.

Bax sent a quick text to Buck. She wasn't sure where he was at that moment, but she didn't want to call him.

CAR THEFT RING BUSTED. CAR AND TEAM SAFE.

She and Paul leaned back against Bax's Jeep and watched as the sheriff took over and loaded his prisoners into several patrol cars for the quick ride back to the county lockup. She patted Paul on the shoulder and smiled.

CHAPTER FIFTY-FOUR

J osh and Louis had found a couple hiding spots on either side of the trail. They had a good view of the trail and of the woods next to it. No one was getting through. The more they talked about the plan, the more Louis was growing concerned. He wasn't keen on what Alicia was doing, but he was having a harder time dealing with the idea of getting into a firefight with police. This was not what he had signed up to do. He wasn't sure he wanted to follow Josh down this road any longer. His hands were shaking as he took up his position behind the rock outcropping and waited. He started to think that maybe when the shooting started, if there was any, he would surrender when the time came. At least that way he wouldn't get killed.

He was still thinking of a way out when he heard a twig snap behind him. Fear filled his eyes as he started to turn his head. Out of nowhere, a hand grabbed the side of his head, and a knife sliced into his neck, below his right ear, and swept across the front of his throat. Louis tried to scream, but nothing came out, and the last thing he saw in this life were the stars above, as his attacker laid him down next to the rocks.

Josh thought he heard something, but Louis was too far away, and he didn't want to yell for him, so he settled in with his AR-15 at the ready and waited behind the downed tree. He was prepared to kill as many cops as necessary to protect Alicia Hawkins. His adrenaline was through the roof, and he wondered if this was how soldiers felt right before the big battle. He smiled and subconsciously ran his hand over the barrel of the rifle. He never heard death as it arrived at his doorstep.

A hand came out of nowhere and grabbed the side of his head. He startled and tried to find the trigger of his rifle as the knife plunged into his neck and swept across his throat. The last thing he felt was the warm blood running down his neck, and he died probably still wondering if this was how soldiers felt.

Alicia Hawkins leaned over the bed and was about to make her first slice when a cool breeze ran up her spine from behind her. She paused with the scalpel, barely touching Maggie Stevens's right breast, and she got angry.

"I told those guys to stay outside and not come near me. What the hell are they doing now?" she said to no one. She set the scalpel down on the edge of the bed, stood up and turned, and was stunned as she looked straight into the gray eyes of a man she had already killed. She stood mesmerized. "How is this possible?" she thought to herself. She had stabbed him in the heart. There was no way he could have survived.

Alicia Hawkins was so fixated on the gray eyes that she never felt the knife slide in under her left breast. She winced when she finally felt the pain, and then the man spoke, with a soft British accent.

"I've stopped the blade before it enters your heart because I want you to be fully aware of what death feels like. Your period of evil is over, and you can now join your grandfather in hell."

PIS slid the knife in another half inch and swept the tip from side to side, slicing Alicia Hawkins's heart in half. He held her close as he watched her life slip away. He slowly laid her on the floor, checked her pulse and stood up. He walked over to make sure Maggie Stevens was still alive and was pleased to see her breathing softly. There was no evidence that Alicia had started her terrible ritual. He left her hands and feet tied to the bed and covered her with a blanket he found balled up in the corner.

He quickly checked the rest of the cabin and found the other victim in the downstairs closet, wrapped in plastic. Even through all the wrapping, the smell was turning the air foul, and he walked back upstairs, shaking his head.

He pulled out the cell phone he had taken from Louis, dialed 911 and gave them the address and hung up. He removed the battery and put the phone back in his pocket. He would dispose of it on his way.

He left the knife with Louis's fingerprints on it stuck in Alicia, stepped out the front door of the cabin, removed his vinyl gloves and headed into the woods. Within minutes he was no longer visible.

CHAPTER FIFTY-FIVE

Buck, Hank and Bob Brady walked through the cabin door and followed the SWAT commander into the bedroom. The first thing they noticed was the smell of death, and the SWAT commander pointed down the stairs.

"We found a body, female, wrapped in plastic. Probably been dead a couple days."

Hank looked at Buck. "I guess we found victim number fifteen." There was no expression on his face as he said it. They stepped farther into the bedroom, and Buck took in the scene.

A SWAT agent who was trained as a medic was sitting on the bed next to Maggie Stevens, who was covered with a blanket, and he was checking her vitals. She was unconscious. He was talking on the phone to someone, and from the sound of the conversation, that someone was most likely a doctor at the hospital.

Buck looked over to where Bob Brady was standing and looked down at the floor. Alicia Hawkins looked almost angelic lying there, except, of course, for the knife sticking out of her chest. The first thing Buck noticed was that there was not a lot of blood. The autopsy would later reveal that most of her blood had flowed into her chest cavity. Whoever had made the cut was exceptionally well trained.

Hank Clancy walked up and stood next to Buck. "Looks like someone stopped her from realizing the tribute to her grandfather. We couldn't save victim number fifteen, but who- ever did this saved Maggie Stevens. What do you make of this?"

Buck didn't answer at first. He was staring at the red piece of fabric that was tied around Ali- cia's neck. It looked like a man's tie or . . . an ascot. He looked at Hank.

"I think someone did us a favor," said Hank. "At first light, we will start searching for Louis. From the looks of things, I'd say if we don't find him dead in the woods, then he is most likely the one who took out Alicia and the guy in the woods. We'll need to dive deeper into his back- ground and see if someone trained him. This was done by a pro."

Buck didn't say anything, but he thought to himself, "I don't think we'll ever find Louis."

"I bet the profilers will have a field day with the red scarf," said Hank. "Must be a subliminal serial killer thing. Part of her ritual, I guess." Hank stepped away, and Bob Brady looked sideways at Buck and nodded. He never said a word.

Buck called the director and filled him in on the situation at the cabin. To say the director was ecstatic would be an understatement. He asked Buck several questions about the scene and listened as Buck described what they'd found. He was silent for a long minute.

"Well, Buck. We'll just have to wait for the forensics and see what the science tells us. Great job on saving the sixteenth victim."

He told Buck about the arrest of the car thieves and that Bax and Paul had done a great job. It had been a busy night in Aspen, with two major crimes brought to a safe conclusion. He was proud of his team. The director hung up, and Buck walked through the cabin and stepped out onto the front porch. He pulled a warm Coke out of his backpack and took a long drink.

He dreaded the next part of the approaching morning. Once the site was wrapped up, he would have to go visit Mrs. Hawkins and tell her that her granddaughter was dead. This was one part of the job he didn't like, but he knew it needed to come from him. He finished his Coke and sat against the rail.

Within minutes a long line of lights appeared down the path as the paramedics and the forensic team entered the cabin site. Everyone was asked to leave the building as the forensic team suited up. The paramedics worked quickly to remove Maggie Stevens from the house, and they headed off to the hospital with a police escort.

Hank stepped out onto the porch. "I've sent out a nationwide BOLO for Louis Thompson. He couldn't have gotten far since we have his van. We'll find him in no time. Buck, you did excellent work on this thing right from the start."

Buck nodded. He didn't do what he did for the credit. It had always been about seeking justice for the victims. He wished he could take credit this time, but he didn't think that was possible.

He pulled out his phone and checked his messages. He had a text from Bax, which he replied to, and a voice mail from his sister. He listened to the message, hung up and wiped a tear out of his eye. He knew he needed to call her back, but once again, that would have to wait. He leaned against the porch rail and, one by one, texted his kids to let them know that he was okay and the danger from Alicia Hawkins had passed. He didn't usually text his kids, but tonight he didn't want to talk to anyone.

By the time Buck left the cabin, the forensic team was well underway with their evidence-gathering routines. The bodies of Josh, Alicia and the unknown fifteenth victim had been removed and taken to the morgue, and Hank scheduled a press conference for ten a.m. Buck saw the sun starting to crest over the mountains, and he knew it was time to handle the last detail of this case. He headed for his car and drove the quick drive to see Mrs. Hawkins.

Buck pulled to the curb in front of the Hawkins home and saw Mrs. Hawkins standing at the front window. She stepped out onto the porch as he walked up the path.

"She's gone, isn't she," she said as Buck stepped up onto the porch. She snugged her shawl around her shoulder and sat down on the porch swing.

Buck nodded. "I'm afraid so. I wanted you to hear it from me before the reporters showed up. Alicia was a big story, and you need to prepare for what's coming."

Tears formed in her eyes as she looked at Buck. "Did she hurt anyone else?"

Buck didn't want to answer, but he had never lied to this woman. He told her the truth, and she took it stoically and without comment.

"I will tell the others. Thank you, Agent Taylor."

She stood up and walked into the house, closing the front door behind her. Buck sat for a minute and then walked to his car. He needed a shower, something to eat and a little sleep.

CHAPTER FIFTY-SIX

B uck, feeling refreshed after a little sleep and a shower, walked through the front entrance of the Aspen Police Department and was buzzed into the back. The reporters had all left, and Buck found Bax and Paul talking with Hank Clancy in the back office area. They shook hands all around, and Buck told Bax and Paul how proud he was of them and what a great job they had done on the car thieves case.

Bax explained that Hank's FBI task force would be taking over the case and trying to figure out how the cars had been moved out of the country. Hank was confident that the arrest of the family was only the tip of the iceberg and that this case would go international in a hurry.

Hank handed Buck a file. He opened it, read it and gave it back to Hank. The initial fingerprint report on the knife that had killed both Josh Kirby and Alicia Hawkins led back to Louis Thompson. Hank had no idea what caused the kid to have a change of heart, but he was confident he would find out. The file also had some background the analysts had pulled off the dark web.

There was a lot of chatter praising Alicia Hawkins tracked back to Josh Kirby, expressing his desire to be like her to the point of almost worship. Some of what they found was downright scary. Here had been another serial killer in the making. Buck wondered how many more of these people were out there in the real world, plotting their first kills.

Buck walked over and grabbed a Coke out of the refrigerator. He shook hands with Hank, and they promised to get together the next time Buck was in Denver for a nice dinner. Hank was on his way to Washington, DC, to close out the Alicia Hawkins case.

Bax and Paul had finished their paperwork and were heading back to Grand Junction. Buck thanked them for all their help on both cases and told them to take a couple days off. They deserved it. He said if they needed him, he would be home, fishing, but he had something to do first. He also wanted to swing by the hospital and see PIS before he left.

Bax asked how things had gone with PIS and his friends from England, and Buck gave them the highlights. He told them he had gotten a voice message from Mac, thanking him for his hospitality and letting him know that they had run out of time and that a plane was waiting for them at the Aspen airport to take them back to England. They were disappointed that they hadn't gotten to see Pheasant before they left, but perhaps another time. Buck thought that would be unlikely, and he deleted the voice mail.

The hospital was quiet as Buck walked through the front door and took the elevator to PIS's floor. He walked down the hall and turned into the room and stopped short. The hospital bed was empty, and the room was clean and waiting for its next inhabitant. Buck stood for a minute, staring into space.

A shadow appeared next to him, and he looked over to see the doctor standing there.

"He checked himself out a few hours ago. I tried to talk him out of it, but you know PIS. Can't stay in one place too long."

He handed Buck a small envelope. "He asked me to give you this the next time I saw you. Have a good day, Buck."

The doctor walked away, and Buck stood for a minute and looked at the envelope. He was no expert on stationery, but he could tell this was a high-quality product. He opened the flap and slid out the note. At the top of the page was a family coat of arms, which confirmed for him that the story Mac and his friends had told was true. He looked at the beautiful script written on the page. Buck admired anyone who could write with a flair, since his script, and even his printing, was hard to decipher. The words reminded Buck of a conversation he and PIS had had one night in the woods, sitting around the campfire, while looking for the missing thirteen-year-old heiress. Buck had seen the picture of the pretty woman in the metal tin that held PIS's tea set and had asked about the picture. The same words PIS had spoken that night appeared on the note in his hand.

MY DEAR AGENT TAYLOR,

SOME THINGS ARE BETTER LEFT UNSAID.

YOUR FRIEND, ALWAYS,

PIS.

P.S. DO NOT WORRY ABOUT ME.

I WILL SEE YOU SOON.

Buck slid the envelope into his pocket and left the hospital. He had one thing left to do.

EPILOGUE

Buck sat in the rental car and watched the people gather at the top of the hill. The morning had dawned beautifully, and the hot desert breeze had held off, making the morning pleasant. From his vantage point, he had a great view of the place, the marble headstones all lined up in perfect rows no matter what direction you looked at them from. Here were thousands of men and women who had made the ultimate sacrifice to fight evil, no matter where it occurred. He looked out over acres and acres of headstones and smiled.

He watched as his son David, his wife, Judy, and their children slid out of the first black SUV. They were dressed in their Sunday best, and he was pleased to see that none of his grandchildren were playing games on their phones. They all looked so grown up in their suits and dresses.

Cassie, his daughter, greeted them all with hugs as they stood next to the cars. It had been so long since Buck had seen her without her green-and-yellow hotshot uniform on that he almost didn't recognize her. He thought she had gained a little weight, but she looked fit and tanned in her black pantsuit and white blouse. With her long black hair hanging down her back, she looked like Lucy standing there.

Buck was surprised to see Lucy's mom, Rosalie, standing next to Cassie. He hadn't expected her to make the trip. Grandma Rose, as the kids called her, stood tall, at a shade over five feet, and hugged everyone as they exited the car, showing them where they needed to stand. Buck wasn't surprised. Rosalie was never shy about taking control of any situation.

Jason, Buck's youngest son, and his wife and kids were the last to arrive, and more hugs were exchanged.

A thunderous sound grew in the distance as a contingent of volunteer honor guards arrived on their Harleys, followed by the hearse and two black limos. The motorcade pulled to a stop at the curb, and the family lined the sidewalk. The volunteer honor guard, in their leather vests full of military patches, formed a line starting at the back of the hearse and waited.

Buck's sister, Beth, her husband, Roger, their three grown children and their families climbed out of the limos and stood with the family. Roger helped Buck's mom get out of the limo. It had been years since Buck had seen his mom, and he was surprised how frail she looked. She stood proudly as she hugged each member of the family and spent a lot of time holding Rosalie.

While the family was meeting on the sidewalk, the Marine honor guard arrived. They unfurled the flags they'd come with and stood at attention, waiting to lead the procession. A gunnery sergeant, in full dress uniform, removed the urn from the back of the hearse, and the family followed the honor guard up the path to the top of the hill. Buck watched as the American flag was marched up the path, followed by the Marine Corps flag, but it was the third flag that caught his attention.

He had grown up seeing that flag all the time, displayed in its place of honor in the Gunnison VFW hall. This morning, the light blue flag with the thirteen white stars in the center glowed in the morning sun. The Medal of Honor flag was . something Buck's dad had always cherished but never spoken about. Tears formed in Buck's eyes.

Buck knew he couldn't put it off any longer, so he turned off the car and slid out into the warm desert air. He walked up the hill alone, wishing that Lucy was here with him. She was so much better at family gatherings than he was. By the time he reached the top of the hill, everyone was gathered around the grave, and a military chaplain had begun the service.

Buck looked at all the family and friends gathered around his mom: the honor guard, friends from the retirement village and from the local VFW. They all listened as the chaplain spoke. He glanced over his shoulder and saw something that made him pause.

Standing on a small hill a hundred feet or so away was a tall, thin man in a dark suit, his long gray hair tied back in a ponytail. What caught Buck's attention was the bright red cummerbund the man wore around his waist. Buck removed his sunglasses, wiped the tears from his eyes and, once the service concluded, looked back towards the hill, but the man was no longer there. He wasn't sure if the vision had been real or not, but it made him smile.

Buck stood next to David and Cassie. He caught his mother's eye, and she smiled. He smiled back and nodded his head. Cassie reached over and took his hand.

"I know Mom is proud of you," she whispered.

ACKNOWLEDGMENTS

A special thank-you to my daughter Christina J. Morgan, my unofficial editor-in-chief. She devoted a significant amount of time making sure the book was presented as perfectly as possible.

Thanks to my editor, Laura Dragonette, whose efforts helped turn my manuscript into a polished novel. Her help is greatly appreciated. Any mistakes the reader may find are solely the responsibility of the author.

Also, I would like to thank my family for all of their encouragement. I have been telling them stories since they were little, and I always told them that someone should be writing this stuff down. I decided to write it down myself.

I want to thank my closest friend, Trish Moakler-Herud. She has been encouraging me for years to write my stories down. I hope this will make her proud.

A special thanks to my late wife, Jane. She pushed me for years to become a writer, and my biggest regret is that she didn't live long enough to see it happen. I love her with all my heart and miss her every day. I think she would be pleased.

Finally, thanks to the readers. Without you, none of this would be important.

ABOUT THE AUTHOR

Chuck Morgan attended Seton Hall University and Regis College and spent thirty-five years as a construction project manager. He is an avid outdoorsman, an Eagle Scout and a licensed private pilot. He enjoys camping, hiking, mountain biking and fly-fishing.

He is the author of the Crime series, featuring Colorado Bureau of Investigation agent Buck Taylor. The series includes *Crime Interrupted, Crime Delayed, Crime Unsolved* and *Crime Exposed.*

He is also the author of *Her Name Was Jane,* a memoir about his late wife's nine-year battle with breast cancer. He has three children, three grandchildren and one dog. He resides in Lone Tree, Colorado.

OTHER BOOKS BY
THE AUTHOR

"*Crime Interrupted: A Buck Taylor Novel* by Chuck Morgan is a gripping, edge-of-the-seat novel. Right from page one, the action kicks off and never stops, gaining pace as each chapter passes." Reviewed by Anne-Marie Reynolds for Readers' Favorite.

"This crime novel reads like a great thriller. The writing is atmospheric, laced with vivid descriptions that capture the setting in great detail while allowing readers to follow the intensity of the action and the emotional and psychological depth of the story." Reviewed by Divine Zape for Readers' Favorite.

"Professionally written in the style of a best-selling crime novelist, such as Tom Clancy, *Crime Unsolved: A Buck Taylor Novel* by Chuck Morgan is a spellbinding suspense novel with an environmental flair. Intriguing subplots of fraud, survivalist paranoia, and murder weave their way through the fabric of the plot, creating a dynamic story. This is an action-filled, stimulating tale which contains fascinating details that are relevant in our present climate." Reviewed by Susan Sewell for Readers' Favorite.

"Chuck Morgan has a unique gift for plot, one that makes *Crime Exposed: A Buck Taylor Novel* a hard-to-put-down book. From the start, readers know what happens to Barb, but they become curious as they follow the investigation, wondering if the characters will find out what happened to her. The descriptions are filled with clarity, and they offer readers great images. The prose is elegant, and it captures both the emotional and psychological elements of the novel clearly while offering vivid descriptions of scenes and characters. This is a fast-paced thriller with memorable characters and a criminal investigation that is so real readers will believe it could happen." Reviewed by Romuald Dzemo for Readers' Favorite.